THE CLOAK SOCIETY

VILLAINS
RISING

Also by Jeramey Kraatz
The Cloak Society

JERAMEY KRAATZ

HARPER

An Imprint of HarperCollins*Publishers*

To Dad, for his unwavering support.

Library of Congress Cataloging-in-Publication Data
Kraatz, Jeramey.
        Villains rising / Jeramey Kraatz. — 1st ed.
            p.   cm. — (The Cloak Society ; [#2])
        Summary: "After leaving the Cloak Society and teaming up with
the Junior Rangers of Justice, Alex Knight must learn to work with the
superheroes who were once his sworn enemies"— Provided by publisher.
        ISBN 978-0-06-209550-3 (hardcover bdg.)
        [1. Superheroes—Fiction.   2. Supervillains—Fiction.   3. Loyalty—
Fiction.]   I. Title.
PZ7.K8572Vil   2013   2012040343
[Fic]—dc23   CIP
                                                                        AC
Typography by Ray Shappell
13 14 15 16 17   CG/RRDH   10 9 8 7 6 5 4 3 2 1
❖

First Edition

CONTENTS

THE CLOAK SOCIETY

VILLAINS
RISING

1

THE HOUSE AT SILVER LAKE

THE CLOAK SOCIETY was written in thick black marker on a sheet of paper pinned to the middle of the wall. Beneath it, on a slightly smaller page, was HIGH COUNCIL. Four index cards were tacked below that, one for each of Cloak's ruling members—Shade, Volt, Barrage, Phantom—with their powers written in Mallory's perfect handwriting. Red yarn stretched out from the High Council leading to other cards and pieces of paper, an adornment that Misty had added one night when dreams of falling ceilings and heroes melting into the shadows kept her awake. To the left, the yarn led to STERLING CITY, which branched out into smaller note cards for government administrators, police officials, and media producers. UNIBANDS, Cloak's non-powered workers living below the Big Sky Drive-In, was another subhead, with a few lists written in Gage's slanting script pinned below. And to the right of the High Council was OMEGAS, Cloak's covert team, the superpowered teens who lived outside the underground base and carried out secret missions only the High Council knew about. The accompanying notes for them were brief. Finally, the path down the center of the wall led to BETA TEAM, now reduced to only two note cards for siblings Titan and Julie, then to GAMMAS, the children of Cloak who hadn't developed powers yet. Alex hadn't had the heart to elaborate on that heading any further.

They hadn't bothered making cards for themselves, the survivors of Justice Tower. Alex, Mallory, Gage, Misty: those who had turned their backs on Cloak, the only world they'd ever known. And Amp, Kyle, and Kirbie: the last of the Rangers not lost in the Gloom.

The wall was in a room they called the Rec Room, but War Room would have been a better name for it now. A map of Sterling City was pinned to the felt top of a pool table and covered in notes and color-coded flags marking important locations like the Big Sky Drive-In, the basement safe house, and possible Cloak targets. The table's cues leaned untouched against the wall beside hand-drawn blueprints of Cloak's headquarters. Still more maps were pinned throughout the wood-paneled room, along with catalogs of the weapons at the High Council's disposal and newspaper clippings from across the country, all looking incredibly out of place among the mounted fish and stuffed ducks beside them on the wall.

The room was on the second floor of a large house located on Silver Lake, a manmade body of water about twenty miles northeast of Victory Park. The small suburb surrounding the lake shared its name, and was a place where people could buy summer homes and vacation without ever technically leaving Sterling City's borders. The house was on the water, with a private beach in a private cove nestled far from prying eyes. It had once belonged to Amp's family, but before he was born—when his father still led the Rangers of Justice—it was turned into a secret retreat for the superheroes. The surrounding properties were bought up and cleared, and the wooded land for acres around was fenced off and marked as a private nature reserve. The house was meant to be a place to regroup if Justice Tower was ever compromised, but it had sat unused for over a decade, all but forgotten.

A "safe house," they all called it, though like "Rec Room," the term wasn't exactly right anymore. None of the seven kids who'd escaped from the collapse of Justice Tower two weeks earlier truly felt safe there, even though the closest buildings were other lake houses located miles away, over the fencing and trees. But then, labels were becoming of less use to them, common words seeming more and more meaningless. They hardly knew what to call *themselves* anymore—hero, or villain, or Ranger, or Beta. They existed in a gray area and felt like strangers in their own world. Like exiles.

Alex sat on a couch, looking at the wall covered in yarn and index cards. Analyzing the wall had become a common practice for all of them, as if by staring at it long enough, they might figure out what they were supposed to be doing. They all hoped that somewhere in the notes and graphs and maps was the key to Cloak's defeat. But so far, that key remained hidden from them.

The morning sun filtered in through a window behind Alex, and he focused on a Polaroid tacked beneath the Beta Team note card. The room seemed to darken a bit as the photograph sparked with blue energy that only he could see. He pulled the pin out and brought the picture forward using his telekinesis, until it hovered in the air a foot in front of him. It was a photo of the Beta Team (or at least, what had *been* the Beta Team before Alex and Mallory became traitors), one of the few items he'd taken with him when he'd left the underground base to meet Kirbie near Victory Park. Right before everything accelerated into disaster. In the photo, he and Julie were grinning. Mallory looked like she'd been caught off guard, her mouth slightly ajar. And Titan smirked, his expression full of self-assurance. Alex studied the picture. The faces staring back at him caused his breath to quicken and dragged up a strange mix of feelings. Shame, anger . . . but also something difficult to place. Something like regret, and a longing to return to the moment the picture was taken, to a time when things seemed much less complicated.

Alex's mind drifted to his mother. He wondered what she might be doing or thinking as he sat in the second-story room. If she was having regrets about leaving her son behind to die as Justice Tower fell apart around him. If she was out there looking for him, even now.

"It's not the best picture." A voice came from behind Alex. "But I get why you can't stop looking at it."

He looked over his shoulder at Mallory, who leaned against the doorway. He offered up a half smile and pushed the photograph back to the wall with his thoughts, reinserting its pin into the worn hole at the top.

"If Amp catches you staring at it like that, he might start up on the whole 'they'll never outgrow their past' thing again," Mallory said. "You should at least think of shutting the door if you're going to get nostalgic."

"I know, I know." Alex sighed. "It's weird. It's not that I miss the underground base, exactly. I mean, there are things I do miss about it, obviously. But . . . I don't know. It just feels like it's been forever since we were there. I never thought I'd want to see the Big Sky Drive-In so badly."

Mallory smiled. She had handled the last few weeks

with her usual poise, even through the arguments, the crying, and the unshakable feeling of helplessness. Alex wasn't sure what he'd have done without her.

"Come on," she said. "Time for a run before the sun gets too high."

Alex nodded. For the first few days after they arrived at the lake house, they'd slept in late and spent most of their time down at the dock, swimming and letting off steam. But they quickly realized that even if they weren't sure what would happen next, the last thing they could do was let their training slide. They needed it now more than ever.

Alex followed Mallory out into the hallway. To his left was the room he shared with Gage, though Gage's twin bed sat empty most nights while he slept on a cot in the detached garage—his makeshift workshop. To the right was Kyle's room. The second bed in there was technically Amp's, but he preferred to spend his time in the house's small, finished attic, a space that his father had apparently used when he wanted to be alone with his thoughts. Alex could sometimes hear Amp pacing above him in the middle of the night.

They made their way downstairs, where there were two more bedrooms: a small guest room where Kirbie slept, and the master, where Misty and Mallory shared an oversized bed.

"Is she still sleeping?" Alex asked, nodding toward Misty and Mallory's room.

"Probably," Mallory said. "She tossed and turned half the night. Bad dreams. But she was completely zonked out when I woke up earlier."

In the living room, Kyle sat in front of the television, his eyes glued to the news. He was much more easily rattled since the fall of Justice Tower. Gone was the fearless Junior Ranger who had once strung Alex up with vines in Victory Park. He'd stopped going by "Thorn" and spent most of his time in front of the TV, jotting things down in a spiral notebook. Kyle told everyone he was watching for clues to help them figure out what Cloak might do next, but Alex suspected he was really waiting for breaking news that Lone Star and Lux and Dr. Photon had miraculously escaped the Gloom, reports that Alex knew would never come. At least, not without their intervention.

"Are they still reporting from Justice Tower?" Alex asked, glancing at the TV. "I thought they made everyone leave so they could finish cleaning up."

"They did," Kyle said. "This is old footage. But you should see the fence they put up around the tower site. Every inch of it's covered with flowers and letters written for the Rangers."

People had flocked to the rubble of Justice Tower

almost immediately after it fell. None could say why they felt compelled to go there, only that they had to see it for themselves. They didn't want to believe what they'd heard. They didn't want to imagine a world without the light of Justice Tower shining as a beacon in the dark night sky.

"There are more of them today," Kyle said to Alex and Mallory. His eyes never left the screen.

"More people?" Alex asked.

"More Powers," Kyle said flatly. "All camped out in the sculpture garden in Victory Park. They're holding some kind of twenty-four-hour vigil."

The Powers were people who had superpowers of their own, though "super" was probably too generous a description for most. They'd begun to show up recently to pay respect to their missing heroes. Some of them wore homemade costumes that related to their code names, or, more often, made them look like second-rate Rangers of Justice. Alex had watched as several of them had demonstrated their gifts on the news— the incredible ability to levitate a few inches off the ground, or the uncanny power to coax a very small flame into a slightly larger one. It was possible that there were real superpowers among them, but mostly they were amateurs, inexperienced and undisciplined. On the TV, a local reporter was interviewing a girl whose long, auburn hair was floating all around her, twisting and braiding with a life of its own.

"What can she do?" Mallory asked.

"Something with her hair," Kyle replied. "She controls it mentally, moving it around and grabbing things."

"Wonderful," Alex said. "Our great hope's big weakness is scissors."

"They're delusional," Mallory said.

"They're dangerous," Amp said, entering from the hallway. "They're untrained and reckless with their powers. If any of them have real talents, they're putting the city at risk. How long will it be before they start showing off to one another and some idiot accidentally sets fire to half the park?"

Amp was only a couple of years older than Alex, but there was a grimness in his voice that made him sound much more grown-up. He'd lost not one, but two sets of parents to the Cloak Society—his mother and father, and his adopted family of Lone Star, Lux, and Dr. Photon—and now found himself on a team with several of its former members. If you could call them a team at all.

"You never know," Alex said. "Maybe they'll end up being helpful."

Amp scowled but didn't respond.

"Where's Kirbie?" Alex asked.

"Outside, waiting for us," Kyle said. "She's fishing again. Or trying to."

Alex peeked out the window. Circling low to the water was a golden bird with an impressive wingspan and an unmistakable uniform. Kirbie. She'd been attempting to catch fish in her talons for several days. She'd had no luck so far, but she kept trying.

"Let's get started," Amp said. Reluctantly, Kyle stood and rubbed his eyes. He left the TV on and followed Amp out the door.

They gathered down at the water's edge. Spotting them, Kirbie landed and took her human form.

"Good morning," Alex said as she approached.

"Hey," she said. She shrugged. "No luck with the fish."

"You shouldn't be wearing the uniform," Alex said. "What if Gage's alarms failed and someone wandered in and saw you?"

"Yeah, well, until he has time to make me something new, I'm stuck in this outfit if I'm taking animal form. It's the only piece of clothing I have that morphs with me, and Gage has more important things to worry about right now than what I'm wearing."

"Are we running?" Mallory asked.

"Of course we are," Alex said. "We have to."

No one challenged his statement. All of them were anxious to do something, anything, that would hinder Cloak. But there wasn't much they could do until Gage found a way into the Gloom. So instead they trained, and went over every detail of Cloak's structure, every facet of its history . . . and they ran.

* * *

When the group returned to the lake house nearly an hour later, they found Misty sitting on the porch, a bowl of cereal in her lap.

"We're almost out of milk," she said, yawning.

"Look who decided to get out of bed," Alex said. He reached out playfully to give her a big, sweaty hug.

"Ew!" Misty said, reeling back. "Don't touch me. You're gross."

"I call shower," Kirbie said as they walked inside.

"No fair, you got all the hot water yesterday," Kyle whined.

"Yeah," she said. "But I was also flying around all morning, trying to catch you dinner."

Kyle groaned and walked back over to the television.

"I think we're almost out of peanut butter and bread, too," Alex said to Misty. "I guess we'll have to go on another supply run tomorrow."

They'd arrived at the lake house with the money Alex had taken from his room in the underground base, then found a stash of emergency cash hidden in a cookie jar. Most of that had gone to Gage to update the security system and start figuring out a way into the Gloom, but they still had plenty of money for the time being. And, if the day ever did come when they found themselves desperate for food, Kyle's ability to control the growth of plants made him a walking produce section.

"Ooh! While you're out, get ice-cream sandwiches, those little frozen tacos you got last time—and does anyone know how to make french fries?" Misty asked.

Alex rolled his eyes.

"Uh, you guys," Kyle muttered. "This might be important. . . ."

On the television, newscasters were cutting in to show some sort of press conference on the steps of city hall. Expecting a statement about the Rangers of Justice, everyone at the lake house quieted. But instead of the mayor, or his press secretary, or the chief of police, someone most of them had never seen stepped up to the podium.

"Oh no," Alex whispered.

"What's wrong?" Kirbie asked. "Who is that?"

The woman at the podium was dressed in a navy suit. Her hair was fiery red, pulled into a tight bun at the back of her head. She wore an expression of deep concern, the corners of her mouth pulled down severely. Text at the bottom of the screen identified her as the head of the Sterling City Council, the governing body second only to the mayor himself.

Alex's eyes darted to Misty, who stood frozen as she watched the television.

"Mom?" she asked, her voice meek and high-pitched.

Alex recognized the woman onscreen from her

infrequent visits to the underground base. She was Misty's mother—Phantom's non-powered sister—who served Cloak's interests in Sterling City while the High Council raised her daughter.

All eyes turned to Misty now. The woman began to speak.

"At approximately four p.m. yesterday, a young girl went missing on her way home from school. That girl is my daughter. Her name is Misty, and she's ten years old. I don't know why she was taken, or what her captors hope for in return, but I come to you now, as a community already mourning the loss of our protectors, to beg for the life of my daughter. To beg that she be returned to me safely. I ask that those who took my daughter turn themselves in. I promise you that we will be merciful, that there will be no punishment as long as she is returned. And Misty, if you are watching out there, be strong, sweetheart. Know that your mother is looking for you. Misty, please, come home to me."

"What's she doing?" Mallory asked, rushing to Misty's side and wrapping an arm around her. "Does she really think we'd be dumb enough to give ourselves up?"

"No," Amp said. "But they're making it harder for us to move around in public. Now if anyone sees Misty, our location will get called in to the police."

"Or they'll try to detain us and cause a big scene," Kirbie added.

"This press conference is just for us," Alex said slowly.

"To tell us that they know we survived. It was only a matter of time before Phantom realized that she couldn't sense any of our Cloak marks in the rubble. This is their opening move."

On the television, the footage cut to a photo of Misty, taken at the underground base. Her smile spread wide across the screen, the perfect poster child for innocence. A note beneath the photo encouraged any sightings of the girl to be reported to a special hotline.

Misty was silent, but the edges of her body were starting to break apart. Her bowl of cereal shattered against the floor.

A BOMB IN THE
TREES

After a quick shower, Alex went outside to the three-car garage that stood across from the lake house. It had a stained cement floor and smelled strongly of old oil. A tarp-covered speedboat sat on a trailer in one corner. Gage had tuned it up and assured everyone that it was water ready, but they figured that a boatful of kids out on the lake in the middle of autumn might draw unwanted attention. Shelving lined the garage's back wall and contained the rusted and gunky hodgepodge that garages tend to collect, like old machinery and tackle boxes and coffee cans filled with nuts and bolts. On another wall, hooks and pegs held all sorts of wrenches and hammers and saws.

The tools were fine for everyday projects, but Gage was

used to his underground workshop, where he had cutting-edge electronics and delicate instruments at his disposal. Still, he was doing his best. On a sun-bleached wooden bench dragged in from the lawn were various drawings and gadgets-in-progress, including the half of the Umbra Gun they'd managed to pry from Titan's hands at Justice Tower, and a box that held the Excelsior diamond. A state-of-the-art laptop that Alex and Mallory had "borrowed" from an electronics store in town sat on a circular patio table.

Taking the computer had been a real problem for the Junior Rangers, but Alex insisted it was their only option. They couldn't afford to *buy* a computer that powerful, and Gage needed something far more sophisticated than the laptop they'd found when they arrived at the lake house in order to update perimeter security. More importantly, the new computer allowed Gage to keep Cloak's headquarters under surveillance. As the one person who had pro-grammed and installed most of the base's electronics, it was easy enough for Gage to hack into their system and pore over any information that crossed the Uniband computers on the first floor of the complex. After plenty of arguing, everyone agreed that the laptop was necessary. Kirbie took note of what store the computer came from and vowed to repay them when the Rangers were back.

Alex found Amp in the garage with Gage, who had taken a keen interest in Amp's control over sound. Amp sat in a lawn chair, wearing bulky headphones that were connected to Gage's laptop by a coiled black cord. The Junior Ranger's body was vibrating slightly, but so quickly that he was almost a blur.

"Taking a music break?" Alex asked.

"Hardly," Gage said. "I'm doing a bit of an experiment."

"What's he listening to?"

"Prokofiev's 'Dance of the Knights' at a very high volume. Watch this."

Gage picked up a small pad of paper, scribbled something down, then held it up for Amp to see: FULL ORCHESTRA. Suddenly music began to pour out of Amp, filling the garage with sound.

"Whoa," Alex said. "That's crazy. How's he doing that?"

"Amp's sonic blasts are made up of concentrated sound energy," Gage said as he wrote on the notepad again. "He absorbs sound from the atmosphere and channels it into a powerful blast. Think of it as crumpling all the sound into a ball and then throwing it."

Gage held up the paper and pointed to the word "violin." Amp narrowed his eyes in concentration. After a moment, the orchestra faded, until the only sound that remained was a shrill stringed instrument.

"That's how he's always used his powers," Gage said, "so now I'm trying to test his ability to store and manipulate sound."

"Looks like he's doing a good job of it," Alex said.

"I think that's actually a viola, but yes, his control is quite remarkable. Watch this."

Gage wrote on the notepad again and raised it once more: CHANGE THE KEY. The viola's tones changed, its pitch lowering until it sounded like another instrument entirely, something deep and ominous.

"What I'm really curious to see is how he deals with all the sound he's been absorbing for the last few minutes," Gage said, walking over to the laptop and tapping on it, stopping the music. "How do you feel?" he asked as Amp removed his headphones.

"Full." Amp's voice absolutely boomed inside the garage.

"What do you normally do when you've consumed so much sound energy?"

"Usually I've absorbed noise for a purpose," Amp said, trying to keep the volume of his words down. "I let it off in a blast, and anything left over just finds its way out through my voice."

"Can you keep it stored?" Alex asked. "For later?"

Amp shook his head. "I don't think so, but I've never really tried."

Sweat was beginning to form on Amp's forehead. Holding in so much energy was clearly straining him.

Gage picked up a pair of earplugs off his workbench

and stuck them in his ears. "You might want to brace yourself, Alex."

Amp began to vibrate more noticeably, and then music rang out from his body—an orchestra blasting out in waves. Alex was knocked back a few steps, and the tools sitting on Gage's tables shook. The sound swelled until it became an unrecognizable cacophony of noise. Finally it subsided.

"Sound waves create pressure," Gage said casually, removing his earplugs. "It's why loud bass notes shake your body. In a way, the manipulation of sound waves isn't entirely unlike your telekinesis, Alex. Amp, if you don't mind, I'd like to test your abilities further at some point. I believe that if we can increase your precision at projecting frequencies, it may be beneficial in disabling opponents during battle. We might even be able to find frequencies that disrupt electronics and communications. I think there's a world of possibilities concerning your talents."

"Cool," Amp said. He shook his head slightly.

"Something wrong?" Gage asked.

"No," Amp replied. "It's just that we never approached our powers from such a scientific perspective in the tower. It would have been helpful."

Gage smiled.

"Did Amp tell you about Misty's mom on the news?" Alex asked.

"I watched it myself," Gage said, nodding to the laptop. "Leave it to Cloak to use a missing ten-year-old as bait. How is she holding up?"

"You know Misty," Alex said. "She'll bounce back."

"It's frustrating," Amp said. "I called every police station and government official I could think of in the past few weeks, telling them who I was and what happened at Justice Tower. I told them exactly where to find Cloak. And they just laughed at me and said they'd been getting hundreds of calls just like that from all over the country. But Cloak can spread all the misinformation they want and no one questions it."

"That's the advantage of having pawns planted throughout the city," Gage said. "An anonymous tip falls through the cracks, but when a public official gets behind a microphone, people listen."

"It'll probably only get worse," Alex said. "How's your work with the Gloom going, Gage?"

"Not well," he said. "I'm finding myself up against the same hurdle as when I was working on the Umbra Gun— the synthesis and manipulation of Phantom's energy. If I had the other half of the gun, I feel certain that I could get us into the Gloom relatively soon."

"Yeah, but that was frozen in Titan's hand when Phantom took everyone out of Justice Tower," Alex said. "It's gone for good."

"Well, not exactly," Gage said, sounding slightly reluctant.

"What are you talking about?" Amp asked. "The gun's what caused this disaster."

"The other half of the gun includes the containment unit where Phantom's concentrated energy is stored—energy I can't easily replicate. Since Titan had that part of the weapon, it would have been taken back to base," Gage said. "The High Council wouldn't have thrown away such a valuable item. . . . It's my assumption that the unit is in my workshop, being examined by the Unibands. I'm sure they're attempting to build a new Umbra Gun. Not that any of them would have the first inkling of how to do that."

"Wait. Are you suggesting that we infiltrate Cloak's headquarters?" Amp asked, his tone serious.

"That's insane," Alex said.

"I'm simply telling you what probably happened to the other part of the gun," Gage explained. "I have no desire to storm the compound, but if it came down to it . . . it *could* be done."

"How?" Amp asked.

"Through manipulation of the artificial environment within the base. Though it would have to be at a time when Phantom was not present. I've been monitoring the High Council's schedule as best I can. It appears that they'll be gone for a few days on their annual—"

"No," Alex said. "It's out of the question."

"Your Cloak buddies may take orders from you, but you are *not* in charge of all of us, Knight," Amp said, his voice rising slightly in annoyance. "If the *Rangers* want to take on a mission, you don't have to follow."

"*Former* Cloak," Alex said. "And you agreed we'd work together. So when I say that trying to steal something from Cloak is suicide—"

"You two are not fighting again," a voice shouted from across the garage.

Misty stood in front of the door, hands on her hips, the outline of her body solidifying. She was practically swimming in a purple sweater that was much too large for her. They'd found the closets of the safe house to be full of nondescript clothing of all seasons and sizes, and the group's wardrobe was now almost completely made up of hand-me-downs from the Rangers. "It's time for lunch."

Alex and Amp looked at each other for a moment. Alex exhaled. The last thing they needed to be doing was fighting among themselves.

"Pizza?" Gage asked with a smile.

"Yep!" Misty said. "It's pretty much the only thing we brought home on the last grocery trip."

"I think I've eaten more pizza in the last two weeks than I have in my entire life," Amp said.

"Come on," Alex said. "Don't tell me you don't like it."

"I'd advise all of you to eat lightly," Gage said. "You're sparring this afternoon."

After lunch, Kirbie, Kyle, Alex, Amp, and Mallory stood together on the front lawn, waiting for Gage, who was in charge of designing the day's training exercise. Other than Kirbie in her Ranger uniform, they all wore shorts and T-shirts they'd found inside, despite the slight chill in the air. Alex stood close to Mallory, who radiated heat thanks to her ability to control temperatures.

"Should we go over strengths and weaknesses again while we're waiting for Gage?" Mallory asked. "Which of us should take on which Cloak member?"

"Let's look at it the other way around," Amp said. "Who they're going to go after."

"That's good," Mallory said. "I'm sure they've talked about the best ways of taking us down individually."

"Julie will come after you, Kyle," Alex said.

"How do you know?" he asked.

"She's best suited to counter your abilities. Her claws are razor sharp. If she's fast enough, she can take out any plant you throw at her."

"And you were her assigned target at Justice Tower," Mallory added. Alex winced. He'd specifically avoided mentioning this, because he knew what the next questions would be.

"You had targets?" Kirbie asked. "So who was supposed to take me out?"

Alex shrugged and looked away. "I was supposed to keep you from getting too close to anyone," he murmured.

"Ha! I'd like to have seen you try," Kirbie said, half grinning. "It's smart, though. Keep the close-range attackers away from the action."

"Is everyone ready?" Gage asked, emerging from the garage with Misty, who carried a tote bag at her side.

"We were just talking about which Cloak members would probably target each of us on the battlefield," Alex said.

"Ah, perfect," Gage said. "That's actually part of the training exercise I've put together for today."

Misty cleared her throat. "With my help," she said.

"Over the last few weeks you've mostly been focused on getting to know one another's powers and establishing some semblance of teamwork," Gage said. "Today, it's time we pit you *against* one another, with some of you acting as Cloak members. Kirbie, let's have you in wolf form, targeting Kyle. Your claws are our best analog to Julie's powers." Kirbie hesitated, glancing over at Kyle.

"It's okay," he said, but Kirbie still looked uncertain.

"Wait," Mallory said. "You *have* sparred with each other before, right?"

"Well, not really," Kirbie admitted. "I mean, we did a *lot* of combat training. They brought in hand-to-hand experts for us to work with, and we would practice with the Rangers all the time. But as far as fighting each other . . ."

"Is this something you did a lot of?" Amp asked.

"You have no idea," Alex said.

"This is actually great training," Mallory said. "Kirbie, Julie's a tough fighter, but she lets her anger get the best of her. So just go berserk."

"If you get freaked out, just tell me to stop," Kirbie said to Kyle.

"You don't have to treat me like a baby," Kyle countered, standing up taller. "Come at me with everything you've got."

"Just be sure to stay in wolf form, Kirbie," Gage said. "Alex, can you use your telekinesis to act like Phantom's tendrils?"

"Yeah," he said. "I should be able to do that." His power to move things with his thoughts wasn't *that* different from Phantom's manipulation of shadows. Apart from her ability to travel through the Gloom, he could be a reasonable substitute.

"Perfect," Gage said. He fished around in the bag Misty held open for him and pulled out a plastic sack containing several dozen cherry bombs. He tossed the bag to Mallory. "I found these in the garage. I trust you can light the wicks yourself. You'll be acting as Barrage, using these to mimic his explosive energy balls. Everyone should assume that if you're hit by debris from the detonation, you've probably been injured in some way. You and 'Phantom' will target Amp."

"Whoa, whoa, whoa," Amp said. "You're throwing *explosives* out onto the field?"

"They're only fireworks," Gage said. "The noise level is minimal, and you'd have to be practically holding one for it to do any *real* damage."

"Explosives," Amp said, more slowly this time, as if Gage hadn't understood him.

"I don't get it," Alex said. "I've fought you guys. You have great defensive moves. You had to have been doing stuff like this at Justice Tower."

"Yeah, but with foam darts and ping-pong balls," Amp said. "You guys really trained this way?"

"Barrage used to follow us around on morning runs, hurling exploding balls of energy at our feet if we were too slow," Mallory said.

"The last time I trained with my parents, they had half a dozen guns stocked with rubber bullets firing at me," Alex added.

"Oh yes," Gage said, turning to Alex. "I never got a chance to apologize for that. I swear I had no idea that's what they were going to be used for when your mother commissioned them."

Alex shook his head and waved his hand. "Don't worry about it."

"All right," Amp said, nodding. "So me and Kyle against the three of you. How do we choose a winner? I'm not going to knock one of you out in the name of training."

"There's a clearing in the woods about a quarter mile from here where there's a petrified tree stump. Do you all know it?" Gage asked. The others nodded. "There's a timer there. Consider it a bomb. Kyle and Amp, you'll have to switch it off in ten minutes, or you lose and the city is destroyed. I'll give 'Cloak' a one-minute lead, then start the timer remotely and send you in after them. Understand?"

"Just ten minutes?" Kyle asked.

"A lot can happen in ten minutes," Alex answered.

"Yeah," Amp said. "We get it."

"All right then," Gage said, motioning to Alex. "Go on."

Alex, Mallory, and Kirbie ran into the wooded area to the right of the lake house, sprinting at first, then slowing down as they entered the screen of trees. Autumn was beginning to take its toll on the surroundings, and their feet crunched on fallen leaves. The foliage above offered varying amounts of coverage.

Mallory surveyed the area. "I'll see if I can climb one of the cedar trees that's still pretty dense and toss out explosives from above."

"No, no," Kirbie said. "If Kyle finds you in a tree, you're helpless. Stay hidden on the ground. Kyle will follow Amp, so I'll try to separate them. If you can put a bomb between them once I've done that, Amp will focus on you."

"Now you're getting into the spirit," Mallory said.

"I'll take cover near the stump," Alex said. "Last line of defense."

Alex ran off, leaving the girls behind. Not far from the clearing, he found a fallen tree. He crouched behind it, then used his powers to raise a veil of dead leaves, camouflaging him. He had a pretty good view of the tree line he'd just come from, as well as Gage's clock, which began to count down. The game was on.

It was quiet at first, only the sounds of birds chirping to break the silence. Then, just as Kirbie predicted, Amp appeared first. After a few seconds, Kyle followed, glancing around nervously. Trees swayed as he passed. Suddenly Kirbie attacked, a blond she-wolf leaping from the brush. Kyle spotted her too late, and the tree branch he sent sweeping down in defense only helped her. She swung on it, her claws cutting deep grooves into the bark, and kicked Kyle backward. Not as hard as she could have, Alex noted.

A sparking cherry bomb landed between Kyle and Amp. There was a pop, and bits of earth clouded the air. Amp staggered backward. More sizzling balls fell onto the battlefield, but Amp knew where they were coming from now and dodged them easily. Mallory began throwing the bombs as fast as she could, until the area around

Amp was so full of dirt that Alex could hardly see him. A bone-rattling blast of sound flew from the Junior Ranger's hands toward the direction the bombs were coming from. Over the sound of splitting branches, Alex heard a small cry from Mallory.

Out of the dust, Amp charged. He ran straight toward the clearing and Gage's timer. In Alex's vision, Amp crackled with blue energy. When Alex was sure he'd locked on to Amp with his powers, he stood, thrusting his arms out. Amp saw him for a split second before being thrown up and back, directly at a large tree.

Alex felt proud of himself until he saw Amp twist his body in midair so that his feet hit the trunk first. Then, like some sort of human spring, he jumped near horizontally off the tree, tumbling into a somersault on the ground and firing a single, perfectly aimed sound-shot as he came out of the roll. Alex was so impressed by this move that he didn't react fast enough, and Amp's shot hit him squarely in the chest, sending him to the ground.

Alex struggled to his knees, his head ringing, as he watched Amp approach. Farther behind him, trees bent unnaturally as Kirbie howled. Amp fired another shot as he passed Alex, ensuring that he was too disoriented to use his powers. The timer continued to count down, but Amp didn't seem concerned about rushing to it: He had plenty of time, and no one stood in his way.

Then something unexpected happened. Dust started to rise up from the ground, as if a breeze was swirling the dirt into the air. But the particles weren't floating along the wind's current. They were coming together, forming the familiar shape of a girl with bright red hair. Now Misty stood between Amp and the stump, her head tilted back and chin jutting out as her eyes zeroed in on Amp.

"Freeze," she said, holding a yellow gun pointed at Amp's face. Before he could respond, she pulled the trigger, and an orange plastic dart flew from the toy and suction-cupped to Amp's forehead.

Misty raised the barrel of the gun to her lips and blew on it, then mimed tucking it into a holster.

"Sorry," she said. "You're dead."

"What?" Amp half yelled. "You're not part of this."

"No," Gage said, stepping out from behind one of the trees. "But she's Shade. Or Volt. Or a Uniband. It doesn't matter who she is. Only that if the toy were a *real* weapon, you wouldn't be here."

"She wasn't part of this exercise," Amp said.

"We're up against people you call supervillains," Gage countered. "Expect them to play by the rules, and you'll end up dead."

On the stump, the timer began to go off.

"I'll say one thing," Alex said as he staggered into the

clearing, one hand clutching his head. "You've got incredible moves, Amp."

"Extensive training in acrobatics," Amp said through a clenched jaw.

"I'm going to go make sure everyone else is all right," Alex said, turning back into the woods.

He walked back toward the house, rubbing his head and trying to shake Amp's attacks. Mallory was leaning against a tree halfway through the clearing. A few leaves were stuck in her chestnut hair. Her face looked pale.

"You okay?" Alex asked.

"Yeah," Mallory said, sliding an arm across her stomach. "Think Amp's blast messed up my inner ear. I feel like I'm gonna puke."

"Do you want—"

She shook her head. "Just leave me alone for a bit."

Alex hesitated, but she shooed him away with one hand.

Close to the edge of the trees he found Kyle and Kirbie, who had reverted back to her human form. They sat on the ground, leaning against an old stump. Kyle's eyes were red, his lips pressed tightly together.

"Everything okay?" Alex asked when he found them.

"Yeah," Kyle said, standing. He turned quickly toward the house. "I'll see you guys inside."

Alex shot a questioning gaze at Kirbie, who got to her feet.

"Did something happen?" Alex asked, confused.

"No," Kirbie said. "I just don't think he was ready for this. He's taking everything really hard. I'm sure it didn't help that it was his sister coming after him like a monster."

She offered a small smile. "Did we win?"

"Yeah," Alex said. "We blew up the city."

A MINOR
INCONVENIENCE

The next morning Alex stood in front of a coffee-shop window, staring at the front page of the *Sterling City Chronicle* someone was reading inside. NO CLUES FOUND IN JUSTICE TOWER EXCAVATION, the newspaper headline read. WITH RANGERS MISSING, CITY FEARS CRIME WAVE. He almost dropped the groceries he was holding.

"Alex." Kirbie's voice came from his right. "Come on. Let's go."

Alex looked over at her, trying to shake off the sudden rush of anxiety. He nodded to the bags in her hands, which were full of different flavors of ice cream.

"Next time, we bring Mal," Alex said. "We're going to have soup by the time we get back."

"I, for one, like ice-cream soup," Kirbie said, looking down at the bag. "But maybe we went a bit overboard?"

"You don't know Misty as well as I do," Alex said. "With the news yesterday, ice cream is exactly what she needs."

"I guess I can't argue with that," Kirbie said, starting down the street. She wore jeans, a blue sweater, and a gray knit cap pulled down over her ears. Large black sunglasses hid her eyes, more to mask her identity than to keep out the sun. Unlike Alex, Kirbie and the Rangers had never shied away from the public eye, so she was more vulnerable out on the streets. She and Alex needed to hurry home before anyone noticed her.

At one time Silver Lake had been its own town, a manufacturing community, but as Sterling City became more prosperous, it grew and absorbed Silver Lake. Slowly the factories and warehouses closed, and upscale restaurants, shopping complexes, and planned neighborhoods began to pop up. The street they walked down now was one of the area's prime retail strips.

"Look," Alex said as they walked by a costume store, the window full of animatronic zombies and fake gravestones. Halloween was only a few weeks away. "Maybe we should stop in and pick up some supplies in case we want to go on patrol incognito."

"Right," Kirbie said. "Because nothing strikes fear into the hearts of criminals like a cheap plastic mask. You'd be surprised how many bad guys the Rangers put away who were wearing things like that."

"I bet the homemade heroes in Victory Park have bought out every mask within the city limits anyway."

Kirbie let out a short laugh.

A few blocks later, while waiting for a light to change, Kirbie jabbed Alex in the ribs with her elbow.

"Ow," he complained. "What was that for?"

"We have a problem," Kirbie whispered. "I think we're being followed. Five o'clock. Green hoodie." She thought for a moment, remembering Alex's blue-tinted vision. "Well, green*ish*."

Alex nodded. He bent to the ground, pretending to tie his shoelace. He let his eyes wander back over his right shoulder, where a figure leaned against a building across the street from them. His face was turned away, his head almost completely hidden by a hood.

The light changed. They continued walking.

"Are you sure he's tailing us?" Alex asked, keeping his eyes straight ahead.

"He's been across the street and half a block behind us for the last five minutes," Kirbie said. As they passed a jewelry shop, she paused, pretending to examine some sparkling necklaces on display. In the reflection of the store window, they watched as the figure came into view, loitering on a stoop across from them. "See?"

"If he's trying to be stealthy, he's really bad at it," Alex said. "Not one of Cloak's."

"An informant, maybe?" Kirbie asked, her voice giving the slightest hint of alarm.

"No," Alex said, peering at the reflection and catching a quick look at the person's face. "He looks too young. Around our age. They would have at least sent someone old enough to drive."

Kirbie sighed, but Alex wasn't sure if it was from relief or dismay. What he did know was that they didn't need any sort of confrontation. It went against the biggest rule they'd established after Justice Tower: *Don't draw attention to yourself.* Their survival depended on staying hidden. At least for now.

"His pants are all worn out at the knees," Alex pointed out. "His hoodie looks old, too. Mugger? He probably thinks we're easy marks, carrying bags full of food. Maybe he's waiting for us to turn off the main road."

"Street crime *is* up in places like Silver Lake, with police so focused on the center of Sterling City," Kirbie said. "Whoever he is, we have to lose him soon, or he'll follow us straight back home."

In the reflection, they watched as the kid in the hoodie crossed the street.

"What's the plan?" Alex asked, turning from the window and walking briskly toward the next intersection.

Kirbie spun the groceries at her sides, the plastic straps twisting until the bags were sealed shut.

"Feel like a chase?" she asked, smiling a bit.

Before Alex could answer, Kirbie was off, the bags cradled under her arms as she dashed around the corner of the next intersection. Alex was behind her in a flash, trailing her by a few yards. The street gave way to a residential neighborhood. Bags of dead leaves were piled up in front of the houses, waiting to be taken away. Carved pumpkins and plastic skeletons looked out at them from front porches. Alex glanced over his shoulder. The boy in green was running after them. Kirbie had been right.

"He's following us," Alex said, coming within a few feet of Kirbie.

"I told you," she said through heavy breaths. "You have to learn to trust my animal instincts."

Alex ventured another glance over his shoulder. The kid wasn't slowing down at all. Alex wondered if he really could have been sent by Cloak. But how? Everyone at the lake house had been so meticulous, so *careful* whenever they left the property. They'd never used their powers in town and only left the house when absolutely necessary. There was no way Cloak could have tracked them so quickly.

Kirbie took a sharp left onto a side street, and Alex almost tumbled over onto the pavement as he followed her. Ahead of them, the row of houses and sidewalks curved, feeding back onto the main road.

"We're going in a circle," Alex grunted. He made a mental note to start carrying weights during his morning run.

"I have an idea," Kirbie said. "Just follow me."

The kid in the green hoodie was gaining on them. Alex looked ahead and focused on several large bags of leaves between two mailboxes. They lit up a brilliant blue in his sight as he ran past. As soon as he was a few feet away, the bags exploded, sending a thick screen of leaves into the air. The mailboxes skittered across the sidewalk. Alex looked back just in time to see one of the posts catch their pursuer, sending him to the ground. So much for not using their powers away from the lake house.

"Alex!" Kirbie shouted, though he wasn't sure if she was angry because he'd used his telekinesis or because of the collateral damage.

"Just buying us some breathing room," he responded.

Their timing was lucky. They bounded across the main street just as the light turned green, putting a line of traffic between them and their tail, and Kirbie managed to wedge herself into the closing doorway of a city bus sitting on the corner. The driver scowled, but opened the door to let Kirbie and Alex on. As the bus pulled away from the curb, the two of them looked across the street, where the boy in green stood, staring at them. Alex thought he saw a glint of something metallic from the shadow of his hood.

"Still think he's just a wannabe thief?" Kirbie asked, collapsing onto a seat and catching her breath as the bus took off.

"Cloak never would have sent someone so sloppy or unarmed." Alex said, taking a seat beside her. "So yeah, I guess so." But he wasn't sure he believed it.

"The city's gotten so weird lately," Kirbie said.

A short ride later, Alex and Kirbie were carefully making their way down an old, unkempt bike trail, then trekking down the slanting embankment of a ravine. Below them a river flowed lazily.

Finally they came to what looked like a drain—two feet in diameter, set inside a cement slab. Kirbie flipped open a rusted metal box nearby, revealing a keypad. She punched at the numbers, and there was a metallic ping inside the grate, then it swung slightly ajar. Alex pulled it open, ushering Kirbie ahead of him, and closed the grate behind them, waiting for the locking mechanism to click back into place before going on.

Kirbie pulled a small flashlight from her pocket. The tunnel was musty, smelling of moss and rank puddles of water. They walked stooped over until the low tunnel opened up to the point that they could stand. Where the tunnel hit a dead end, there was another metal box positioned near the ceiling. Inside this one was a generic-looking electrical outlet. Kirbie held down the button marked TEST.

"*Lux Aeterna*," she said in a clear but quiet voice. The wall in front of them shifted, opening, and as soon as they were through, it closed behind them. Kirbie breathed out long and slow, relaxing for the first time since she'd noticed the hoodie kid.

They stood on a platform within another tunnel, this one large enough for an oversized van to drive through. Dim overhead bulbs lit the corridor. It had been built by the Rangers of Justice well before either Kirbie or Alex was born. On one end was access to Victory Park. On the other, the lake house. When Amp first brought them here, Gage had scoffed at the simple two-step security system that protected the passage, vowing to upgrade it to something impenetrable. But the route was safe enough. After all, it had been unused for over a decade, pushed so far into the back of the Rangers' minds that even *they* had all but forgotten about it. So long as no one followed them to an entrance, they were safe.

The air was dank, but it didn't bother Alex. He felt at home underground. Kirbie set down her bags and stretched a bit. Alex saw something crawling on her sweater.

"There's a giant bug on your back," he said calmly.

Kirbie let out a small yelp and jumped, causing the insect to flit into the air. She turned and saw it, and punched Alex on the arm.

"It's just a dragonfly," she said. "I thought you meant a big spider or something."

"Spiders don't count as bugs, though."

"You *know* what I mean."

At the end of the platform was a metal booth, like something from a space-age diner. They sat across from each other. Kirbie tapped on a console sticking up from the floor, and the booth began to move, rushing them through the tunnel. She shivered and pulled her arms in tight as the air blew over them.

Several minutes passed before the shuttle began to slow, and they found themselves stopped at another platform. Stone steps led up to a thick metal wall where, once again, Kirbie tapped a long series of numbers into a keypad and whispered into a hidden microphone. A panel in the wall slid aside, revealing a metal ladder, which they climbed until they opened a hatch and emerged in the basement of the lake house.

"Can we get a little help down here?" Kirbie yelled up into the house as they stacked grocery bags on the stone floor.

They heard the sound of footsteps on the floor above them.

"What took you guys so long?" Misty asked, making her way downstairs. "Do you have any news?"

"Nope. We just took the long way home," Alex said, not wanting to worry her with the story of the chase.

"Where's the candy?" Misty asked.

"I've got something even better for you," Kirbie said, holding out a bag of ice cream.

Misty's eyes lit up, and she lunged for it. Then she and the bag were gone, drifting in a haze up over the stairs and into the main floor of the house.

"Save some for the rest of us," Alex called up to her.

He closed the hatch in the floor. Behind him, he heard Kirbie snicker.

"What is it?" he asked.

"You have a giant bug on you."

"Oh, very funny," Alex said. He turned his head to pretend to look over his shoulder, only to find the same very large dragonfly perched there, two big eyes staring into his own. He yelped and jumped back. The insect flew away, out into the upper floors of the house. Kirbie tried in vain to hide a mischievous grin as she headed for the stairs.

BUG

The next morning, Alex had hardly gotten out of bed when there was a knock at the door. Misty burst into the room as soon as Alex turned the knob.

"We need to have a very serious conversation," she said, pointing to a chair in the corner. She had a bundle under one arm.

"Morning to you, too," he muttered. He sat down, yawning.

"We need a name." Misty began to pace back and forth. "I've been thinking a lot about it. We're not a part of Cloak anymore. And we're not Junior Rangers. Not *really*. I mean, we could probably call ourselves that if we wanted to, but I don't know. . . . That's just kind of weird, isn't it? And

Kirbie and Amp and Kyle *definitely* aren't Betas. We need something to call ourselves that fits everyone. I started thinking about what we are now, but Outlaws and Exiles and the Hidden don't sound right. And then I realized that we have the perfect name already. We just hadn't thought about using it as *all* of our names."

She looked at Alex with anticipation, as if her pitch might have forced the name into his brain. He stared back at her.

"Alex . . . Knight . . . ," she said, leading him. "We could be the Knights! It sounds cool *and* it makes sense, right? Like, the Rangers are there to protect Sterling City but the Knights are the ones who actually get stuff done and go on awesome missions. And you're *kind of* like our leader, so . . ."

She dropped a drawing into Alex's hands. It was a basic uniform, not unlike what they had worn as Cloak members, but lighter in color.

"Is this a sash around the waist?" Alex asked.

"Yeah. I thought it needed some decoration so it wasn't so plain. If you don't like red, we can change it to another color, but it's not like you can tell the difference anyway. I drew some possible symbols for the chest on the other side. I think the sword is probably the coolest, but the horse head that looks like the chess piece—that was Gage's idea—would be really neat if someone who could actually draw a good horse head did it. Unless you think that people might call us 'the Ponies' or something."

"This is . . . really great," Alex lied. "But I think it may be a little too soon to start thinking up new team names. And even though I think it's awesome that you want to use my last name, I think that Kirbie and the others might not want to give up being Rangers right now. You know?"

Misty sighed loudly.

"What's the point of us all being here together if we're not a team?" she asked.

"It's more complicated that that, Misty. You can't just put a name on a handful of people and suddenly have us be something like Cloak. These things take time. But we're all working together toward the same cause. As long as we're doing that, we don't need a name or a symbol on our chests."

"It's just . . . ," she said, looking down at the ground. "I know we can't ever go back to the way things were. And I know we *shouldn't* go back to Cloak. But sometimes I miss it. I miss the Gammas, and I miss wondering when I'll get an actual Beta uniform. I even miss the Tutor."

"I know," Alex said. He understood where she was coming from. Since birth they had *belonged* to something. They knew their places by the bands on their shoulders. Now they were on their own, and with that freedom came the feeling of being lost in some way. "But you're right when you say we shouldn't go back. It's hard now, but we're doing the right thing. And no matter what, you've always got me."

"Thanks," she said, taking the drawing from his hands. "It's dumb, but one of the reasons I want us to have uniforms and a name is so when we face Titan and Julie and the others again, we look like a team. Like we know what we're doing."

"That's not dumb at all," Alex said. "In fact, it's really smart. But you shouldn't worry too much about that. We're going to get the Rangers back. They'll be there to help us."

"And if we don't? What then?"

"Then the High Council will tremble in fear of *the Mist*," Alex assured her.

Misty grinned. She tossed the bundle from under her arm onto Alex's lap. A silver skull grinned up at him.

"Is this—," he started.

"The Beta uniform I wore the night of Justice Tower. It's too big for me, and I thought you might need it if we end up going on secret missions or something where you need to move around easily and blend into the shadows." She looked away from him. "Plus it kind of creeps me out now. Like it's watching me every time I open my closet."

Alex smiled. "Thanks."

There was a knock at the doorway, and Gage walked

in, wearing his white lab coat, goggles pushed up on top of his head.

"I need you to leave the room," he said to Misty.

"What?" Misty asked, her moment of happiness now completely replaced by frustration. "I was here first."

"This is *my* room," Gage said. Misty understood the stern look in his eyes.

"Fine," she said, stomping out into the hallway. "But don't think this conversation is over, Alex. We have a lot of planning to do. I'm going to work on better horse heads and then I'll need a decision."

She closed the door in an exaggerated huff. Alex smirked.

"Thanks," he said to Gage. "It was a little early for talk about costumes and team names."

"I need your help," Gage said, his voice serious. "There's something I'd like to test on you."

Alex sat in a lawn chair inside Gage's workshop, staring at the odd device in his hand. The base was a metal cube that fit perfectly in his palm. The top was a convex bubble made up of several smaller pieces of metal. On one side of the cube was a light switch, and on the opposite, a dial that looked like it had been taken off a kitchen timer.

"It's not my most aesthetically pleasing design," Gage said with a small frown, "but I'm doing the best with what I have."

"What does it do?" Alex asked. Gage had been quiet about his reason for bringing Alex to the garage, and Alex was starting to get a little freaked out.

"Using some of the pieces we recovered from the Umbra Gun and my admittedly rudimentary knowledge of Phantom's powers, as well as a few theoretical formulas pertaining to dark matter—not to mention the work I did with analyzing Lone Star's powers, my father's transporter, and basic principles of attraction when dealing with powerful sources of energy . . . ," Gage stopped talking, noting Alex's blank expression. He paused for a moment. "It's basically a magnet tuned to Phantom's energy signature. If it works, I should be able to use it to collect Phantom's energy, which is the key to opening a doorway into the Gloom."

"Great," Alex said dryly. "So we have to get close enough to Phantom to steal some of her energy, then get away before Cloak realizes we're there. No sweat."

"There's another way." Gage took back the device and placed a finger on Alex's palm. "Phantom's energy courses through you," he said. "If I can draw it out, I'll have something to work with."

"You don't sound as sure as you usually do," Alex said warily.

"I'm cobbling devices together with spare parts and whatever I can find lying around. I don't miss working for the High Council, but I certainly miss their resources."

"Is it safe?" Alex asked.

"I believe so, yes," Gage said. "But I don't know what the experience will be like. I would test it on myself, but I'm not marked."

Alex stared down at his palm. Somewhere beneath his skin, a dark skull was waiting to surface—a reminder that the power of the Cloak Society still coursed through his veins. A brand, but also a tracking device of sorts, since being marked with Phantom's energy meant that she could sense him when she was close by, and could drag him through the Gloom.

"Okay," he said. "Let's try it."

"You'll lose your mark. And I must stress to you that this might be painful. If you prefer that we—"

"Do it," Alex said. "I promised everyone that we'd find a way into the Gloom. If this helps, I can take a little pain. Besides, it may be helpful in the future if Phantom can't detect my presence."

Gage stepped back a few feet, lowering goggles over his eyes.

"If it feels like something's going wrong, tell me to stop," Gage said.

Alex nodded and braced himself.

Gage flipped the light switch on the side of the cube, and a high whining sound started from somewhere inside. Alex felt nothing.

"It's not working," he said.

"I haven't activated it yet," Gage said quietly.

Slowly he began to rotate the dial on the side of the device, and the bubble on top opened, the individual pieces of metal sliding apart from one another. The hair on Alex's neck and arms immediately pricked up. He flinched. Gage looked concerned, but Alex nodded for him to continue.

Gage turned the dial more, and a chill caused Alex to shake. It felt like an icy liquid was running through him, freezing his circulatory system. Gage kept turning, and the dark power within Alex began moving rapidly, concentrating in his right arm and causing him to gasp, then clench his jaw. He turned his right palm upward in time to see the dark mark of Cloak roiling to the surface, gleaming like oil in the garage light. It burned cold and pulled toward Gage's device.

"Is everything okay?" Gage asked.

"It feels like my hand is about to fly off," Alex said through gritted teeth. "But I can handle it."

"Okay. I'm dialing to the maximum current now. Hold on."

Alex nodded. At first it seemed like nothing had

changed. Then the dark energy began to emerge, tearing itself away from Alex's palm. The feeling was completely foreign to him, both painful and oddly relieving, as if a great stress was being removed from his body. He watched with wide eyes as an inky substance rose slowly out of his hand, hovering just above his palm. But before the energy moved any farther, something strange happened. Alex's eyes flared a visible, brilliant blue—bright enough to illuminate the dark corners of the garage. The tools on Gage's tables and along the walls began to shake.

"Alex," Gage said quietly, able to see the telekinetic energy himself. "What are you doing?"

"I . . . ," Alex started, but he couldn't finish. It was as if his powers had taken over his body. He could hardly move. Tools were flung from the shelves and walls, and the makeshift workbenches slid across the floor. Alex's lawn chair rose slowly off the ground, until it hovered a few feet in the air. But his eyes never left his right palm, where a gleaming ball of crackling blue was forming.

"Alex?" Gage asked with marked concern. "Let go of it. You're trapping Phantom's energy."

The ball flickered for a moment before collapsing in on itself.

"GAAHH!" Alex screamed as the dark energy shot back into his palm.

The resulting aftershock of telekinetic power pushed

both boys backward through the air. Alex was still seated in the lawn chair when he landed, its plastic frame splintering around him. Gage's flight through the air was broken by one of the metal garage doors.

They picked themselves up and stared at each other. Gage stepped toward Alex, the device still in his hand. Alex shook his head and backed away.

"Don't worry," Gage said. "It's disabled now."

"What just happened?" Alex asked, catching his breath. "What did it do?"

"What did *you* do?" Gage asked. "Your telekinesis kept me from collecting anything. For a moment I thought you might take out the entire garage."

"It wasn't my fault," Alex said. "I couldn't control it. All I could do was watch."

Gage was silent, his brow wrinkled. After a few moments he spoke.

"I can think of two reasons for this reaction. One, subconsciously you didn't want to part with your Cloak mark."

"That's not true," Alex started. "You know I—"

"Yes, I know. Which is why I think the more likely answer is that your *powers* don't want to be separated from the mark. Phantom's energy and the Gloom are tied to the Umbra that gave your ancestors powers in ways no one really understands. Your telekinesis went into overload to protect the dark energy. To keep it inside you."

Gage sighed. "The device is a failure."

"Maybe as a way to get Phantom's energy," Alex said. "But it had me completely incapacitated. We might be able to use that as a weapon against anyone else who's been marked."

"Possibly . . . ," Gage said. "But we'd have no way of knowing how other powers would react to the stimulation."

Alex opened his mouth to protest, but before he could speak, an alarm sounded within the garage. One of the perimeter sensors had been breached.

"Which one was tripped?" Alex asked as he rushed to look out the windows.

"Southwest," Gage said, picking his computer off the floor, exhaling in relief to find it unbroken. "Heat imaging shows a single person. Male, I think. Maybe a bit taller than you."

"Titan?" Alex asked, his eyes scanning the line of trees to the south.

"No. Not bulky enough."

There was a crackling of static from the walkie-talkie Gage kept in the garage, followed by Amp's voice.

"Gage, are you there? What's going on?"

They'd been over this before. A trip in any of the sensors around the perimeter of the property resulted in alarms sounding both in the garage and the house. Everyone had their stations. Misty would be waiting in the basement with

Mallory, preparing for escape through the underground passageway if necessary. Kyle would be at a second-floor window, ready to use the plants and trees outside against any would-be attackers, while Kirbie waited at the front door, ready to transform at a moment's notice should brute force be needed. And Amp would be on the walkie-talkie, ready to give orders.

If Alex had been inside the house, he'd have been right beside Amp, ready to disarm any attackers. Instead he picked up the walkie-talkie in the garage.

"Single male intruder," he said. "He should be approaching the house entrance any moment now. From the south."

Alex could make out Amp's face pressed against the glass of one of the front windows. He nodded back at Alex, and they turned their attention to the approaching danger.

"I can see him," Kyle radioed in from the walkie-talkie in the Rec Room. "He's coming up fast."

A figure appeared, jogging up the overgrown dirt road that led to the lake house. Gage had been right about the boy's height and build. His jeans were dirty and ripped at the knees. His hooded, zip-up sweater was faded, and a duffel bag was slung over one shoulder. There was something shimmering as it fluttered around his head.

Alex recognized him immediately as the kid who'd followed him and Kirbie after their grocery run.

"Is he Cloak's?" Amp asked.

"I don't think so, but consider him hostile," Alex barked into the walkie-talkie. "It's the guy who chased me and Kirbie."

"Then we need to incapacitate him before he has a chance to make a move," Amp said. "Lock him down, Alex. Kyle, secure him. On three. One . . ."

Alex focused on the kid, who had made his way to the center of the front yard, looking around curiously.

"Two . . ."

Everything around the boy faded, until he was the only thing in Alex's sight. A blazing blue silhouette.

"Three."

Alex thrust his hands out and clenched his fists. The kid jerked forward for a moment before rising several inches off the ground. The duffel bag fell to the grass. His arms shot out, held by Alex's telekinetic powers, while he shouted and kicked his legs in the air. His hood fell back, revealing tan skin and wavy black hair that fell almost to his shoulders.

Amp burst through the front door, his hands outstretched and vibrating in front of him, ready to release a sonic blast if the kid broke free of Alex's hold. At the same time, ivy from the lattice that ran alongside the house snaked across the front yard and rooted itself in the ground before looping around the intruder's wrists and ankles. Alex hurried outside.

"Who are you?" Amp demanded. "What are you doing here?"

"It *is* you," the kid said to Amp, his face lighting up. "I knew you weren't dead. I knew it was Kirbie I saw on the street."

"Have you got him?" Alex yelled up to the window.

"Yeah," Kyle replied. "You can let him go."

Alex slowly lowered the boy to the ground. He was slightly taller than Alex, and on the lanky side. Kyle's vines tightened around the intruder.

"Who sent you?" Amp asked.

"No one," the boy said. "I came looking for you once I saw Kirbie. Sterling City needs you. You have to go back. Where are the others?"

"Why are you here?" Kirbie asked, from the doorway of the lake house. She was half crouched, ready to leap forward and attack at a moment's notice.

The kid looked at her and grinned sheepishly.

"I always wanted to be one of you," he said. "I came to Sterling City to see if you would take me in as a Junior Ranger. Hitchhiked from Oklahoma. But by the time I got there, Justice Tower was gone."

He looked back and forth between Kirbie and Amp, trying to read their expressions, before continuing.

"I camped with the mourners for a while. Then all the supers started showing up with their strange powers, talking about avenging the Rangers. . . . It just didn't seem right. It didn't seem like what Lone Star would want. So

I left and was heading north to go back home when I saw you, Kirbie. On the street."

"That doesn't explain how you found us here," Alex said. "We lost you. There's no way you could have followed us."

"Oh. That," he said. "This is Zip."

From inside his hood, a huge bright-green-and-blue dragonfly emerged and landed on his shoulder.

"I . . . kind of had her follow you guys back here."

"You mean to tell me you can talk to dragonflies?" Amp asked.

"Not just talk," the kid said. "I can see what they see. Control them if I have to. And not just dragonflies."

The boy closed his eyes for a moment. When they opened again, his irises were a metallic mixture of green and yellow, shining in the sun. All around them, insects began to appear. Dragonflies and moths and beetles darted to him, swirling in circles around him for a few moments. Then his eyes slowly began to fade, and the insects dispersed, all but the dragonfly on his shoulder.

"So you've got powers," Amp said.

"Why should we believe you?" Alex asked.

The kid looked over his shoulder at Alex and then back at Amp and Kirbie.

"I just want to help," he said. "Seeing you on the street like that . . . I knew I had to find you. I don't know what else to say." He struggled to move his arm, but Kyle's plants held him tight. "If someone could get to my wallet, it might help show that I'm not lying."

Alex walked toward the kid, focusing on his back pocket and pulling out a worn leather wallet with his mind. He let it drift into his hands as he joined Amp and Kirbie on the patio steps. There wasn't much inside, but Amp immediately saw what the boy wanted them to find. He took the wallet from Alex and pulled out a yellow, laminated ID card. The photo on the card was obviously the boy now entangled in ivy, though several years younger. HONORARY MEMBER OF THE RANGERS OF JUSTICE, the card said at the top. And beneath, a name and an Oklahoma address.

"Tyler Benally?" Kirbie asked.

"Most people call me Bug," the kid responded. "For obvious reasons."

"Right," Alex said, unmoved. "What is this supposed to prove?"

"Just that I'm who I say I am."

"What's in the bag?" Amp asked.

"Clothes. My toothbrush. Basically everything I own."

"Where's your family?" Kirbie asked. "Do they know you're here?"

"I doubt they even realize I'm gone," Bug said.

"And you've got nowhere else to go?"

Bug shook his head.

Kirbie frowned and took a long, hard look at Bug. Finally, she gave in.

"Loosen up on him, Kyle," she called up to her brother. "Radio down to the basement and tell Mallory and Misty they can come up."

"Wait," Alex whispered to her. "We're just going to trust this kid because he has a novelty ID card in his wallet? He had us followed yesterday. Here. To our *secret safe house*."

"To the *Ranger* safe house," Amp said. "To my family's house. Where you are a guest."

"What else are we supposed to do?" Kirbie asked, her voice hushed. "He knows who we are and where we are. If we force him out of here, he becomes a loose end."

"You're putting us in danger," Alex said. "I know the Rangers were all about helping others, but this is not a good idea."

"It's because Lone Star took us in that Kyle and I are here now," Kirbie said.

"We don't know what he really wants," Alex said, his voice rising.

"I think he's telling us the truth," Kirbie said.

"What would you have us do, Alex? Kill him?" Amp added.

Alex hesitated before answering. Of course he wasn't recommending that they kill him, but he was sure there was another way. Kirbie grabbed his right hand.

"What's this?" she asked.

Alex looked down at his palm. A bruise had formed: a deep purple, hooded skull bleeding into shades of yellow around the edges.

"I . . . ," Alex started, looking back to the garage, where Gage stood in the doorway. "Gage and I were trying to—"

"It's funny," Kirbie said. "Of everyone here, *you* should trust my judgment the most, Alex. After all, I believed in you, didn't I?"

Slowly Alex nodded. "You're right."

Mallory walked cautiously out onto the patio. Misty ran to Alex's side, her eyes wide with excitement.

"Is it true what Kyle said on the radio?" she asked. "Can this guy *really* control butterflies and stuff? Is he here to help?"

Alex wasn't sure what to say. He turned to Mallory, who was looking to him for some sort of explanation.

"Bug," Amp said, "come inside. I want a full report on what's happening in Sterling City."

Kyle's vines fell away. Bug nodded his thanks at the window and picked up his bag. He started inside, pausing in front of Alex on the patio.

"Thank you," Bug said. Zip remained on his shoulder, staring at Alex. "I didn't catch your name."

Alex looked from the dragonfly to Bug, his expression blank.

"Leave the bag on the porch," Alex said. "I'm sure you understand that we'll have to search it."

Bug nodded slowly, dropping the bag at his side. Kirbie looked as though she might argue with this but said nothing. Misty held out her hand.

"I'm the Mist," she said. "Don't let anyone tell you differently."

"Come on in," Kirbie said, standing beside the front door. Bug smiled and stepped inside. Misty, Amp, and Kirbie followed behind.

Mallory and Alex stood alone outside the Ranger safe house.

"So, what's the deal?" Mallory finally asked. "Some long-lost hero we didn't know about?"

"No," Alex said. "Just some wannabe with a really convenient backstory."

S'MORES

At Alex's suggestion, they kept Bug in the dark about some of the things that were going on—like where the Rangers were, exactly, and the truth about the Betas' past. Bug offered a wealth of information about Victory Park and the Powers. There were loose factions forming, he told them, growing more vocal with every day that went by without news of the Rangers. There were some who believed that if the Rangers didn't return, it was their responsibility to take up the heroes' job, ensuring the safety of Sterling City, a concept that made Amp groan in disapproval. The last thing they needed was a bunch of amateurs fighting one another for power.

The group talked well into the night. Alex and Gage searched Bug's bag but returned it after finding nothing but clothing and a few odds and ends. The metal cube that Gage had used on Alex had no effect on the intruder, which proved he wasn't marked by Phantom's energy. Amp gave his bed to Bug, moving permanently into the attic. Alex maintained his distance but kept a close watch on the new arrival.

A few days after Bug showed up, Alex found himself sitting cross-legged on the front lawn along with the other housemates as Kirbie led the afternoon's training exercise.

"When I was first taken in by the Rangers," Kirbie said, "I didn't have any control over my transformations. All kinds of things would set them off, even in my sleep. Meditation helped me get in touch with my powers. Helped me gain control over them."

"So, we just sit here and . . . not think?" Misty asked.

"That's the gist of it, yeah."

Alex imagined how easily Titan or Julie would have turned that into a joke. Misty didn't look convinced, and Alex couldn't blame her. It was an odd sort of training, one that the former Betas were unfamiliar with. They weren't being pitted against one another, or having their powers tested under extreme circumstances, or being yelled at and threatened by the High Council. This was the exact opposite. It was all about quiet and calm, and peace.

"Usually I do this alone in the morning, but I'll try my best to help you all with it," she said. "Start by closing your eyes. Clear your mind. Listen to the wind in the trees. Let that be the only thing that fills your head."

Alex couldn't help feeling that this whole exercise was silly and would be useless in a fight against Cloak. They sat in silence for a while before Alex allowed himself to open one eye and glance around. Everyone else looked like they were enjoying themselves. Bug had a smile on his face, as if he had never been more content than he was sitting there, his insect companion on his shoulder.

When Alex looked at Kirbie, she stared back at him, raising one chiding eyebrow. He closed his eyes again and tried to concentrate on nothing.

"Okay," Kirbie said. "Now envision all your stress, all your worries, as a ball in your mind. Push all your anger and sadness and confusion into that ball."

Now *this* was something that sounded familiar to Alex, though not exactly as meditation. He'd spent the last few years focusing his thoughts into hard, palpable forces. He was good at moving his thoughts, whether by pushing them out of his mind or hiding them deep inside a shining blue box where no one, not even his mother, could find them. So he gathered all his stresses and fears—that he was partly responsible for their current situation and the safety of those around him, the knowledge that he would one day have to face his family in battle, that they were out there somewhere even now, looking for him and his friends.

"Now," Kirbie continued, "let those feelings drift away. Feel them leaving your body through your fingertips, flowing out into the wind and becoming nothing, until the only thing left in your head is your power. Not something separate from you, but a part of you. Something you have complete mastery over. And just breathe."

Alex felt as though he really *could* sense the stress leaving him. It was nice. He felt light and energized. And in control.

He opened his eyes again, curious to know whether the others were feeling a similar sense of calm, and he was met with a vision of Kirbie in full color, a sight he had longed to see since they'd escaped from Justice Tower. Her bright hazel eyes were open, and she smiled at him. But it wasn't just Kirbie who was in color—the whole world was a spectrum of vivid hues. Out of the corner of his eye, there was movement, and he turned to see Bug beside him, surrounded by various winged insects, his jeans crawling with little ants and maroon millipedes, and Kyle, sitting in a patch of overgrown grass of an impossibly green color.

It took Alex a moment to notice there was something strange about the size of everyone around him, as if they'd shrunk slightly. It wasn't until he looked down that he realized *they* hadn't changed, but his vantage point had. He was floating a foot off the ground.

He let out a startled cry, and his vision went blue once

more as he fell back to the ground. Around him, every-one opened their eyes. They looked relaxed, more assured than they had been earlier in the day. Except for Misty, who yawned, and might actually have been napping through the entire exercise.

"All right," Kirbie said. "That's it for now. I think Gage wants to go over Cloak weaponry with us in an hour or so."

Everyone stood and stretched. Alex took his time, thinking about what had happened. His mother had told him once that when he had full control over his powers, he'd be able to see color again. And while his unconscious floating was proof that he still didn't have a firm grasp on his telekinesis, it gave him hope that he was improving.

"Could we start meditating together in the morn-ings?" Mallory asked Kirbie. "I've spent years working on keeping my temperature in check, and I think this might really help."

"Of course," Kirbie said, smiling. "I'd like that."

"You guys, I was thinking," Misty said. "Since Bug is new here and all, we should have a party or something. I mean, not like a *party*, but . . . a night off. Where we don't worry about Cloak or anything for a little while."

"You guys don't have to do that for me," Bug said, his cheeks flushing.

"No," Kyle said, "that's a great idea."

"Misty," Alex said, "we don't want to draw attention to ourselves."

Misty ignored him. "We could make s'mores! I've never had them before, and they're in, like, *every* lake and summer camp movie I've ever seen."

"You've never had a s'more before?" Bug whispered incredulously.

"S'mores mean a fire," Amp said. "Smoke's the last thing we need."

"Alex can hold marshmallows with his mind, and I'm a walking heat source," Mallory said. "No smoke. S'mores wouldn't be a problem."

"Besides," Kirbie said, "Misty's right. We could use a night of relaxing. It'd be good for us all."

Alex turned to find Misty looking up at him, eyes wide and pleading.

"Okay," Alex said finally. "Let's do it."

Misty let out an excited squeal. "I wonder if I can find some streamers or something!" she shouted as she ran inside. Amp and Mallory headed in after her, discussing what supplies they'd need to pick up before the night.

"Back to the news," Kyle said, starting inside.

"Uh-uh," Kirbie said, pulling him back. "You're starting to look way too pale. Spending a little quality time in the trees will do you some good."

"I guess I could catch up on all the news later . . . ," Kyle said.

"I was going to go on a walk myself," Bug said. "Can I come?"

"Of course," Kirbie said.

"Huh. Between the three of us, we're like some sort of nature supergroup," Kyle mused.

"You're right," Bug said. "Maybe there's some kind of link between our powers. This probably sounds crazy, but I kind of feel like we're all connected in some way."

Alex frowned.

Or maybe you're just good at blending in and fooling everyone.

"Oh, Alex," Bug said, as if only just realizing that he was standing there. "Did you want to come?"

"No thanks," Alex said coldly. "I wouldn't want to intrude on your nature party."

"You guys go ahead," Bug said to Kirbie and Kyle. "I'll catch up with you in a sec."

Kyle and his sister headed for the trees, leaving Bug and Alex alone on the lawn.

"Hey," Bug said. "I just wanted to make sure everything is cool between us."

"Cool?" Alex asked. "You chased us through town, followed us with your little friend, and then showed up on our doorstep uninvited."

"I know, but like I explained—"

"I don't care about your membership card or your story," Alex said. "Until you prove to me that you're not a threat to us, I'm going to keep my eyes on you."

Bug opened his mouth to protest, but stopped. There was really nothing he could say.

"Sure," he managed.

"And Bug?"

"Yeah?"

"Don't ever follow me again," Alex said.

Bug nodded, his face falling. At the tree line, Kyle and Kirbie called his name.

"Better not keep them waiting," Alex said, and turned away.

When the sun began to set, they dragged the picnic bench and folding chairs from Gage's lab out onto the lawn and set them next to some tall stools Kyle had created out of a seemingly endless supply of ivy and other strong plants he wove into thick, intricate structures. Bug kept the season's lingering mosquitoes away, while Kirbie and Misty laid out a feast of chips and hot dogs on the table, courtesy of a quick run into town by Amp. Alex and Mallory cooked hot dogs before moving on to the main event—s'mores. At first Alex held a few of the marshmallows with his thoughts while Mallory roasted them, but soon they were all tossing the white puffs high into the air as target practice. Mallory scorched them with searing blasts, while Alex caught them between graham crackers and hunks of chocolate, assembling s'mores in the night sky.

"You know, I think this might be the best s'more I've ever had," Amp said, devouring his third one.

"Seriously," Alex said. "We should have been doing this at the underground base for years."

A buzzing blur shot across the table before landing on Bug's shoulder. Zip. He raised a finger and rubbed the underside of the dragonfly's head.

"So, what's the deal with Zip?" Kyle asked. "Is she . . . special or something? I mean, there have to be hundreds of dragonflies around here."

"I don't know," Bug said. "The day I left Oklahoma I was walking by the water, and she landed on my shoulder. I'd always had a connection with insects, but something was different with Zip. Usually my abilities are limited to a pretty small area, but Zip can fly for miles and miles and I can see perfectly through her eyes. I guess we just kind of clicked, you know?"

"So, can she eat a s'more?" Misty asked Bug, a gooey mixture of marshmallow and chocolate coating her fingers.

"She's a predator," Bug said. "She eats other insects."

"Ugh," Misty said. "Now I'm done eating."

"Oh, good." Gage pulled a long, faded box out of his pocket and placed it on the table in front of Misty. He smiled. "I found these with the cherry bombs we used in training. They're small enough that they shouldn't draw any unwanted attention our way."

Misty opened the end of the box and pulled out a long, skinny gray stick. She held it in front of her, perplexed. Mallory reached over and placed her finger on the tip of the object, which burst into a shower of brilliant white light.

"Sparklers!" Misty said. She ran farther down the lawn, away from the others, creating loops of light that lit up the air before fading away.

Dusk became full-on night. It was cool, but pleasant. None of them wanted to go back inside, so they brought out a few lanterns from the garage and placed them about the lawn on their dimmest settings. And they played.

"The ground is lava," Bug said. On his finger, he twirled an old volleyball that Gage had found in the garage. "Keep the ball in the air. After you hit it, call out someone's name, and they're up next. You can only use your hands. If the ball hits the ground, you're out."

"No powers," Gage said. "I'm at enough of a disadvantage against all of you already."

"Don't worry," Alex said. "We'll take it easy on you."

Bug tossed the ball high into the air, and they began. The first ones out were those without years of training in agility and focus—Gage soon retreated back to his make-shift workshop, and Bug stuck around for a while as the others played before going inside for a glass of water.

From there, the game went on for a while, the ball never touching the ground. And so they became more ruthless, spiking the volleyball at one another instead of hitting it into the air. Kirbie sent a particularly powerful serve to Alex, who leaped across the grass, narrowly catching the ball and sending it bouncing off Misty's shoulder.

"No fair!" Misty said. "You're using your telekinesis."

"Am not!" Alex said.

"I don't believe you," Kirbie said, grinning. "You're out this round."

"Fine," Alex said. "I wanted another hot dog anyway."

"Oh!" Misty said. "If Mal gets out, will you make me another s'more?"

Alex rolled his eyes and headed back to the table. Behind him the game resumed. He was halfway through his hot dog when something in the corner of his eye caught his attention. Bug was moving briskly through the yard, keeping to the shadows with impressive stealth, visible only in the few spots where the moonlight broke through the clouds and leaves. Soon he disappeared into the trees.

Alex looked around. No one else seemed to have noticed. The game continued—the game *Bug* had insisted they play. Did he realize that they'd be so good at it that he could slip away into the woods alone? Alex feared that Bug had tricked all of them. He shoved the rest of the hot dog into his mouth and started for the trees. This was his opportunity to see what Bug was *really* up to.

Alex kept his distance, careful to use the darkness to his advantage, his skills as a former Cloak member serving him well. He moved quickly but made almost no sound. Bug didn't seem to notice him and continued deeper into the wooded area. He finally stopped in a small clearing, where the moonlight filtered down through the trees. Alex crouched behind some brush, watching. Bug's lips were moving, but Alex couldn't hear what he was saying. Who was he talking to? Was there someone else lurking out of sight, or did he have a communicator that he was using to report back to someone? He could imagine what Bug was telling them. *I know where they are. Now's the time to move in on them. They're eating s'mores.* It was lucky that Alex had seen him. Now he could save the others, could warn them of impending danger.

Bug stopped speaking. He turned his head slowly but deliberately, until his shining eyes stared directly at the bush Alex was crouched behind.

"You found me," Bug said.

Alex's mouth fell open. He was genuinely shocked he'd been discovered. That was impossible. He'd been trained since birth to disappear in the shadows. There was no way

Bug could have found him, unless . . .

"Who are you talking to?"

"Just making a few new friends."

Alex gathered energy around his fists, ready to attack if necessary.

"Who? Where?" Alex asked.

"It's kind of a surprise," Bug said, his eyes growing brighter. He smiled. "I don't want to spoil it."

"So that was your plan?" Alex asked. "Distract us and then disappear into the woods and rat us out?"

"Wait," Bug said, his face crinkling in confusion. "What are you talking about?"

"Who sent you here?"

"Alex, you've got the wrong—"

"Save it," Alex said. "I'm not as gullible as the others."

"Not as gullible as who?" Kirbie asked from the edge of the clearing.

They both turned to look at her. Neither of them spoke. Kirbie's eyes narrowed at Alex for a moment before she continued.

"I noticed you were both gone, so I tracked your scents out here." Her eyes drifted slowly back and forth between the two of them.

"Our scents?" Bug asked.

"Yeah. The perks of being part animal. I try to get a

scent off anyone who might be important. Is everything all right here?"

"Yeah," Bug said. "Alex was just helping me with something."

"He wandered off out here alone," Alex said, pointing a finger at Bug and turning to Kirbie. "He was talking to someone and—"

"Oh, wow," Kirbie whispered, staring over Alex's shoulder.

Alex turned. Emerging from the trees all around Bug were dozens of tiny lights fluttering through the air, hanging around him like constellations. Fireflies.

"I needed to concentrate to find this many," Bug said sheepishly. "I thought you guys might like it. . . ."

Kirbie smiled.

"Let's bring them back to the others," she said. "Misty's going to die when she sees them."

Bug nodded, his eyes glowing bright, and started back toward the lake house with a swarm of blinking insects in tow. Kirbie started after him.

"Kirbie," Alex began. "I—"

"I get that you're trying to look out for us," she said. "But cut Bug some slack, okay? If you don't make him feel welcome here and he leaves, we're going to have a civilian running around, knowing where we're hiding."

She left Alex standing alone in the clearing, trying to

sort out what had happened. Was he really supposed to believe that the kid who randomly showed up on their front lawn had disappeared into the woods to mumble to a bunch of flies?

Alex noticed a glint of silver in the moonlight. On a tree stump in the middle of the clearing, Zip sat staring at Alex. Her silver wings twitched. Alex stared back at her, certain that somewhere on the lawn, Bug was watching him. He narrowed his eyes and let everything fade away, focusing on the blue energy crackling around the insect. *It would be so easy to get rid of her. Just one squeeze.*

The moment passed. Alex shook his head, letting the clearing fade back into view. He turned away from the dragonfly and headed to the house.

On the lawn, the others were gathered, looking on with awe as the glowing insects danced through the air. Alex leaned against the garage, watching them.

"Our parents used to call them lightning bugs," Kyle said. "Remember that, Kirbs?"

"Yeah," Kirbie said. "I do."

"I've never actually seen them before," Mallory said.

"Really?" Amp asked.

"Well, we didn't exactly spend a lot of time in nature," she said wryly.

"Awwww," Misty whispered as one landed on her

open palm. She held it to her eyes. "Oh. They're not as cute up close."

Someone tapped Alex's shoulder. He turned to find Gage, a finger over his lips. Gage nodded toward the garage door. Silently Alex followed him.

"There's something you should see," Gage said once they were inside. He went straight to his laptop, turning it to Alex.

"What is it?" Alex asked.

"I have a program set to notify me of any news regarding Cloak or the Rangers," Gage murmured as he scrolled to the top of the page. "Usually it's nonsense and speculation, but this just appeared on the *Sterling City Chronicle*'s website. . . ."

BREAKING NEWS, the headline read. NEW DEVELOPMENT IN RANGERS' DISAPPEARANCE POINTS TO INSIDE JOB.

Below were photos of Kirbie, Kyle, and Amp, along with the caption: WERE THE JUNIOR RANGERS WORKING IN LEAGUE WITH OUTSIDE FORCES TO BETRAY THE CITY'S PROTECTORS?

"The High Council," Alex muttered. "Why would they do this?"

"They're instilling fear," Gage said. "Even if the story has no truth behind it, now the people will doubt the Junior Rangers. Anyone who might have allied with us before will think twice before trusting us now."

"They're turning them into public enemies," Alex said. "Making it harder for us to move around. Just like with Misty."

"This isn't going to go over well with the others."

"I know," Alex said. He turned to the window, catching a glimpse of Kirbie and Kyle both grinning wildly as fireflies spun in circles around them.

"Cloak is accelerating things, Alex," Gage said. "We need to get into the Gloom. Now."

LIFE
RAFT

"This is a bad idea," Alex said for the tenth time in the last hour. The others didn't even bother to look over at him. Only Mallory made any indication that she'd heard, with a slight bob of her head.

They stood together in the Rec Room, staring at one of the hand-drawn blueprints of Cloak's underground base. Through the side window, Alex watched as Bug and Misty played in the front yard amid the dim lanterns. Bug's eyes were shining in the darkness. Katydids and moths that looked like leaves and buckeye butterflies fluttered around Misty en masse. She practically danced in delight. Kirbie had suggested they stay outside and enjoy the night. Neither of them needed to know what everyone else had gathered to talk about.

"Cowards," Kyle said, banging his fist down on the billiard table.

"Kyle . . . ," Kirbie started.

"No, that's all Cloak is," he insisted. "Cowards. They're trying to get Sterling City to turn on us so they don't have to fight their own battles."

"Tactically it's a pretty good plan," Mallory said.

"Let's get back to the task at hand," Amp said, turning his attention to Gage. "If we can retrieve the other half of the Umbra Gun, we can bring back the Rangers, and Cloak's lies won't fly anymore. That's our goal."

Gage stood closest to the blueprints pinned to the wood-paneled wall.

"There are three entrances to the base," Gage said. "The easiest way in would be through the emergency transport running through the Gloom, but since this was how Alex snuck out to meet with Kirbie, I think it's safe to assume the High Council has taken measures to block it."

"No telling what would be waiting for us at the safe house apartment either," Mallory added.

"Right," Gage said. "And, worst-case scenario, they've somehow rigged the transporter to trap its user within the Gloom."

"But that's what we want, right?" Kyle asked. "Can't we just use that to get in and find the Rangers?"

"Not unless we have a way out," Alex said. "Which we don't."

"We could use the several miles of tunnel connecting Cloak's underground garage at the base to the surface," Gage continued. "But that option is by far the most time-consuming, and leaves us trapped should something go wrong."

"So we take the main elevator," Mallory said.

"Right. There's an elevator that goes through the center of the base, accessible from the surface. The entire facility is basically run from the first level. That's where all security systems are set up, as well as the monitoring instruments for the artificial environment—the temperature and oxygen levels. My workshop is here," Gage said, circling a spot on the blueprints. "This is where they would be keeping the other half of the Umbra Gun. We get in, grab the container and anything else helpful, and leave. We go out the same way we came."

"And you're sure that will work?" Amp asked.

"Positive," Gage said. "I did upkeep on most of the systems myself, and I can't imagine that Cloak would revamp their entire base when they're not even sure that I survived the Justice Tower ordeal."

"All right," Amp said. "But how do we get in and out without battling Cloak henchmen or the Betas?"

"I can hack in remotely and reboot the security system without much issue," Gage said, a hint of pride in his voice.

"As I said, the three levels are connected by the elevator, and that will be easy enough to disable once we're there. As for the Unibands—the 'henchmen' you're referring to—my plan is to adjust the oxygen flow to the first level of the base, where they live and work. There are several gases that make up the artificial environment underground. It's merely an issue of adjusting the mixture to knock out any occupants."

"Is that safe?" Kirbie asked. "I mean, it wouldn't kill them, right?"

"They'll pass out. But I'll make sure they have enough oxygen to prevent any permanent damage."

"What about the kids?" Mallory asked. "The Gammas who are living below."

"They wouldn't be affected."

"But neither would Titan and Julie," Amp said.

"Right. We'd have no way of knowing where they are within the base."

"Which is part of what makes this too dangerous," Alex said. "One thing goes wrong and we're trapped down there."

"We're trapped up here," Amp said. "We can't take Cloak out without the Rangers. And those monsters—your *family*—are looking for us. It's only a matter of time before they find us. We can't just sit around waiting for that to happen. They're already using the media against us. Who knows what's coming next?"

"He's right, Alex," Mallory said. "I don't want to go back there any more than you do, but we're no match for Cloak alone."

Alex grimaced but didn't respond.

"You're sure the High Council will be gone in two days?" Kirbie asked.

"According to the schedule I've intercepted from the Uniband computers, yes," Gage said. "It's an annual black-tie affair in New York City they've gone to every year for as long as I can remember. Some party thrown by a gang of criminal kingpins called the Guild of Daggers. The former High Council allied with them."

"After their victory over the Rangers, I'm sure they wouldn't miss the chance to gloat," Mallory said.

"Let's hope they're not recruiting new members," Kyle said.

"Even if they're alerted that we're there, Phantom's transportation through the Gloom isn't instantaneous," Gage continued. "It would take them hours to get back that way. I'm not even sure it would be possible to travel so far through the Gloom. They'll probably take the jet, anyway."

"Of course they have a jet," Amp muttered.

"This is a one-time opportunity," Gage said. "Right now we have the element of surprise. They won't expect us to infiltrate the base, but once we've made this move, they'll no doubt realize that I'm alive and watching them. I'm sure they'll black out my observation."

There was silence as they stood around, letting this sink in.

"Then we don't fail," Alex said finally. "But we can't all go, in case something happens and we get trapped or run into the Council."

"So who, then?" Kirbie asked.

"Me, Alex, and Mallory," Gage said. "The base was our home. We know it. And we've dealt with Julie and Titan before, if it comes to that."

"No," Amp said. "It can't be all the Betas who go."

"What?" Alex asked. "Do you think we're going to get inside and realize that we wanted to be Cloak members after all? I thought we were past that."

Amp frowned. "No. It can't be all Betas because if something happens and you're captured, we lose our inside knowledge. Kirbie and I will go with you and Gage. If we run into trouble, you and Kirbie will handle it while I cover Gage. Kirbie's been there before, so at least she knows what to expect."

"Those are excellent points," Gage said, nodding. "But I would remind you that I'm not completely helpless."

"Maybe not," Amp said. "But you're the only one who has any idea how to get us into the Gloom. If we lose you, we're done for."

Gage had looked ready to argue his ability to defend himself but remained silent. He wasn't used to being considered such a valuable asset, much less by his former enemy.

"So the four of us will go," Amp said.

"Mal, is that okay with you?" Alex asked.

"Yeah," she said. "It makes sense."

"Kyle?" asked Kirbie.

"Sure," he said.

"The question is, how do we get there?" Amp asked, staring at the map of Sterling City pinned to the billiard table. "We can take the bus out to the edge of the city, but that leaves miles of highway and open space between us and the elevator."

"We could take a car," Alex suggested.

"You mean *steal* a car," Amp said.

"We would bring it back," Alex explained.

"There are so many things wrong with that idea," Kyle said.

"Would you prefer we hitchhike?" Alex asked. "Or take a cab? Having it drop us off at an abandoned drive-in wouldn't be hard to explain or anything."

"The Betas *did* go through extensive training in operating motor vehicles," Gage said.

"Forget it," Amp said. "A car is out. Lone Star would never be okay with us breaking so many laws and risking our lives like that."

"Lone Star isn't here," Alex said, his voice rising. "And he won't be unless you're willing to bend a few rules."

"I'm not becoming one of the villains in order to save the heroes," Amp said, his voice booming as he took a step toward Alex.

"Kirbie," Mallory interjected, "what about you? Could you carry the three of them in your bird form?"

"No," Kirbie said, biting her lip. "I mean, I'd have to take them one at a time. I'd need both talons to secure them."

"What if you had some sort of box to carry them in or something?" Mallory said. "Could you handle the weight?"

"I'm not sure."

"There's an inflatable raft in the garage," Gage said. "I could rig some rope to one of them."

"We can try it," Kirbie said. "I've never carried that much weight before. I'd want to test it out here."

"Over the water," Amp said. "And at night. The cove is private enough, but a giant bird carrying a raft full of people is asking for trouble. And we'd have to figure out a way to camouflage it."

"Let's not worry about that until we know I can do it," Kirbie said. "One step at a time."

"There is another option," Gage said. He turned to look out the window at Misty.

"No," Alex said. "We're not bringing Misty into this."

"She carried all of us three times that distance the night of Justice Tower," Amp said.

"And it knocked her out for half a day."

"She's been training aggressively," Gage said. "A few days ago she moved a boulder across five acres and barely broke a sweat."

"It's too dangerous," Alex protested.

"I agree," Kirbie said. "She's just a kid."

"A kid who's been training for things like this since before she even had powers," Mallory said.

Alex shot a look at Mallory, surprised to hear *her* defending Misty's inclusion.

"She wouldn't have to enter the base," Mallory continued. "She could stay topside, away from the action. I'm not saying I'm happy about the idea, but it might be our best bet. Besides, we can't keep hiding things from her and leaving her out. If we keep telling her she's not ready, it's only a matter of time before she tries to prove herself on her own."

Alex was quiet. He turned to look out the window at Misty, then at Kirbie, his eyes pleading.

"All right," Kirbie said. "It's late. Let's sleep on all this and regroup in the morning. Maybe we can come up with something better by then. Amp, we'll need to make sure we know these blueprints by heart before this goes down."

Amp nodded, and they dispersed. Alex remained behind, staring at the blueprints of the base, wondering what it would feel like to be back inside. Not as someone who lived there, but as an intruder. An enemy.

After dinner the next day, Alex left Amp inside to keep Bug occupied while he went down to the water. Everyone else seemed satisfied that Bug meant them no harm, but Alex felt it would be best to leave the boy out of the loop as far as their raid on the underground base was concerned, just in case. He found Kirbie on the dock with Gage, where they stood around a bright yellow inflatable raft. Mallory and Kyle were a few yards away, concentrating on the surface of the lake. Every few seconds, a small mound of moss rose from the water—Kyle's doing—and Mallory's hands shot forward, destroying it with a single blast of heat. Target practice.

"How's it going?" Alex asked.

"Okay," Kirbie said. "I flew with the straps Gage attached in my talons, but the wind resistance was killer. We're about to try a test flight with people in the raft to see if the added weight will help balance it in the air."

"It's good you're here," Gage said. "You can help keep the raft stabilized."

"Should I get in?" Alex asked.

"Eventually, yes," Gage said. "For now I'm hoping you'll

just keep me from getting wet if I end up falling out of this thing. We'll try it with three people if this trial works. Kyle, you can take your place now."

Gage climbed over the side of the raft and took a seat. Kyle jogged over and followed suit.

"You guys ready?" Kirbie asked. Gage nodded.

She jumped off the dock, her body changing into her bird form in midair. Her golden wings spread wide just above the lake, talons dragging across the surface of the water. She made a quick turn before grasping the two handles that Gage tossed above his head. When the ropes attached to the handles pulled tight, the raft flew off the dock with a jerk and swung out over the water.

"I have to admit," Mallory said, stepping up beside Alex, "if that's how you're getting to the base, I definitely don't mind staying behind."

Alex let out a short laugh but kept his thoughts focused, trying to keep the raft steady. Even without being inside, he could feel the air pressure pushing down on the inflated vessel and the slight tremble in Kirbie's talons as she turned at the end of the cove. Her wings flapped with increasing swiftness, but the raft was dropping slowly, weighing her down. Gage and Kyle clung to the sides, the wind rushing through their hair, afraid to move too much.

As they neared the dock, Kirbie let out a screech, the

added pounds finally getting the best of her. The handles slipped from her grip. Alex slowed the raft down, but it was Kyle who provided them with a soft landing, summoning a bed of thick moss to the surface of the water. They sank into it like a pillow. Alex pulled the raft in as Kirbie landed on the dock and morphed.

"I'm sorry," she said, breathing heavily. "Let me rest for a minute, then maybe I can try again with just one person and work my way up."

"I could feel the strain," Alex said as he helped Gage and Kyle onto the dock. "It's not your fault—it's just too much weight."

"Perhaps I could fashion a nylon covering to go over the top," Gage suggested. "We could use Mallory's powers to heat the air and cause it to float."

"You want to make a hot-air balloon?" Kyle asked. "Isn't that a little . . . easy to see coming?"

"I would *camouflage* it, of course," Gage said.

"What are you guys doing down here?" Misty asked, materializing beside Alex. She'd appeared out of nowhere. As usual. "Where are you going in a hot-air balloon?"

"It's nothing important," Alex said, not wanting to rouse her suspicions. He still hoped they wouldn't have to get her involved. Besides, it would be better to tell her about it after they returned safely, or else she'd fear for their safety while they were gone.

"You're going on a mission, aren't you?" she asked. "You're going out after Cloak."

"It's nothing you should worry about, okay?" Alex insisted.

Misty clenched her jaw, the edges of her hair beginning to break apart. She reached out and grabbed Alex's arm, and before he knew what was going on, he could feel himself floating. He could see the sky rushing overhead, but he didn't have control over his body—he couldn't even *see* his body. Then in a flash he was back, and he dropped, plunging into the middle of the private cove.

Alex surfaced, sputtering. "Misty!" She was back on the dock, arguing with Mallory about something. He began a clumsy stroke, his clothes and shoes heavy in the water, when a set of talons grabbed onto his shoulders and lifted him into the air, carrying him to land and dropping him on the shore. Kirbie transformed from her bird to human form as Alex caught his breath.

"Alex could have drowned," Mallory yelled at Misty as they ran over to him.

"It would take more than a little lake water to hurt Alex," Misty said, refusing to apologize.

"Are you okay?" Kirbie asked.

"Y-yeah," Alex stammered. "Just a little cold."

"Here," Mallory said, holding her hands out. Heat enveloped Alex and dried him almost completely after a few moments.

"You guys can't keep doing this!" Misty said. Her voice was angry, but her expression was sad. "You can't keep me in the dark about what's happening just because I'm a little bit younger than you. If I don't know what's going on, then it's like I'm not really a part of this not-team."

"I know," Alex said. "I'm sorry."

"What if you went on a secret mission and something happened and you never came back? What would I do then? This is serious, Alex. You treat me like I'm just some little kid, but you keep forgetting that *I'm* the one who always ends up saving you guys."

"You're right," Alex said.

"Now," she said. "What's going on?"

Alex looked at the others. Kirbie gave him a slight nod.

"Okay," he said. "You up for a challenge tomorrow night?"

"Well . . . ," Misty started, then stood up tall. "Of course I am."

"Good," Alex said. "Because you're going to be transporting four of us over a long distance. From the edge of the city to the underground base."

"Five," Kyle said, before a stunned Misty could respond. "I'm sure Misty would be fine waiting for you guys outside by herself, but it wouldn't hurt to have some backup."

"What about the house?" Alex asked. Kyle had fallen into the role of guarding the lake house anytime the others were gone, since his powers were perfect for defending a base surrounded by plants and trees.

"I'll be here," Mallory said. "Any intruders show up, and they're toast."

Misty started in on a long list of questions.

"Why are we going to the base? Are we attacking the High Council? How are we getting in without being caught?"

"Let's all get back inside and we'll talk everything out," Alex said.

Everyone turned and started back to the house. Alex put his hand on Mallory's shoulder, holding her back for a moment as the others followed Misty's excited sprint toward the patio.

"What's up?" Mallory asked.

Alex paused.

"It's going to be strange being back there," he said.

"You don't have to do this," she said. "I can go instead of you. We both know I've had luck taking on Titan before."

"Thanks," Alex said. "I'll be fine. But Mal, promise me something."

"What?" she asked.

"Don't let Bug out of your sight while we're gone. And if we don't come back—if something goes wrong—don't try to rescue us. Take Misty and Kyle and the diamond and get as far away from Sterling City as you can. Because if the High Council captures us, we're either corpses or brainwashed soldiers, and the last place I want any of you to be is within their reach."

Mallory stared at him long and hard. Reluctantly, she nodded.

7

THE UNDERGROUND
BASE

Late the next afternoon they took a bus to the outskirts of Sterling City to make sure they didn't tire Misty out with an unnecessarily long sublimation. They loitered around an empty construction site until the sun finally set. Kirbie wore Alex's old Cloak trench coat over her Ranger uniform, which Alex might have found amusing under different circumstances. Gage carried a black backpack that held his laptop and several other supplies. Misty practically vibrated with excitement as they joined hands and began to break apart in the light evening breeze.

They reconstituted in a field about a mile away from the Big Sky Drive-In, at the base of a small hill, far enough away that any Cloak security systems would be unable to detect them. By then the sky was dark, a half-clouded moon their only light.

"How are you feeling?" Alex asked Misty.

"I'm okay," she said. She stood tall, but her breathing was heavy, a sheen of sweat on her forehead.

"You did great," Alex said, smiling at her. "Now you can just relax and rest up for the trip back."

Kyle walked over to one of several mesquite trees dotting the area. He reached out to the tree, and it leaned toward him, one of its limbs stretching out toward the ground.

"You two will be okay here, Kyle?" Kirbie asked.

He grinned. "These branches are covered in two-inch thorns—and that's without my powers causing them to grow. Don't worry about us. If anything goes wrong, I'll live up to my code name."

Gage removed a walkie-talkie from his bag and handed it to Misty.

"Keep this on, but only use it if there's an emergency," he said. "We'll meet you back here when we're done."

Alex stepped up beside Gage and pressed a watch into Misty's other hand.

"If we're not back in an hour, you and Kyle get out of here, okay?"

"But—"

"We'll be fine," Alex said, to himself as much as to

Misty. "If that happens, we'll just meet up at the lake house later."

Misty looked down at the watch and nodded.

"Okay," Amp said. "Let's get going."

Kirbie handed over Alex's coat and changed into her bird form. She took to the sky, making sure to fly high enough over the base to be undetectable. She was looking for stray Unibands or anyone else who might have been topside. Meanwhile, the others headed toward the base on foot. As they walked, Alex used his powers to hold Gage's laptop up in front of the inventor, who was typing furiously on the keyboard. After a few minutes, he closed the computer and pulled it from Alex's mental grasp.

"All right," he said. "The oxygen levels are adjusted and on a timer, so they'll be back to normal once we arrive. The Unibands should stay knocked out. Security is rebooting, and all the cameras are on loop. I believe that means we're a go."

They continued, crossing through empty fields and ducking under barbed-wire fences. They were at their most vulnerable in these moments, in the open, and Alex was relieved when they reached the line of trees that kept the Big Sky Drive-In hidden from the highway. They moved slowly, keeping their eyes darting about, looking for anything out of the ordinary. Only Gage seemed calm, positive that he'd disabled all the security systems.

When they got to the old parking lot in the center of the theater, Gage quickly headed over to the projection booth and pried off a side panel, exposing the maintenance box for the elevator that would take them underground. Kirbie landed and took her human form once more.

"So this is it?" Kirbie whispered, looking around at the dilapidated ruins.

"Don't go into the snack bar," Gage murmured as he twisted a few wires together. "That's where they trained the Betas to make and disarm booby traps. There are probably a few live ones still set up."

Alex looked around. So little time had passed since he'd stood among the rusted speaker poles and rotting screen, but it felt like it had been ages. For years he'd spent every morning jogging around the deserted parking lot. He'd learned to harness his powers on the ground they were now standing on. He would never tell the others—he barely admitted it to himself—but he felt proud of the place, of the afternoons and energy he'd spent there. Of what he had accomplished.

"All this time," Amp said, "and you were right here outside the city. I told Lone Star over and over that our priority should have been to search for the rest of Cloak and put you away. But they wanted to believe you were gone for good, and that Cloak was so wounded they'd never resurface. We should have known better. We should have found you."

"*Them*," Alex corrected. "And it wouldn't have done any good. How do you imprison someone like Phantom, who can sink into the shadows? Or Barrage? Or my mother? Anyone with a brain would be her slave. I hope Lone Star and the others have a plan to contain the High Council."

"One step at a time," Kirbie said. "We'll worry about that once we've rescued them."

"Kirbie. Gentlemen," Gage said, as he replaced the metal siding. "I give you the underground base of the Cloak Society."

Instantly Amp took a grounded stance a few yards from the projection booth, his hands in front of him, pulsing slowly. But when the door slid open, there was nothing but the gleaming silver interior of the elevator, impossibly sleek compared to the Big Sky's shabbiness. Gage entered, and the others filed in behind him.

They rode in silence to the first level, all three crouched and ready to attack—but again, the doors opened to nothing but a pristine lobby of darkly stained cement floors and metal walls. Gage tinkered with the wiring, and the lights inside the elevator went dark.

"Okay," he said. "We should be alone."

"I wouldn't say 'alone,' exactly," Alex said quietly.

Right outside the elevator a Uniband lay on the ground, sprawled out as if he'd been overcome very suddenly with the urge to nap. Kirbie rushed to his side, her fingers feeling for a pulse at the man's throat. She looked up at the others and nodded.

"He's fine," she said quietly. "Just passed out."

They followed Gage into a room to the right of the elevator, where the base's security and environmental functions were monitored. Two more Unibands lay hunched over on the desk, one of them drooling, both breathing softly.

"Oxygen levels are stabilized now," he said. "But if any of you feel faint, try to take deep breaths and stay calm. We've got about fifteen minutes before our sleepers start to wake up."

"Let's get what we came for," Kirbie said. "Being back here is giving me the creeps."

They hurried down the hallway. It was strange for Alex how *familiar* everything was. Not just the look of it all, but the sound of footsteps reverberating through the halls, the scent of recycled air—he even thought for a moment he could smell whatever it was that his mother used on her hair floating in the corridor, a scent he'd never given much thought to until now.

The workshop also had a recognizable smell, the acrid scent of machines and electronics. Gage stopped in front of his old workstation, below the oversized Rembrandt painting his father had cherished.

"It's weird being here, isn't it?" Alex asked.

"You have no idea," Gage said. "I thought I'd never see this place again. Or these half-finished projects. Or this painting . . ." His voice began to trail off as his eyes focused on a boxy metallic object. "Or this."

Sitting right there on the counter was the containment unit for the Umbra Gun.

"Is that it?" Amp asked.

"Yes," Gage said, stroking one side of it. He picked up a few loose papers and notes from the table. "It seems they've had my former assistants trying to figure out its functionality. But by the looks of these notes, they've barely begun to understand its most basic elements."

"Good news at last," Alex said.

"Amp, keep guard at the door," Gage said, pulling a rolled-up black duffel bag out of his backpack. "Alex, grab all the notes on that workspace, whether they're mine or not. They may give some hint as to Cloak's next move. Kirbie, will you help me gather a few things we could use back at camp?"

Kirbie rushed to Gage's side as he tossed his backpack to Alex.

"And grab the Umbra Gun, too, of course," he added.

Alex carefully placed the container of Phantom's distilled energy into the bottom of the backpack and then began shoving all the journals and loose papers he could fit inside. Gage directed Kirbie around the workshop as he gathered shiny tools and specialized equipment.

"All right," Gage said, zipping up his bag. "Let's get back to the elevator."

"Wait." Amp said. "Just a second . . ."

"Amp," Kirbie said. "Let's go."

"The War Room," Amp continued. "If the High Council is gone, the War Room is empty, right? That's where anything that might clue us in to Cloak's plans would be."

"We don't know that for certain," Gage said.

"But it's the best lead we have," Amp said. "If we can get to the War Room, we might be able to find out exactly what Cloak is up to next."

"That's not the plan," Kirbie said.

"The elevator would take us straight down there, right?" Amp asked.

"Well, yes," Gage said.

"You guys, this is our *one* chance," Amp said. "You said it yourself, Gage. We're here. Let's take some initiative."

"Amp's right," Alex said grimly. "It's our best bet."

He looked at Kirbie, who clenched her fists at her side and nodded.

"Okay," Gage said. "Two minutes down there. That's all. I don't want to have to deal with any Unibands waking up and causing a commotion."

They hurried back to the elevator, and in seconds were heading down into the heart of Cloak's operation. As they passed the second level, the place Alex had called home, his heart thumped. He didn't realize he was holding his breath until they reached the bottom floor, and as Gage disabled the elevator once more, he slowly exhaled.

They walked carefully, listening for footsteps, but the floor seemed deserted. Kirbie's eyes darted around. She was clearly anxious at being so close to the cell where she'd been held prisoner.

Inside the War Room, there was a faint scent of charcoal—a sure sign that Barrage had been in the room earlier that day. The Junior Rangers looked around with a combination of curiosity and disgust at the stacks of weapons, papers, and electronic devices littering the walls and shelves. Alex let his fingers trail along the side of the long, dark table, his eyes focused on the inlaid mark of Cloak, a gleaming skull that matched the one on his bruised palm.

Gage found an electronic pad and stood in front of a screen on the wall. Not long ago he'd used it to pull up blueprints for Cloak's attack on Justice Tower. Now he hoped it might give them insight into Cloak's newest mission. He paused for a moment, narrowing his eyes at the electronic pad as he tapped away.

"They've changed the security measures on *this* device, at least," he said. "Let's see if I can bypass them."

"What else should we be looking for in here?" Amp asked. "Any ideas, Alex?"

"Guys," Kirbie said, picking up a set of papers off a nearby counter. "Look at these."

Amp came to her side and looked down at renderings of a structure that was not quite a tower, though a portion of it jutted into the sky with an angry point. It was a dark gray, with silver accents along the tall, thin windows. The building was triangular, almost like a craggy pyramid, and had an undeniably insidious look to it.

"What is this?" Amp asked. "It's no place I've ever seen in Sterling City."

"Not yet," Kirbie said as she sifted through more renderings of the building. She held one up for Amp to see. "Look at the skyline around it. They're going to build it on top of Justice Tower."

Amp grabbed the paper from her and glared at the structure.

"Alex." Kirbie turned to him. "Come look at this."

But Alex was lost in thought, standing at the end of the long table behind a chair he'd sat in countless times while discussing missions and the future and the glory of Cloak. His eyes were fixed on a map of Sterling City that was laid out on the table. Notes were scribbled all over it, with pins and small stickers dotting every few inches. There was a cluster of markings in the area surrounding Silver Lake, though thankfully nothing pointing directly to the lake house. But the notes were damning enough. *Unusual bird reported to Parks and Wildlife Department,* one line read. *Possible Amp sighting,* read another.

There was something else weird in the Silver Lake territory: a small horseshoe-shaped pin. There were two more identical pins on the map—one in Victory Park, and another to the south.

"This is bad," Alex murmured.

"What is it?" Kirbie asked.

Before Alex could answer, an alarm was blaring, filling the room and echoing out into the halls of the third floor. The screen on the wall in front of Gage was now white, a black skull grinning back at them from the center.

AN UNWELCOME
REUNION

"Oh no," Gage said over the noise.

"Make it stop!" Alex yelled.

"I'm locked out," Gage said, tossing the electronic tablet away and moving to a computer terminal against the wall.

The decibel level of the alarm fell as Amp rubbed his hands together. His body pulsed in time with the noise, absorbing as much of it as possible.

"Is this the source?" Amp asked, pointing to the computer terminal beside Gage.

"Yes. Give me a moment."

Amp shot his palm forward, unleashing the stored-up sound energy in a single blast, destroying the equipment. The alarm stopped. For a moment, they were all very still, as if any motion might set it off again. Finally Kirbie spoke.

"Move," she said.

They darted for the door, but Alex stopped and ran back to the table. He rolled up the map, the pins scattering onto the floor, and shoved it into his backpack, along with several of the blueprints Kirbie had been looking at.

"This is bad, this is bad, this is bad, this is bad," he chanted.

Outside the War Room, he froze. He could swear he'd heard a noise coming from the hallway where he'd once been held prisoner. Alex couldn't be sure, but it had sounded like a shout—like something human.

"Alex!" Kirbie yelled. "Come on!"

He ran to join the others. If there was someone in the cells down the hallway, they'd have to wait for the Rangers to save them.

"Stay calm, everyone," Gage said as he fiddled with the elevator wires. "Outgoing communications should still be jammed. Even if they aren't, we'll be out of here before the Council returns."

"Okay. So we get to the surface, disable the elevator, and break for Misty," Alex said, going over their exit strategy one more time.

"I'll fly ahead," Kirbie said. "Follow my lead."

As the elevator began to rise, there was a light thump on the ceiling. Before any of the passengers could respond, a second, much heavier object hit the top of the elevator, causing the entire carriage to shudder. The four-some stared breathlessly at one another, but the elevator continued to rise past the second level, heading toward the surface.

"Someone's up there," Kirbie whispered.

"But they'll be crushed if we reach the top," Amp said.

"Not necessarily," Gage said softly.

The elevator passed the first level. Alex held tightly to the straps of his backpack, watching the ceiling, willing the elevator to continue. But just when it looked like they would reach their destination, they stopped abruptly.

"That's what I was afraid of," Gage said.

"It's Titan," Alex said. "He's wedged himself between the elevator and the surface, blocking our exit. The other thud must have been—"

Five long, clear talons broke through the top of the elevator, causing everyone inside to duck down and cry out. They tore parallel gashes along the ceiling, until Alex could make out a narrowed eye squinting through the torn metal, and a hint of black hair.

"You should have stayed dead," Julie said, before shoving her clawed hand back down in another attack. But before she could slice criss-cross patterns into the ceiling and shower bits of metal down on them, her claws stopped. Alex had managed to hold her in place with his mind. She cursed as she pulled against his thoughts.

"We've got to get out of here," Amp said. "They'll break through any minute." His fingers searched the smooth metal floor for an escape hatch. No luck.

"I'm taking us back down to the first level," Gage said, his hands once again in the wires. "It's our only way out now."

"I thought you said the transporter was suicide," Amp said.

"It is," Alex said, as the elevator began to descend. "We head for the garage through the entrance in Gage's workshop. We'll take a car. It's the only option now."

"We shouldn't be driving—," Amp started.

"Not the time, Amp," Alex said. "It's that or the Gloom."

Julie's claws began to shrink down and turn flesh colored, disappearing from view and slipping out of Alex's grasp. The others stayed huddled near the floor, listening for signs of movement above them. Then a fist broke through the center, accompanied by a shout of rage. The metal bent down on either side of the thick hand, scraping it from thumb to forearm, exposing a shiny silver layer beneath the skin. Before anyone could react, Titan was peeling back the top of the elevator, as if it were nothing more than an oversized aluminum can. Alex pulled down on the metal with his thoughts, but Titan's brute strength overpowered him.

When part of the ceiling was ripped away, Julie looked down through the hole, her face a scowl of pure hatred.

Her hair—usually twisted up in twin balls on either side of her head—shot out wildly on either side. She wore a black T-shirt and pink fleece pajama bottoms. She must have sprung straight from bed at the sound of the alarm. The High Council would have been proud of the pair's prompt response. Titan was dressed in a black tank top and gray mesh shorts. His blond crew cut was longer than Alex remembered it being the last time he saw him, frozen in Justice Tower. Alex was surprised to see not anger, but satisfaction on Titan's face. He smiled at Alex, his grin wide and toothy.

"Welcome home, Knight," he said.

The elevator door slid open.

"Go!" Amp yelled. He thrust a vibrating palm into the air and shot a blast of sound upward, catching Julie by surprise and sending her reeling backward, falling out of view as the others rushed out of the elevator.

They ran as fast as they could down the hallway, but Titan trailed behind them by only a few yards and was gaining on them with every step.

"Incoming!" Amp shouted from the back of the group. Alex looked over his shoulder just in time to see Titan hurling a torn-off chunk of metal from the elevator toward them. Amp dodged its trajectory, and Alex feebly pushed energy toward the object, but the metal was moving too quickly. It struck him in the back, the backpack absorbing most of the impact as he was sent sprawling onto the ground, sliding across the smooth cement floor.

The Umbra Gun! Alex hoped it was okay, but now wasn't the time to check. Titan rushed toward him and for a moment, the scene felt very familiar, one that had played out countless times before. Alex's mind knew just what to do. He focused his powers on Titan until he sparked with blue energy. Then Alex pushed, fear and anxiety fueling his telekinetic power. Titan flew backward through the air, letting out a frustrated yell. He hit the ground in front of the elevator, bounced once, and smashed against the wall with a resounding clang.

Julie stepped out of the elevator, but a sonic burst hit her in the stomach, taking her to the ground. Alex was back on his feet and running to the others in no time. For some reason, everyone was gathered outside the doors to Gage's old workshop. By the time Alex joined them, Gage was prying the door-control mechanism off the wall. Amp stood beside him, his eyes narrowed in extreme focus as he fired off blast after blast of energy down the hall at Julie, who'd ducked back into the elevator.

"What's wrong?" Alex asked, catching his breath.

"We're locked out," Gage said. "Whatever new security they've installed downstairs locked this place down remotely."

"But the elevator—"

"I manually bypassed it from the beginning, which I'm trying to do now," Gage said, pulling wires out of the new hole in the wall.

"How much time?" Kirbie asked.

"I'll need a few minutes," Gage said. "And a few more once I'm in, assuming the garage door is similarly affected."

At the end of the hallway, Titan was back on his feet. He sprinted toward the group, his top lip raised in a snarl. One of Amp's blasts landed directly on Titan's chest, but it just bounced off, not slowing him a bit.

"I can hold off Julie," Amp said, his eyes never leaving his targets. "But Titan is pretty much immune to my powers."

"Then we'll keep him occupied," Kirbie said.

"I can't keep pushing him back," Alex said, a flood of past failures against his former teammate filling his mind. "It takes a lot of energy to stop him."

As Titan ran by the elevator, he scooped Julie out with one hand and said something to her. Julie's face twisted in confusion, but before she could say anything, her brother planted his feet and tossed her as a human projectile toward the group.

"Everybody down!" Amp said.

Julie flew above their heads. As she passed over them, Alex got his first good look at her. Her entire arms were crystal clear now, with razor-sharp spikes jutting from her elbows and shoulders, ripping out of her T-shirt. Her training was showing results. She landed neatly on the other side of them, crouched, ready to attack.

"Clever boy," Gage muttered, realizing Titan's strategy as he pulled wires from the exposed panel. "He's been paying attention in class."

Alex nodded solemnly. Titan was dividing their powers.

"We're fighting on two fronts now," Amp said as he turned to face Julie. "You two take Titan and buy Gage some time. I've got Spikey over here."

"Get in close," Alex whispered to Kirbie as he slipped off his backpack and set it down beside Gage. "I'll bring him to the ground."

Kirbie nodded, her human form melting away as her body morphed and grew taller, her face and teeth extending into a beastly snout. A she-wolf on two legs, she raised her head to the ceiling and roared, a sound that Amp absorbed until, smiling, he let off a tremendous sonic boom that sent Julie tumbling head over foot down the hallway, her claws gouging into the cement floor in an attempt to stop herself.

"What's the matter, Alex?" Titan asked as he stepped toward them. His voice was confident, his arms spread wide in mock confusion. "No 'hello' after all this time? You have no idea how glad I was when Phantom told us she couldn't sense your presence in the ruins of Justice Tower. How *happy* I am that I get to face you again."

"Talking always got you into trouble," Alex said, his thoughts wrapping around Titan's feet. "Don't you ever learn?"

Titan sneered. Kirbie charged.

Alex waited until Titan reared back, preparing for a mighty punch, then pulled the boy's legs out from under him. Titan began to fall backward, and Kirbie jumped, her feet catching his shoulders. He landed on his back with a loud *crack* as Kirbie leaped off. She twisted around in the air and landed on the other side of him, ready to strike again.

Not giving the Beta a chance to recover, Alex thrust his arms across his chest and sent Titan sliding sideways, across the hallway and through double doors that served as the entrance to the Uniband cafeteria. The metal doors were torn off their hinges and flew backward into the room as Titan crashed through them. If they were going to keep Titan at bay, they would have to get him somewhere more open than the hallway. The cafeteria was perfect.

Kirbie was inside before the doors hit the ground, still in wolf form. Alex followed. Titan's body knocked several metal tables and chairs skittering across the floor. He was up fast and grabbed a table, swinging it wildly and knocking Kirbie across the room.

Titan hurled the table at Alex, who just barely avoided it by falling to his knees and pressing his back to the floor, sliding across the cement.

"Give up, Knight," Titan said as Alex scrambled to his feet. "I was always the strongest of us and you know it."

"Really?" Alex asked, focusing his thoughts on one of the metal doors on the ground behind Titan. "Tell me: How long did it take you to thaw after Justice Tower?"

Titan's mouth tightened in anger as Alex brought the door rushing forward, ramming into Titan's back and wrapping around him like a silver cocoon.

"Is that all you've got?" Titan asked, already prying his way out of the trap.

There was a growl on the other side of the room as Kirbie ran forward, grabbing a metal chair off the ground with a clawed hand. She leaped on top of one of the few standing tables, then used her momentum to flip high into the air, bringing the chair down on top of Titan's head.

Titan blinked, then fell to the floor unconscious in a great, heavy heap.

Kirbie tossed the chair aside and shrank down to her human size. Alex stood awestruck.

"Are you, like, a former acrobat or something?" he asked.

"The Rangers brought in an Olympic gymnast to train us one summer," Kirbie said as she headed out of the room. "You should see Kyle's aerials."

They found Amp at the now-open doors to the workshop. Julie was practically on top of him, moving with incredible speed. She swiped at him, talons coming within millimeters of his throat, but a sonic boom sent her flying back. She disappeared down the hallway.

"Are you okay?" Kirbie asked as they reached him, her eyes fixed on several shallow cuts on his forearms.

"I'm fine," Amp said, but his breathing was heavy. "She just got a little too close."

"What's the status?" Alex asked.

"Gage is working on the inner door." He began firing more blasts down the hallway. "Julie's good. Every time I let up, she's in front of me again in no time."

Alex envisioned his former teammate crouched in wait, ready to strike. She was at an advantage here. This was her home; she knew the hallways well. But so did Alex.

"Gage must be almost done," Alex said. "You two keep him and the bags safe. I'll take care of Julie."

"But . . . ," Amp started.

Alex shook his head.

"Trust me," he said. "I got this. I'll meet up with you in a second. Don't leave without me."

Amp nodded. He faltered slightly as he began to walk, and Kirbie helped him into the workshop.

Alex walked in Julie's direction, his eyes narrowed, watching for movement. As he passed one of the doors, he held his right hand up to a square box beside it. There was a flash on the box's electronic screen, and the door slowly slid open, exposing a small, dark room—the transporter room that served as a link between the underground base and Cloak's safe house in the city. *At least this lock still works,* Alex thought, though he shuddered to think of where the transporter might send him.

"Julie?" he shouted. "What's the matter? Don't you want to play?"

A figure rounded the corner of the hallway faster than Alex expected, and she was on him in no time.

"You. Stupid. Idiot." Julie snarled as she slashed at Alex's face. He managed to duck and dodge her attacks, but her talons were close enough that he could hear the high-pitched sound they made as they sliced through the air. "Why do you keep ruining everything?"

"I—," Alex started, but the back of her hand slammed against his jaw, sending him reeling backward.

Julie charged, leading with the spike jutting out of her right elbow. Alex barely had time to hit the floor and dodge. The spike embedded itself in the metal wall. Julie pulled at it, but she was stuck. Alex stepped away from her slowly and stood in the middle of the hallway.

"I guess you haven't worked out the kinks in your shiny elbows," he said. Out of the corner of his eye, he kept watch on the open doorway behind him.

"They're new," Julie muttered. "Don't act like you're some untouchable hero now. I'd be holding your head if it weren't the High Council's orders to take any of you alive."

"Huh," Alex said, genuinely thankful for the information—at least he now had some idea of the Council's intentions. "I guess my mother hasn't given up on the whole brainwashing thing yet."

"You'll never escape us, Alex." Julie shook her head. "Sooner or later you'll end up back here. Even a traitor can be retrained. And just wait until you see what we have planned for Sterling City."

"Oh yeah? What's that?"

"Ha. Nice try." Julie grinned. "I can't wait to see your face when Sterling City falls at our feet and you realize that even though you know the truth about what's going on, no one will believe you."

In his peripheral vision, Alex saw movement. The door was sliding shut automatically. It was time to make his move.

"Poor Julie. Always such a big talker, but never really any good in a fight."

Julie's face contorted with anger as she placed her feet against the wall and launched herself at Alex. He stepped out of the way and, using his powers, sent her flying claws-first into the small, dark room. Before Julie could scramble to her feet, Alex pulled at the electronic screen beside the door. The entire box flew off the wall, leaving wires spitting electricity into the hallway. The door stopped moving, stuck with only a few inches of open space between it and the wall, a space that was quickly filled with diamondlike claws and Julie's shouts. Alex smiled.

"Say hello to my mother for me," he said as he hurried down the hallway.

He met Kirbie in the middle of the workshop.

"There you are," she said as they jogged toward the door to the garage. "Julie?"

"She's trapped for now."

"Good. Gage is working on getting the tunnel door open, and Titan hasn't resurfaced. Amp already radioed for Misty and Kyle to meet us where the tunnel empties out at Phil's Fill-Up."

The garage itself was a cavernous room that made Alex feel insignificant no matter how many times he'd been in it. But it was the fleet of vehicles inside that was really awe inspiring. There were the standard black SUVs and cars Cloak used for everyday needs, but also dozens of classic and exotic automobiles lined up against the far wall, the spoils of looting and decadence spanning generations.

Gage's fingers were flying over a computer terminal near the door. Alex stopped beside him, looking over his shoulder.

"Come on, Gage," he whispered. "Tell me we can get out of here now."

Gage stopped tapping. The screen was nothing but

an illegible mess of numbers and letters to Alex, but Gage smiled.

"Apparently they didn't think intruders would get this far," he said. "I've overridden the controls for the gate at the end of the tunnel. It will stay open until one of the Unibands wakes up and figures out how to reprogram it."

"Brilliant," Alex said. "Let's get—"

Something heavy hit the side of Alex's head, sending him flying into one of the nearby SUVs. Before his vision settled, he heard Titan's voice.

"No one moves or powers up unless you want Gage's windpipe crushed," he sneered.

Alex blinked, shaking his head. Titan stood just inside the garage. Metal gleamed at his hairline from Kirbie's earlier attack. His fingers were wrapped around Gage's neck.

"Now," Titan continued, "everyone play nice. Start by telling me where my sister is."

Alex started to talk, but something about the look on Gage's face stopped him. Gage had stopped kicking and looked perfectly calm. There was even a hint of mischief in his eyes, which Alex almost never saw from his friend.

The inventor slipped his hand into his pocket and pulled out something long and red. It looked like a normal click-top pen, but Alex knew better. Gage held it up in the space between himself and his captor. Titan let out a snort.

"What?" he asked. "Are you going to write me to death?"

As Gage clicked the end of the pen, Titan's face showed a hint of worry. But it was too late. A cloud of near-translucent gas shot out of the end of the pen, filling the air around the two boys.

"Stupid . . . ," Titan managed before collapsing. Gage fell beside him, the two sleeping peacefully on the floor of the garage.

"What just happened?" Kirbie asked cautiously.

"A Gasser," Alex said. "Titan will be out for hours. Here, help me get Gage into a car." Alex looked down at his friend, sleeping on the ground. "You dumb genius," he murmured with a laugh.

Kirbie and Alex carried him into the backseat.

"That could have gone better," Amp said.

"We're making it out alive and with the container," Kirbie said. "We can't ask for much more. I just want to be back at the lake house."

"Silver Lake," Alex murmured to himself. "We're not safe there."

"What do you mean?" Amp asked.

"The map I found in the War Room . . . ," Alex started. He'd been so preoccupied with getting everyone out of the base that he'd forgotten all about it.

"The one with the notes?" Kirbie asked. "There were a lot in Silver Lake, but nothing looked like it pointed them directly to us. We just have to lie really low."

"No," Alex said. "Not the notes. The pins."

"The horseshoes?" she asked. "What do they have to do with anything?"

"They aren't horseshoes," Alex said. He took one last look back at Titan and the door leading into Gage's workshop.

"They're Omegas."

THE FORMER
BETAS

Amp pulled the card marked OMEGAS off the wall and tossed it onto a coffee table, where Cloak's map from the War Room was spread out.

"What do we know about them?" he asked.

"Not much," Alex said. "That's kind of the point of the Omegas."

Alex, Mallory, and Gage sat on the couch, with Kyle and Kirbie in chairs beside them. Misty, exhausted from their return trip, slept downstairs. The sun was just beginning to rise, light streaming in through the windows. Bug had not yet emerged from his room. Gage, having only recently awoken from his Gasser-fueled sleep, rubbed his eyes groggily.

"A secret society's secret team," Kyle said. "Great. Things are looking better every day."

"Why don't you just start with what you *do* know?" Kirbie said. "And we'll work from there."

"Okay," Alex said. "After the Victory Park battle ten years ago, there were a lot of newly orphaned Cloak kids running around the underground base. Eventually three of the kids whose parents were killed in Lone Star's blast developed powers. They were older than me by four or five years. They became the first Beta Team. I don't remember when they made it official . . . maybe when I was seven or eight. I just remember looking at them and thinking *that's* what I wanted to be when I grew up."

"It was the first junior Cloak team," Gage said, fighting a yawn. "Before them, the powered kids in Cloak had no formal training. They basically had to figure out their powers on their own. But the new High Council demanded discipline. Shade wanted them to know their powers inside and out. The first Betas were trained rigorously. They were the perfect soldiers. Angry, bitter, and wanting very badly to avenge their fallen mothers and fathers."

"So what happened to them?" Kirbie asked.

"My generation started to emerge," Alex said. "Titan developed powers as a toddler. Mallory was brought to the base when she was six, after the High Council . . ."

"Killed my parents." Mallory finished Alex's thought.

"Right. Then Julie and I got our gifts. Once it became clear that there was another line of trainees who would soon be coming of age, the High Council thought of a better use for the older three. They graduated them and anointed them 'Omegas.' And one day, they were just gone. No one would tell us where they went, only that they were now serving Cloak in an outside capacity."

"I remember that," Mallory chimed in. "I think I was . . . nine?"

"That sounds right," Alex said. "It was about a year before I got my powers."

"It wasn't *that* long ago, then," Kirbie said.

"No, but growing up we didn't have much interaction with the Betas," Alex said.

"The Council sent them to who knows where," Gage said. "They were taught by a network of underground mentors in the ways of stealth and infiltration. And killing. The Betas you know were trained to be soldiers and strategists and the future High Council, but the Omegas were trained in the ways of death."

"They're assassins," Amp said.

"That label doesn't do them justice," Gage warned. "They're extremely intelligent spies as well. They've handled countless jobs around the world, and not a single one has ever been linked to them."

"Like what?" Kyle asked.

Gage turned to Kyle. "Have you ever wondered why there were no other great teams of superpowered heroes that rivaled the Rangers of Justice? Think about it. Every time you'd hear about a group forming, something would go wrong and the team would disband. Or the members would just disappear."

"That's true," Kirbie said slowly.

"And the Omegas are that 'something,' I take it?" Kyle asked.

Gage nodded.

"Okay," Amp said. "So what else can you tell us about them? We need descriptions and powers."

"Ghost is the oldest," Mallory said. "He has this strange, silvery-white hair. He would be around seventeen now. Very thin. Pale, even for someone who lived underground."

"In a way his powers are like Phantom's," Gage said. "Ghost is able to transfer most of his body mass into the Gloom. When he does that, he's virtually intangible in our world."

"So what?" Amp asked. "He can walk through walls?"

"He can walk through anything," Alex said. "When he's ghosting in our world, he's nothing but a shadow. You can hardly even see him. I remember walking down the hallway, and all of a sudden he'd just sink in from the ceiling and fade into view. You can imagine how useful he is as a silent killer. He appears out of nowhere and is only physically in our world when he wants to be. If we end up facing him, he's vulnerable only when he's solid, and if he's solid, it means he's attacking."

"Wait," Kyle said. "So he could be a way for us to get into the Gloom if we captured him, right?"

"Doubtful," Gage said. "He has to stay anchored in our world, never going a hundred percent into the Gloom. The times he tried to cross back and forth between planes, Phantom always had to go in and bring him back."

Kyle sat back, sighing.

"Novo is the only girl," Mallory said. "She's very tall. Blond. And quiet. But unnerving. When she looks at you, it's like she's dissecting you. I was always a little creeped out by her."

"What kind of a name is Novo?" Amp asked.

"Latin," Gage said matter-of-factly, as if this was obvious.

"What can she do?" Kirbie asked.

"Not much in terms of offense," Alex said. "But she can turn into a liquid and move around, then reconstitute herself. Kind of like Misty. It makes her pretty much impossible to harm. If she's injured, she can just melt down and re-form herself."

"Her real power is her brain," Gage said. "Novo is smart. Incredibly so. The other Omegas looked to her for leadership, even at a young age. From what I understand, she mostly did behind-the-scenes work during their missions, directing the other two."

"Then there's Legion," Alex said. "Sixteen—same age as Novo. Shorter than the others, but stocky. Brown hair. He has this amazing power where he'll be walking and suddenly there are two of him. Another person will just *step out* of him. And his clone can move around and fight—basically can do anything Legion wants him to until it gets too hard for him to concentrate, and then the copy just kind of fades away."

"Alex used to follow Legion around the halls, talking and talking," Mallory said. "Only to realize that he was following a duplicate and not the real thing."

"Thanks a lot, Mal. I just thought his powers were really cool," Alex muttered. "He was the muscle of the Omegas. Like Titan, but someone you could stand to be around for more than five minutes."

"You all have to remember that these were the Omegas as they were when they left the base years ago," Gage warned. "We have no idea how much further their training may have enhanced their powers since then."

"And you think they're in Sterling City now?" Kyle asked. "Looking for us?"

"Yeah," Alex said. "I do."

"Great," Amp said. "So in addition to a bunch of villains plotting to take over the city, we have to deal with highly trained covert operatives, who, for all we know, are closing in on us at this second."

"I don't understand why they were called in," Alex said, staring at the note card on the table. "The Omegas have always been used for missions outside Sterling City."

"Because they are trained at finding people," Gage said. "Tracking us down must be more important to the High Council than we expected."

"Or they just can't be bothered to look for us themselves," Alex said. "So they've brought in their dogs to track us down."

He found himself slightly disappointed that his parents had called in the Omegas instead of looking for him themselves.

"The High Council must be working on something big," Mallory said. "Think about it. We stopped the bomb at Justice Tower, but that's a minor setback for them. So right now they're plotting, recalculating. They're bringing in all their resources. Setting up for something."

"Like this?" Kirbie asked. She held up one of the blueprints stolen from the War Room. "What do we think this is?"

"I don't know," Alex said. His eyes burned from lack of sleep. "I can only guess that it's the future headquarters of a Cloak-run Sterling City. They'll want a base aboveground, and where better to build it than on the ashes of their biggest victory?"

"They're getting a little ahead of themselves," Kyle said.

"No, they're not," Alex said. "I mean, look at this." He waved an arm at the cluster of notes and red yarn connecting Cloak to the inner workings of the city. "They control practically everything already, and who is there to stop them? Us? Seven kids who were enemies a month ago against the High Council, the Betas, the Unibands, everyone in Sterling City who Cloak has influence over, plus three highly trained superpowered assassins? How do those odds sound to you? This city is practically theirs already."

"Alex . . . ," Mallory started, sounding unsure of what to say. Kyle looked at the ground, sulking. Kirbie stared Alex down angrily.

"No. We can win this," she said. "We got the container Gage needed, so we're close to being able to rescue Lone Star and the others. They'll know what to do."

"You don't know that for sure," Alex said.

"Yes I do," Kirbie argued.

"Then you're in denial," Alex responded. "Your faith in the Rangers is blinding you to just how bad this is."

"What would you know about the Rangers?" Kyle interjected, his voice raised. "What *Cloak* told you? You have no idea what they're really like."

"They've been stuck there for almost a month now. We don't even know what shape the Rangers will be in if we find them," Alex said quietly.

"*When* we find them," Kyle added.

They were all silent for a moment.

"Eight," someone said from the doorway.

Alex looked up to see Bug walk into the room. He wore a tattered brown henley, and his hair was all skewed toward one side. His eyes were puffy from sleep. Alex didn't know how long he'd been standing there, but it was obvious that he'd heard most—if not all—of his rant.

Great.

"What?" Kirbie asked.

"You said there were seven of you up against everybody else," Bug explained. "You forgot me."

"This isn't your fight," Alex said.

"Of course it is," Bug said. He furrowed his eyebrows slightly, as if he couldn't understand why Alex would say such a thing. "From what I can tell, it's everyone's fight. I just don't understand why you're wasting energy arguing with each other."

"It's complicated," Kyle said.

"No," Amp said. "It's not. He's right. Fighting like this is probably exactly what Cloak wants us to be doing right now."

"I ran away from home to try to help the Rangers of Justice because I believed in what they stood for," Bug said. "I thought . . . I *hoped* that when I found you guys,

I would get a chance to do that. I always thought that the Cloak Society was more legend than anything else, but I guess I was wrong. And if they're back, then they have to be stopped. No matter what it takes. You can't give up now. Not when the people need you most."

Alex glared at Bug. His speech may have sounded nice, but he had no idea what he was really talking about.

Amp turned to the wall. His eyes scanned the note cards and photos and yarn.

"What's our next move?" he asked.

"Right now the Council is probably furious," Gage said. "They'll be trying to piece together what happened at their base. From there, it will be a swift security overhaul and a redoubling of their efforts to find us. It wouldn't surprise me if they retaliate in some other way as well. They've made clever use of the media thus far, so we can expect to see our names and faces popping up next."

"They'll know we have the container," Mallory said. "They'll assume that Gage is working on a way to get the Rangers back."

"Or on a new Umbra Gun," Gage said.

"We still have a few advantages," Kirbie said. "Even if they think we're in Silver Lake, they don't know our exact location, or even how many of us survived. For all they know, it's just those of us who raided the base."

"So what do we do?" Kyle asked. "Are we stuck here

waiting for Gage to find a way into the Gloom while they're closing in on us?"

"We can't just keep waiting here, holed up," Amp said. "They know we're alive. They know we're after them. There has to be something we can do in the meantime."

"There were three Omega pins on this map. One in Victory Park, one somewhere in the south, and one here," Alex said, putting his finger down on the map, "on the edge of Silver Lake. If one of the Omegas is operating out of this area, we might be able to surprise them. They may be highly trained, but it'd be one against all of us."

"It's not much to go on," Kyle said.

"But it's a start," Amp said. "We'll take them down one by one."

"We'll have to do recon work before we strike," Mallory chimed in. "We may be able to learn more about what Cloak is up to if we can observe one of the Omegas. They won't be telling us anything willingly."

"I can help with that," Bug said. "I can have eyes everywhere."

"Obviously," Alex muttered.

"And then we attack," Kirbie said. "*We* strike first. We catch them off guard."

"Agreed," Amp said. "Once we find them, of course. And we're useless if we're not in peak condition. Everyone should take the morning to sleep. Keep up your personal training this afternoon. We'll reconvene tonight and go over the details of the mission. Bug . . . I'd better fill you in on everything you don't already know."

Bug nodded and shuffled out of the room with the others.

Gage picked up the stack of notes Alex had emptied from his backpack. "Sleep?" he murmured with a slight laugh. "I'm going down to the garage to sort through these and start work on the container."

Alex suddenly felt very tired, the battle-filled night catching up to him. He sat on the couch for a while, staring down at the map and yawning. There was something bothering him, but he couldn't pin down what it was. He almost didn't believe that he'd been back at the underground base just hours before. That he'd been back at his home, and fought his old teammates, the people he'd grown up with. Julie and Titan were power-hungry Betas, sure, but they'd also blown up balloons for Alex's birthday parties and spent movie nights eating popcorn together.

Something Julie had said kept coming back to him. The High Council wanted them alive. Did they want Alex and the others so that Shade could strip away their minds and turn them into Cloak drones? Or was it just so the High Council could make sure that they suffered until the very end, or that they lived to see Sterling City fall the same way Alex's mother had once hoped that Lone Star would watch the Junior Rangers melt into the Gloom?

And there was something else. The Omegas were out there looking for him, but his mother was not. She'd left his fate to someone else, just as she had in Justice Tower, when she disappeared as the sky was falling down around him. Despite all the terrible things she stood for, knowing this made Alex ache somewhere deep inside.

DESTINY

Alex slept off and on throughout the morning, his dreams littered with faceless Omegas and his mother's voice whispering the old Cloak nursery rhyme:

For the Glory of the Society,
I will grow mighty and strong.
For we were born to rule the weak,
And right a world that's wrong.
Hail Cloak.

He woke up in the early afternoon but was slow getting out of bed and brushing his teeth, still sluggish from the night before. When he stretched, he could feel sore muscles. There was a tender spot on the side of his head from Titan's attack in the garage and a bruise on his back from the hurled piece of metal. He shuddered to think how much worse he would have been injured if he hadn't been carrying the backpack stuffed with papers and half the Umbra Gun.

He went downstairs and found Kyle on the ground in front of the porch, huddled over a small pile of seeds. The afternoon light was bright, but the breeze off the lake was chilly. Alex shivered, wrapping his arms around himself.

"Hey," Alex said.

"Hey," Kyle replied.

"What are you doing?"

"Growing tomatoes," Kyle said. He was deep in concentration, his hands placed on either side of the seeds. Slowly they began to sprout, roots digging into the hard earth. Before a minute was over, thick vines holding plump, fist-sized tomatoes were standing upright in the air. Kyle knit his brow as his palms passed over a few of the tomatoes, reddening them, then he lowered his hands, the fruit falling softly onto the ground in response.

"Is it harder to grow things now that it's getting colder?" Alex asked. He'd seen Kyle control whole walls of plants with the flick of a wrist, but the tomatoes seemed to take extra energy.

"Not really," Kyle said, gathering the tomatoes in a big

bowl. "Tomatoes are just tough. You have to be careful not to over-ripen them."

"Huh," Alex said. He hadn't thought about this facet of Kyle's powers before. "Are you planning on making spaghetti or something?"

"No," Kyle said. "Just keeping up with my training. The more in tune I am with the plants . . ."

Suddenly the tomato vines flew into the air, twisting around one another until a thick spike jutted several feet above Kyle's head, decorated with oversized tomatoes.

". . . the easier they are to control."

Kyle plucked one of the new tomatoes off the vine, rubbed it on his shirt, and bit into it as he walked past Alex and toward the house.

"Wait," Alex said as the boy passed him. "I'm sorry if I sounded defeated talking about the Omegas. I was just really tired, and being back at the base was . . . weird. I know this has all been really hard on everyone. The Rangers especially."

Kyle turned around, his eyes meeting Alex's.

"It's been twenty-five days," Kyle said. "Twenty-five days since Cloak attacked us. I know what you did for us, and that Justice Tower could have been much worse if you hadn't been there. And I know Kirbie trusts you. She doesn't hesitate to fight beside you. But until you live up to the promise you made to us that night—until you get the Rangers back—I can't help but remember that it's because of you that my sister was locked up in a cell and had her mind hacked. And *that's* how they got by our security so easily."

"Kyle . . . ," Alex started, but he wasn't sure what to say.

"Just get them back," Kyle said. "Prove to me that in the end, all this will have been worth it."

He turned and walked inside, leaving Alex on the porch with goose bumps crawling up and down his arms from the cold.

In the garage, Alex collapsed into a lawn chair near Gage, who was leafing through the notes from the underground base.

"Find anything interesting?" Alex asked.

"Well," Gage said, drawing out the word. "Nothing I would note as surprising. The High Council was trying to replicate the Umbra Gun. They were further along in the process than I expected. They took copious notes on how it works. I'm sure we didn't manage to take them all."

"You think they have another Umbra Gun in development?" Alex asked.

"Of course they do," Gage said. "Wouldn't you, if you were on the High Council? But taking the container will definitely set them back. And they figured out how we were able to monitor them. The base has gone dark, as far as my surveillance is concerned. We've got all the information we can from them."

"Wonderful." Alex sighed. "So what about the container? Can we get into the Gloom with it?"

"I believe so," Gage said. "But it will take some time. I've been working on designs that look promising, but I want to be completely sure that whatever gateway I can create will work before I even consider any form of experimentation."

"Can't you just build one of the designs and test it out?"

"We're talking about tearing a hole in the fabric of our world, Alex," Gage said. "There are fail-safes that have to be put into place. The last thing we need is to create a portal into the Gloom that we can't close. Or worse, one that grows out of our control. Not to mention I'll have to make sure that using it won't immediately alert Phantom of our whereabouts."

"Right. Of course." Alex was starting to feel discouraged. "How long do you need?"

"A week," Gage said. "Give or take. It's hard to say exactly when I'll have a breakthrough."

"Okay. We can deal with that. We can survive until then."

"I *do* have news that will interest you, though." Gage moved over to his computer and began typing, then spun the laptop around to Alex. The screen showed a satellite view of what seemed to be a warehouse district. "I took the liberty of looking into real estate in the area of Silver Lake where you saw the Omega pin. All these buildings appear to house legitimate businesses, except for this one." He pointed to a building in the center of the area. "It's a derelict warehouse that was purchased two weeks ago. I don't recognize the name, but the buyer paid in cash."

"That's our target, then," Alex said. "This is great, Gage. Thanks. I'll let everyone know."

"Alex," Gage said, reluctance in his voice. "I know the others are set on taking action, but do you really think going after the Omegas is the best plan? Even if we manage to capture one of them, they'll never talk. And we'll be exposing ourselves in the process."

"I know," Alex said, shaking his head. "But if we don't go after the Omegas, it feels like we're giving up, as much as I hate to agree with Bug. Like we're just waiting for them to take us. And who knows, maybe if we do capture one of them, we can find out a little bit more about what Cloak is doing. Maybe save a few people. At least we'll be showing the Council that we're not giving up without a fight."

"Valid," Gage said.

"Besides," Alex said with a sigh, "I think if we stay here at the lake house and don't go after the Omegas, we'll all go crazy."

They ate dinner late on account of the day's odd sleeping schedule, a mixture of sandwiches and microwaved pizzas and bags of chips strewn across the dining room table. After

Alex filled them in on the suspicious warehouse, the conversation picked up where it had left off that morning.

"Timing-wise, I think it would be best if we investigate tomorrow," Amp said, "before Cloak has a chance to fully sort out the details of what happened last night."

"Shouldn't we go at night?" Mallory asked. "For better cover?"

"Good idea. But Bug can do recon during the day," Kirbie said.

"Sure," Bug said, happy to be useful for a change. Zip's wings fluttered on his shoulder, as if in agreement. "Anything you need."

Kirbie smiled in thanks.

"I took a full set of radio communicators that double as tracking devices from the underground workshop," Gage said. "I'll make sure they're charged and ready for tomorrow."

"Mallory and I should go with Bug," Alex said. "We've got the lowest profiles."

"No, I'm coming with you," Amp insisted.

"Amp," Kirbie said. "People are looking for us. It's too risky for us both to go out. Besides, they're trained at stuff like this. Right?" she asked, turning to Mallory.

"Probably more than you've been," Mallory said. "Once we have an idea of what to expect, we'll radio back. If we all think it's doable, we'll raid the building after dark."

"Are you sure Bug's ready?" Misty asked teasingly. "He

hasn't had as much training as someone like me."

"Oh yeah?" Bug asked, holding up a slice of pizza. "Watch out, or you might wake up in a bed full of roaches."

"Hey," Mallory chimed in, "that's my bed too."

"*You* should be careful, Bug," Kyle said, grinning. "Or you'll wake up and find yourself in the middle of nowhere."

"It's true." Misty lowered her voice to an exaggerated whisper. "I'm kind of superpowerful."

Mallory almost choked on a gulp of water.

"Hey," Misty said. "Why are you laughing?"

"Seriously, guys, Misty has a point," Alex said, staring across the table at Bug. "He hasn't had training like us."

"I was just kidding, Alex," Misty said. "Stop being such a downer. What Bug does is amazing. He could be a professional . . . I don't know, what do people do with bugs?"

"Exterminate them," Alex muttered.

"I'm sure Bug will be fine," Kirbie said, munching on a sandwich. "Misty's right. He's incredible with insects, and they're perfect for recon."

"Thanks for having so much faith in me, guys," Bug said. "It means a lot to me. I think it's my destiny to have found you."

"Of course," Kirbie said, smiling.

Alex stared down at his plate. Everyone had taken to Bug—even Mallory, who'd been keeping an eye on him at Alex's request. Their new housemate wasn't going anywhere, and Alex would just have to accept that. But he didn't have to believe that Bug had been *destined* to meet them. After all, according to Cloak, it was Alex's destiny to be among their ranks again one day. Fate was something he couldn't afford to believe in.

After dinner, Alex climbed the lattice on one side of the lake house and sat cross-legged on the roof. He thought back to all the times he'd snuck out of the underground base with Gage's help to spend a few precious minutes on top of the snack bar at the Big Sky. It had always been so calming up there, so easy to sort out his thoughts and feelings. But on top of the lake house, Alex just stared into the sky. Somewhere the Omegas were looking for him and his friends. He couldn't shake the feeling that the worst was yet to come.

There was a rustling on the side of the house as someone made their way up the lattice. Amp's head poked up over the edge of the roof.

"Mind if I join you?" he asked.

"Sure," Alex said. "How'd you know I was up here?"

"My room is in the attic," Amp said, climbing onto the rough shingles. "Someone walking around on the roof isn't exactly stealthy."

He took a seat beside Alex. The two of them were quiet

for a while, staring out into space. Eventually Amp broke the silence.

"You doing okay?" he asked.

"Yeah," Alex said. "Of course. What do you mean?"

"You just seemed a little hopeless when we were talking about the Omegas this morning. I headed the Junior Rangers. I learned a few things about leading. If one of the team members starts to feel defeated, it affects everyone."

"Amp, you're not stupid. You have to see that we're facing crazy odds, right? I mean, the High Council alone is so powerful. . . . How can you be so sure everything will work out in the end?"

"Because I have to be," Amp said. "If you don't believe there's a possibility of winning, why even bother fighting?"

Alex stared down at the shingles on the roof. The breeze picked up slightly, and he shivered.

"I asked Gage how Cloak knew that the Rangers had the Umbra Gun," Amp said, staring out over the water. "Do you know?"

"Yeah," Alex said. "Phantom felt it. She said it must have been turned on for some reason."

Amp nodded. "I told you back at the drive-in that I'd urged the Rangers to look for Cloak. But what I didn't tell you was the weird way they didn't want to talk about it. Lone Star especially. If I brought up Cloak or Victory Park, he'd go really quiet and get this sort of far-off look in his eyes. So one day, I was looking around in our storage and archives and I found it. The Umbra Gun. And I was so furious. Why hadn't they told me? Why weren't we studying it, trying to find a way to get everyone back? So I turned it on. I don't even know why. And it was just for a few seconds. Later, when I confronted Lone Star about it, he told me that they'd been trying to figure out how it worked for a decade. That all kinds of scientists had analyzed it. I apologized for messing with it, but I guess by that time it was too late. I'd already tipped Phantom off."

Amp stopped speaking, lost in his thoughts for a moment.

"None of this is your fault," Alex said. "Cloak would have come for the Rangers even without the Umbra Gun. It was only a matter of time."

"You're right," Amp said, turning to look at Alex. "It doesn't matter whose fault *any* of this is. What matters is that we fight. That we make it right. And to do that, we have to think we can win. We have to *know* we can win. All of us have to believe."

11

WAREHOUSE
INVESTIGATION

A busy coffee shop was located a few blocks away from the suspected Omega building. Mallory and Alex ducked into it while Bug continued on, pulling his hood up to conceal a small communicator hooked over his ear.

Inside the coffee shop, Mallory got in line at the counter and tried to look as natural as possible, while Alex slid into a corner booth. He pulled a small electronic tablet from his bag and clicked it on. The screen lit up. He took a long look around, pretending to be searching for Mallory, making note of the shop's customers and workers. It was early afternoon, and customers were sparse. There were a handful of teenagers scattered about in small groups, a few adults typing away on laptops, and a tired-looking barista wiping down the milk-and-sugar station. No one paid any attention to Alex.

Perfect.

He looked back down at the device in his hands. Grids began to appear onscreen, and the image zoomed in, until Alex had a clear aerial view of the blocks surrounding the coffee shop. There was a green blip moving slowly across the screen. Bug. Alex plugged in a set of earbuds and put one into his right ear. A small microphone was located a few inches down the wire.

"Can you hear me?" Alex asked.

"Yeah," Bug's voice came through the tiny speaker. "No problem here."

"I've got you onscreen," Alex said. "We can start whenever you're ready."

Mallory slid into the booth next to Alex, setting a mug topped with whipped cream in front of him.

"Hot chocolate," she said, raising an identical mug in her hand. She smiled broadly, acting as if she didn't have a care in the world, and slipped the other earbud into her ear. To the rest of the coffee shop, the two of them were just a couple of kids watching a movie or playing a video game together.

"I've picked up a housefly along the way," Bug said. "I'm sending it out along with Zip, just in case I can find a way inside. I figured it would be less noticeable flying around."

"That's great," Mallory said.

"Make as big a circle as you can while you're walking," Alex said. "Don't get close to the building until you're on your way back. Try to look lost."

"That's not a problem," Bug said. "Have you ever tried to see through the eyes of multiple flying insects while navigating streets you've never been on?"

"Point taken," Mallory said as she sipped her hot chocolate.

"Okay," Bug said, "I got the fly inside through a vent in the roof. It's circulating the top floor now. It looks pretty dead to me. A lot of open space and garbage. It looks like there might have been squatters living here. Careful, little guy, there are lots of spiderwebs."

"Anything unusual so far?" Mallory asked.

"Unusual?" Alex asked, his hand covering the microphone. "He's talking to a housefly like he's an old friend."

"Not really," Bug said. "I've got Zip outside, looking for other entry points. So far all the street-level windows are barred from the inside. There are a few boarded up on the higher levels. A fire escape on the . . . southern side, I think."

"Look for basement access as well," Alex said. His eyes followed Bug onscreen. "You're about to come to a series of side streets that dead-end into one another. Take your next left, then another left. It should take you right back in front of the building."

"Okay," Bug said. "There are two big loading docks at the back of the building that are both locked down, and a normal door beside them, but nothing that looks like it goes underground. The fly is heading down to the first floor. Wait. This is weird. . . ."

"What is it?" Alex asked in a whisper.

"There are two cars parked down on the first floor. Black. Shiny. They look expensive. And it's definitely cleaner down here, nothing like it was upstairs. There's a light coming from a room in the corner. It looks like it used to be an office."

"Send the fly in," Alex said.

"Okay. There's definitely movement. The fly is going in now. I see four guys. All wearing what look like black motorcycle jackets or something. It looks like they're . . . packing?"

"Packing what?" Mallory asked.

"I don't know. Papers. Maps. Some computer equipment. Oh man, that's definitely a gun. And . . . uh . . ."

"What?" Alex and Mallory asked at the same time.

"These guys . . . they all look exactly the same. Identical haircut and hair color. Same sunglasses. Short but buff. Everything."

Alex and Mallory looked at each other. Mallory

mouthed the word "Legion." Alex nodded.

"All right," Alex said, looking back down at the screen. Bug was still a few blocks away from crossing in front of the building. "Just keep talking. Tell us everything you see."

"There's not much else. Wait. One of the guys is on the phone now. He's looking down at his watch and seems angry. The other guys are moving faster and GAHHH—"

The line went silent. The green blip stopped. Mallory and Alex froze, listening intently. It was Mallory who spoke first, trying to remain calm, though Alex could feel her temperature rising beside him.

"Bug, is everything okay?"

There was a pause.

"Yeah," Bug said, his voice markedly upset. "I lost the fly. One of the guys just snatched him out of the air. He moved so fast. . . ."

Alex leaned back in the booth, fighting the urge to yell at Bug for scaring them over a housefly. Mallory exhaled slowly and continued to coach him.

"Keep moving," she said. "Have you found a way to get Zip inside?"

"Not yet," Bug said, his blip on the screen continuing down the street. "Give me a few seconds. She's too big to go through the roof vent, but I'll get her in somehow."

Almost a minute passed before Bug spoke directly to Alex and Mallory again. During the rest of the time he was murmuring quietly to Zip, coaxing her along until she found a broken pane of glass in one of the second-floor windows.

"Okay, she's in and heading toward the office, but I'm going to keep her at a distance."

"That's fine," Mallory said. "Just tell us what you see."

"There are more of them," Bug said. "Six now. All identical. They've all got boxes in their hands except for one of them, who's looking around. I think he's making sure nothing is left behind. And . . . uh, there's a car coming."

"Inside the building?" Alex asked, leaning forward.

"No, it's outside. A big black SUV, stopping right in front of the building. I'm going to turn around."

"No!" Alex whispered loudly, staring at the map. "You're already on the block. Turning around will just look suspicious. Keep going."

"There's someone getting out of the car," Bug said, whispering now. "Oh man, I'm going to die, aren't I?"

"You're fine," Mallory said. "You're just someone walking down the street."

Once again, Mallory and Alex looked at each other. They listened carefully, but all they could hear was the slight rustle of Bug's clothes. Then, suddenly, a girl spoke.

"Hey, kid," she said.

The rustling stopped, as did Bug's green blip, positioned directly in front of the entrance to the building.

There was a pause, then, "Yeah?"

Alex and Mallory waited breathlessly. There was noise in the background and the sound of another voice, though they couldn't make out what anyone was saying.

"Never mind," the female said dismissively.

Once again, there was the rustle of Bug's clothes as his pinpoint on the map began to move. When he was farther down the block, he began to whisper again.

"The guys are loading the back of the SUV. Now they're climbing into the backseat . . . but it looks like they're vanishing once they're inside. The guy who wasn't carrying anything is getting into the front with the girl. They're driving away."

"Have Zip follow them," Alex said quickly. "We need to know where they're going."

"It's no use," Bug said. "Zip is still inside. She'll never be able to catch up with them. I'm sorry."

"It's okay," Mallory said. "You were perfect. Can you leave Zip there so we know if anyone comes back before tonight?"

"Sure," Bug said. "It's pretty gross upstairs. There should be plenty of bugs for her to eat."

"They know I took the map and they're moving camps," Alex said to Mallory. "I should have just left it."

"Alex," Mallory said, "because you took the map, they lost their notes on our location. That probably set them back at least by a day or two. That's worth it, wouldn't you say?"

"Describe the girl," Alex said into the microphone.

"She was tall," Bug said. "Blond. Maybe sixteen, but kind of gave off an older vibe. She didn't really say anything, just stared me down. She must have seen my eyes glow, even though I tried to keep them hidden. Once the guy came out, they were in a hurry to get out of there."

"Did they say anything to each other we can use?" Alex asked.

"No, I don't think so." Bug said. "They just talked about everything being packed up."

The green blip on the screen was nearing the coffee shop. Alex started to power down the electronic screen.

"Oh, there was one thing," Bug said. "He called her 'Novo.'"

"Here's what we know," Alex said, leaning against the wall in a narrow alley beside the warehouse. "Until today, Legion was using this warehouse as his base of operations. This afternoon, he packed and left with Novo. The Omegas are definitely in Silver Lake. They're looking for us."

Night had fallen. Amp stood across from Alex and Mallory, next to Kirbie, who was once again dressed in her Rangers uniform under Alex's dark coat. Bug squatted near some trash cans a few yards away from the others, his eyes glowing a golden green in the darkness. A small swarm of flies circled around the building, serving as sentries, their many eyes on the lookout for anyone who might bring trouble. Kyle, Gage, and Misty remained behind at the lake house, keeping watch over their base.

"There were three pins on the map you took," Kirbie said. "If they're each trying to find us in different areas of the city, why were two of them here today?"

"The map definitely had the most notes in this area," Alex said. "Legion's powers would come in handiest covering lots of ground fast. He could check up on half a dozen leads at the same time. Maybe more. For all we know he can make a whole army of himself now."

"So why was the girl here?"

"Novo's the backbone of the Omegas," Mallory said. "She probably wanted to oversee the transition to a new base herself. In person."

"They probably don't want to talk about any sensitive information over the phone or internet after we used their tech against them to get into the base," Alex added.

"That's a good thing," Amp said. "It means we scared them. Or at least made them look over their shoulders."

"Yeah," Kirbie said. "And it made them angry."

"So we scour this warehouse for any information we can get on Cloak, just in case Legion left something behind in the rush to move out of here," Alex said. "Then we head back to the lake house and plan our next move."

"I doubt he left anything behind, with twelve eyes at his disposal," Amp said.

"Yeah," Alex agreed. "But only one brain controlling them all. That's a lot of information to take in at once, no matter how skilled he is. Just look at *him*."

Alex pointed with his head at Bug, who didn't seem to notice that anyone was talking about him. His bright eyes were wide and darted around spastically.

"All right," Kirbie said. "How do we get in?"

"We already used Zip to check for any sort of alarm system. It appears to be clear," Alex said, stepping away from the wall. "There's a door in the back. Simple dead-bolt locks. Easy to pick."

"The perks of working with former criminals," Amp said under his breath as he walked toward Bug. Alex started to retort, but stopped when he realized Amp had said *former* criminals. Progress.

The door's locks took only a few seconds for Alex to pick telekinetically, his mind feeling out the pins and levers inside with relative ease. Before they entered, Mallory stood in the doorway, hands outstretched. Freezing air swept into the building like a fine mist. She lowered her arms.

"All right," she said. "Just checking for any laser alarms that Zip might not have seen. We're good."

They filed one after the other into the building. Alex

waited for his eyes to adjust while Kirbie pulled a few LED flashlights out of a bag she'd brought from the house and passed them around. Zip zoomed in a circle overhead before landing on Bug's shoulder.

"Good girl," Bug cooed.

The first floor was almost completely open—one big room with a cement floor and exposed brick walls. It was easy to imagine its former use as a warehouse. Two identical black cars were parked by the loading doors just like Bug said, their sleek exteriors completely out of place in the building.

"Why would he leave these here?" Kirbie asked.

"They want a completely clean slate," Mallory surmised. "New base. New cars. Cloak can afford it."

"Bug, the area is still clear, right?" Amp asked.

"Yeah," the boy replied softly, his mind lost among his insects.

"Good. Keep your eyes on our perimeter," Alex said. "Kirbie, will you help me check out these cars? Mal and Amp, you guys take the office over there in the corner."

Mallory nodded, and took off with Amp. Alex circled one of the cars and found the driver's-side door unlocked, the key sitting in the ignition.

"He must not have been too worried about security," Alex murmured. He nodded to Kirbie, who opened the back passenger door and got to work looking for anything left behind.

"This car looks totally new inside," she said.

"It probably is," Alex said as he opened the car's center console, finding nothing. "Hey, could you get his scent? Maybe we could track him or something?"

Kirbie slowly raised her head from the back floorboard, where she'd been searching beneath the passenger seat. She stared at Alex.

"Are you suggesting I act as the team bloodhound?"

"Oh no, no," Alex said, quickly trying to backtrack. "I just thought that—"

Kirbie cut him off with a disarming smirk.

"Relax," she said. "I'm kidding. It's not a bad idea. I don't even have to fully wolf out. I won't be able to track him from here, but it may help later if I know his scent."

Kirbie closed her eyes, and Alex watched as her face started to contort, her ears pointing slightly and her mouth and nose pressing forward. She opened her eyes, showing off diamond-shaped pupils, and inhaled deeply several times.

"I've found a distinct scent that's not ours," she said, her voice almost a growl. "But it's faint. Not much to go on."

Her face went back to normal.

"Anything up there?" she asked.

Alex opened the glove compartment. Inside, he found a small laser pistol like the one his mother carried and a few slips of paper, most of which were receipts or addresses with notes like *possible Misty sighting* on them. His eyes grew wide as he came to the last one.

"What is it?" Kirbie asked.

"A receipt from a gas station just a few miles from the safe house," he said.

"Is there a credit card number? Could Gage track it?"

"Cash," Alex said. He slipped all the papers and the weapon into his pocket. "I'm done up here. Why don't you take the other car and I'll check the trunk?"

Kirbie nodded and left, hopping inside the driver's seat of the next car. Alex popped the trunk, finding nothing but a spare tire and jack beneath the carpeting.

He started to close the trunk, when he heard the sound of breaking glass from somewhere upstairs. Kirbie didn't seem to have noticed, as she continued digging around inside the car beside him. He looked around and spotted an open door, which led to a set of stairs. It would be a good idea to check out the second floor, even if Bug had cleared it earlier. Bug wasn't trained like they were. Kirbie could finish scouring the cars.

There was a thick, undisturbed layer of dust covering the stairs. As Bug had said, the second floor was covered in trash and makeshift bedding, as if several people had been living there before Cloak bought the building. Remnants of a fire pit sat near the center of the room. A few sets of shelves were covered in empty bottles and discarded food containers.

Alex was halfway across the room when he heard a click

behind him. He jumped and spun around, shining his flashlight in the direction of the noise. The door to the stairwell, which had been propped open earlier, was now shut.

He froze, listening for any hint of noise or movement. The flashlight swept over the room, but Alex didn't see anyone lurking in the shadows. He'd just begun to gather energy around his right hand as a cautionary measure when something struck him in the middle of his back, sending him onto the dirty floor, the flashlight skittering away.

There was a dark-clad figure moving around the room with stealth that both impressed and terrified Alex. He would have cried for help, but the fall had taken his breath away. He struggled to regain it and counter, but the figure was too fast for him. It struck him with precision in several pressure points, keeping him off balance and unable to get to his feet.

"Stay quiet and I won't rough you up too much before calling the police," a girl's voice said with exaggerated toughness.

Police?

Alex was surprised how authoritative—but young—the voice sounded. For a moment, it reminded him of Kirbie's. His training took over. He blocked his attacker's next move, while at the same time sweeping her feet. She jumped backward and landed in a defensive crouch.

Finally Alex got his first good look at her. She had a

slight build and was dressed in dark colors, with a cropped black jacket and tall boots. There was something wrapped around her head, obscuring her entire face—except for dark eyes.

She leaped forward but, clearly not expecting her opponent to have superpowers, was caught off guard by a powerful telekinetic blast. She flew upward and back but didn't fall. Instead, what looked like a rope shot out from her body and pulled her up into the shadows of the rafters.

Alex wasted no time pulling his flashlight to him with his thoughts. He shot the beam of light around the ceiling, but nothing was there. He took a few deep breaths, listening for his opponent while gathering energy, getting ready for her next attack. He cleared his mind and focused on his breathing and the air around him.

The attack came from his right. Alex felt the disturbance in the air, just before the girl's boot made contact with his side. He twisted, and pushed his thoughts forward, wrapping her body in energy and holding her securely in the air. She tried to struggle, but it was useless. Alex shone the light on her.

It wasn't cloth wrapped around her face, but *hair* that looped around her several times. Her eyes narrowed in the light, her pupils growing small. And then her hair began to move, uncoiling itself, until it flared out in all directions around her. Their gazes locked, and for a moment, Alex saw her in color. His jaw fell open in surprise at her stunning hues. She was about his age. Her eyes were dark brown. Her hair was a deep auburn with hints of red, and it seemed to be in constant motion, serpentine locks defying gravity.

He'd seen that hair before. She was one of the Powers who'd gathered in Victory Park.

Behind him, someone pounded on the door. The girl must have locked it. Alex blinked, and his world turned blue again. It was then that he noticed that the hair at his captive's waist was pulling small, sharp-looking metal triangles from her belt: throwing knives.

Suddenly the girl's hair shot out at him, wrapping around his wrists and twisting his arms one over the other, causing him to flip and land hard on the ground, breaking his hold on her. She was on top of him in an instant, holding one of the knives up to his cheek. A rope of hair wrapped around his neck, choking him.

"Move, and you're dead," she said.

Alex struggled to speak, but it was impossible. The pounding at the door grew louder. The girl had two more knives held in her hair, ready to strike. Alex tried to get a grip on her hair with his mind, but there was something about her powers that made it resilient to his telekinesis, as if it were too slippery to hold on to.

There was a loud bang, and the door swung open. The girl crouching over Alex let out a noise of surprise. The knives clinked on the floor beside her. She unwrapped her hair from Alex's neck and rushed toward Kirbie, who stood in the doorway in her Ranger uniform.

The girl in black fell at Kirbie's feet, hair braiding itself down her back.

"It's you," she said, sounding as if she might break into tears. "I knew the Rangers weren't really dead."

She looked up at Kirbie, whose face was twisted in confusion.

"Where are the others?" the girl asked. "Where's Lone Star?"

DEL

"Alex?" Kirbie asked, taking a few steps back into the stairwell. Her nostrils flared as her face threatened to take animal form. "What's going on?"

"She attacked me," Alex managed to say. He was on all fours on the dirty floor, still trying to catch his breath.

"No, no, no," the girl with the auburn hair said, getting to her feet and shaking her hands in front of her. "I mean, yeah, I *did*. But I didn't know he was here with *you*. I thought he was robbing the place."

"Who are you?" Kirbie asked, her voice a confident growl. "What are you doing here?"

"My name's Del," the girl said. "I'm . . . well, I don't know what you'd call me. I always thought of myself as a one-day Ranger. I guess I'm really just a vigilante."

"You were in Victory Park," Alex said, getting to his feet. "You were one of the Powers who came to pay tribute to the Rangers, right? I saw you interviewed on the news."

"That's right," Del said. "I think they picked me because my hair makes for good TV. That and there aren't many people with real powers down there. Nobody has any training, and their talents . . . Well, the most promising candidate for the New Rangers is a guy with a homemade heat ray, and he spent most of his time making grilled cheeses for people."

"New Rangers?" Kirbie half growled.

"There's a group of people down in Victory Park who think that it's their job to pick up where the Rangers left off, as the protectors of Sterling City," Del continued. "It's ridiculous. It's like they've given up on the Rangers coming back at all. They asked me to join them, and that's when I came home to Silver Lake, to get away from all the craziness for a while."

"Wait. Back up. Why are you in this building?" Alex asked.

"Silver Lake is my home," Del said. "Since I came back a few days ago, I've been trying my best to protect it. It's usually a really boring part of the city, but since Justice Tower fell, crime has been getting bad everywhere. So I've been listening to the police scanner and going on patrol. I saw you guys breaking in." She paused for a moment, looking back and forth between Alex and Kirbie. "Wait. It's not true, right? What they said on the news about the Junior Rangers betraying—"

"Of course not," Alex said. "Kirbie and the others would never do something like that."

"So the other Junior Rangers *are* okay. Thank goodness." She focused her attention on Kirbie. "Is he a new recruit? Where are the others? What's going on? Oh my gosh, I have so many questions for you."

"I'm not really a Junior Ranger," Alex said. "There's a lot more going on here than you or anyone else knows—"

"Where are your parents?" Kirbie asked, cutting Alex off before he could give Del any more information. "They just let you play hero and hang out in Victory Park all day?"

Del looked taken aback by Kirbie's questioning, as if she'd been expecting the Junior Ranger to welcome her help. Kirbie was going through the same line of questioning she had when Bug showed up at the lake house, only her tone was much harsher with Del for some reason. But then, Del *had* just attacked Alex, so he couldn't really blame her.

"My dad disappeared about a year ago," Del said softly. "My mom . . . hasn't really been the same since then. She spends most of her time traveling for work anyway. I kind of take care of myself."

"Disappeared?" Kirbie asked.

"Yeah," Del said softly. "He was a reporter. He'd been obsessing over this big story for a while, and then one day he just wasn't there. All his notes and research were missing. And the police gave us some story about how he'd probably just skipped town, but that couldn't be true. He loved us. He was a good man."

"What was the story?" Alex asked.

"I'm not sure, exactly," Del said. "Something about corruption on the Sterling City Council, which was linked to a bunch of shady businesses—and how some unknown corporation basically ran everything. He was going to blow the whole thing wide open. Then he was gone."

Alex felt as though Titan had just punched him in the stomach. Standing in front of him was a girl whose father had been murdered by Cloak. That's what had to have happened. No wonder she had taken matters into her own hands. Who else was there for her to turn to? Alex wondered if the Council had sent a Uniband to do the job, or if one of them had done it themselves. Maybe his parents. He shuddered and felt such guilt, not only that this had happened to Del, but that it probably happened all the time and he'd never realized it. In some way, *he* felt partly responsible for her father's death.

He looked at Del with sympathy. Kirbie continued her questioning.

"And your training?" Kirbie asked. "You took down

Alex, and I know that's not exactly easy."

"I've been in martial arts my entire life. I know this probably sounds dumb, but I was hoping that one day I could be like you. One of the Rangers. I love this place. I just want to keep it safe."

Finally Kirbie seemed to relax.

"You shouldn't be patrolling," she said. "There are worse things running around Sterling City right now than robbers and petty criminals."

"Like what?" Del asked. "And where are Lone Star and Lux and Dr. Photon?"

"They're not able to be in Sterling City right now," Kirbie said. "Their current whereabouts are . . ." She struggled for the correct word.

"Classified," Amp said from behind her. He stepped out of the stairwell, followed by Mallory. Trailing behind them was Bug, whose eyes still glowed in the dim light.

Del smiled when she saw Amp, whispering his name to herself.

"It's an honor to meet you," she said to him, bowing slightly. Her waist-length braid flicked to one side like a tail. "And . . . you're Bug, right? I think I remember seeing you at Victory Park."

"Hmmm?" Bug asked. When he focused on Del, his eyes widened somewhat. "Oh, hi. Yeah. What are *you* doing here?"

"Who is this?" Amp asked Kirbie, never taking his eyes off Del.

"My name's Del," the girl said. "Superpowered prehensile hair. Apparently terrible at first impressions. Really glad to see you guys."

Amp looked confused.

"I'll fill you in later," Kirbie said. "Did you finish your search downstairs?"

"Yeah," Amp said. "We're ready to go when you are."

"Great. Well, it was nice to meet you, Del."

"Wait," Del said. "You can't go yet. I have so much to talk to you about. I don't know what's going on, but with Justice Tower falling . . . It's obviously bad. I can help! Just tell me what to do. Let me join your team. I'm a great fighter. Alex can attest to that." She nodded to Alex, her eyes pleading with him to agree.

"That's true," he admitted.

"I don't think that's a good idea," Kirbie said. "But thanks."

"Well, you're coming to the memorial tomorrow, right?" Del asked. "I mean, it would be great for everyone's morale if you could be there and clear up all the stuff in the news about you guys. I'll be there."

"Memorial?" Kirbie asked.

"Yeah, didn't you hear?" Del asked. "The mayor is speaking at the park tomorrow." She lowered her voice, talking slowly. "The city is losing hope. It would mean a lot to everyone if you were there."

Kirbie and Amp looked at each other.

"I . . . ," Kirbie started. "We'll see." She turned and headed down the stairs.

Del looked defeated. She stepped to Alex, as two lengths of hair unbraided themselves and pulled a card and a pen from her pockets.

"Here," she said, taking the items from her hair and scribbling down a phone number. She handed the card to Alex. "This is my cell number. If they change their minds, or if I can be of any help, call me. Day or night."

"Thanks," Alex said, taking the card. "I'm sorry if Kirbie came off as harsh or something. It's been a rough couple of weeks."

"That's okay," she said. "I'm sure whatever is going on must be especially hard for them. *I'm* sorry I kind of beat you up earlier."

She smiled mischievously. Alex couldn't help but grin.

"I was just letting you get in a few punches before I took you down," he said.

"*Sure*," Del replied. "Well, hopefully I'll see you around."

With that, she walked to an open window on the side of the room and climbed through, out onto the fire escape.

Alex felt bad for Del. There was something likable about her that he couldn't put his finger on, despite the fact that she'd attacked him. And she was the only person besides Kirbie who Alex had seen in color since his powers emerged. He wasn't sure what that meant, but it had to count for something.

"Alex," Bug called from the stairwell. "Are you ready?"

Alex stared at the card and slipped it into his pocket.

"Nice job on keeping the perimeter secure," he said, passing Bug. "If she'd been an enemy, I could have been killed."

"I don't know what happened," Bug said, his face marked with confusion. "I had eyes all around the building."

"Right," Alex said, heading down the stairs. "Good to know you've got my back."

He met the others on the first floor, beside the cars.

"Can't we take one of these home?" Mallory asked. "We've got a long trek back."

"It's too risky," Amp said. "Besides, for all we know they're bugged or being tracked, left here as bait."

Alex sighed. "Then we'd better start walking," he said. "It's a long way to the tunnel."

"Shhh," Kirbie said. "Is she still up there?"

"No," Alex said. "She left through the window, out onto the fire escape."

They exited into the alley and made their way to the street, keeping to the shadows. Alex and Mallory were naturals at blending in with the darkness, but the others would definitely need more training in that area.

Kirbie kept her head up, her eyes watching the rooftops. When they came to the main street, Alex looked around, searching for signs of Del. He finally saw her, swinging between two streetlamps and onto the top of a building, moving gracefully.

"You've met her before, right, Bug?" Kirbie asked.

"Yeah, sort of," Bug said. "She was kind of a big deal down at Victory Park, always milling around, trying to figure out what powers and training people had. I think she was putting some sort of group together. That's about all I know, though."

"What's the deal, Kirbie?" Alex asked. "When Bug showed up, you practically rolled out a welcome mat for him, but you treated Del like she was an enemy."

"She might be," Kirbie said. "And Bug's situation was completely different. He found where we lived. We couldn't just let him walk away and risk him telling half of Sterling City where we were."

"I would never—," Bug started.

"I know," Kirbie said. "You've been incredibly helpful so far."

"Yeah," Alex said. "By completely screwing up his job tonight. His lack of training is a *liability*."

"I—," Bug started.

"Del had some serious skills," Alex said, ignoring Bug.

"She might be a good asset to have."

"Really, Alex? You spend all this time telling me stories of superspies and assassins and then wonder why I don't want to bring the girl who attacked you back home?" Kirbie asked.

"Enough," Amp said firmly. "What would Lone Star say if he heard the Junior Rangers bickering like this? And in *public*."

"There's something off about her, Amp," Kirbie said. "Of every person I've ever met, she's the first one with no scent."

"What?" Amp asked. "How is that even possible?"

"I don't know," Kirbie said. "Maybe she was masking it somehow. But I don't like it."

"Well, there was nothing in the office," Mallory said, changing the subject.

"Yeah, not a scrap of paper," Amp said. "The place had been completely cleared out. Did you two find anything in the cars?"

"Not really," Alex said. "A weapon. Some notes that I think were probably leads on us. There was a receipt for a gas station not too far away from the lake house."

"It's only a matter of time until they find it," Mallory said quietly.

They walked for several blocks in silence, all of them wondering what was coming next. They were tired, desperate, and once again empty-handed, without a clue to go on. Finally they came to a bus stop where they could pick up the line that would take them close to one of the entrances to the underground tunnel.

"Are you guys . . . I mean, would you want to . . . ," Alex started. He wasn't sure how to frame the question on his mind. "Do you want to go to the memorial tomorrow?"

"It'd be a really stupid move," Kirbie said. "For all we know, it's a ploy set up by Cloak to lure us into the open."

"Besides," Amp said, "memorials are for the dead. And the Rangers are still alive."

Alex nodded. He stepped out into the street, looking for the bus.

"With all our powers," he said, "I wish one of us was a teleporter."

They were all exhausted by the time they crawled out of the tunnel and into the lake house. Kyle was pacing in the living room and looked relieved when they walked through the basement door. Misty sat on an overstuffed chair in a deep sleep, her mouth hanging open, head tilted awkwardly to one side.

"She insisted on staying up to make sure you all got back okay," Kyle said. "But I don't think she made it past the eleven o'clock news. Speaking of which, there's going to be some sort of memorial tomorrow."

"We heard," Kirbie said.

Kyle looked as though he wanted to say more about it, but just nodded.

"I take it the investigation didn't turn up good news," he said.

"It didn't turn up anything," Amp said. He yawned. "We should get some sleep. We'll go over everything in the morning and come up with a new plan."

They shuffled off to their rooms, Mallory stopping to toss a blanket over Misty.

In his room, Alex put the gun on a side table and sat down on the bed. He began to go over the scraps of paper, recording the addresses and phone numbers and notes, making a catalog of the receipts.

After he was done, Alex looked at his right palm, where the skull-shaped bruise was beginning to fade away. He closed his eyes and lay back, wanting to rest his eyes for just a moment before transferring the receipt locations to one of the maps in the Rec Room. Instead he fell into a deep sleep and found himself dreaming of the night he'd been marked with Phantom's energy.

He was ten years old when he was officially initiated as a member of the Cloak Society, standing with his chest puffed out in the formal dining room on the lowest level of the underground base. A raging fire was the only source of light in the room, the reflection of the flames licking at the silver skull mounted on the wall above him. The High Council stood in a cluster, wearing heavy hooded robes that he had never before seen.

It was the proudest moment of his life.

"Alexander Knight," Phantom said, her voice low and cold, "fourth-generation member of the Cloak Society. You have been blessed by the Umbra—by our ancestors—with extraordinary power. You are something more, something *better* than human. And tonight, the High Council has a gift for you."

Alex tried to remain still, but his body was practically shaking in anticipation. He had waited for this his entire life.

Phantom continued.

"Do you, son of the Umbra, pledge yourself to the Cloak Society? Do you submit yourself to the will of the High Council just as your parents have, and their parents did before them, even in the face of death, vowing to avenge the memory of those who fell before you? Do you vow to put the good of the Society before all else, before your own needs, knowing that when the time is right, you will lead this broken world into an age of glory?"

"I do," Alex said as firmly as he could.

"Hold out your right hand."

Alex did as instructed. A breeze entered the room, though this was technically impossible so far underground.

The flames flickered violently in the fireplace behind him, and their light faded. The darkness that framed the room closed in tighter. The shadows moved unnaturally, tendrils of black energy seeping over the ground and swirling around the four hooded figures, gleaming slightly, like wet ink. A black pool rose into the air, circling Phantom before forming a small vortex above Alex's open palm. The energy shot down into his hand, a freezing black blot. His eyes grew wide as he tried not to flinch. Slowly the dark energy formed a familiar shape. The hooded, grinning skull. The mark of Cloak.

"Your fate is forever entwined with Cloak," his mother said, removing her hood. She smiled at him. "The Society's blood and power flows within you. You belong to us, and through us, you will take your destined place as the ruler of this world."

Then, in Alex's head, *I am so proud of you, my son.*

Shade raised her right hand up until it was even with her head, the others mimicking her action. Alex could see their marks even in the darkness.

"For the glory," they said in unison.

"Hail Cloak," he said, raising his hand to the side of his head and beaming.

THE FUTURE LEADERS OF
STERLING CITY

"It's not one of mine," Gage said, turning the gun Alex had taken from the car over in his hands, "but the design practically screams Cloak. It looks like it's an updated version of an electric-discharge model my father created."

"It's not a laser pistol?" Alex asked.

"No," Gage said, pointing the gun at one of the lawn chairs nearby. He pulled the trigger, and a bright electric charge shot from the barrel. It hit the seat of the chair, sending electricity snaking over it with a crackling hiss, leaving a faint scorch mark where it landed.

"It's a taser," Gage explained. "Made to stun, not kill."

"Huh," Alex said, taking the gun back from Gage. "Do you mind if I hold on to it? It might come in handy."

"Be my guest. It looks like it has a few dozen bolts left, but if you run out, I can recharge it for you." Gage paused for a moment before continuing. "So this Del from last night—you think her story was legitimate?"

"Yeah," Alex said. "I mean, I saw her on TV. Bug recognized her from the park, too. I think she just happens to be one of the Powers at the park who has *actual* powers. And her dad . . . Well, it doesn't really seem far-fetched that Cloak would do such a thing."

"Statistically speaking, one day we're bound to meet a budding superhero with a normal, living set of parents," Gage mused. "But Del's situation must be different from Bug's, since you haven't exactly made him feel welcome among us."

"That's not true," Alex said. Then, frowning, he amended his statement. "Not completely, anyway. I just got the feeling she really did want to help out. Plus, she's definitely much more talented than Bug. Plus, she didn't just show up at our safe house, and didn't try to follow us or anything. *Plus*, Gage . . . I saw her in color. I don't know what that's about, but it seems important."

"I feel as though we had a very similar conversation not too long ago," Gage said, raising an eyebrow. "I'm beginning to suspect that you have a weakness for girls who want to beat you up."

"This is nothing like things in Victory Park," Alex

said. "I just don't get why Kirbie was so quick to nix the idea of her helping us. I mean, look at how fast she let Bug into our circle."

"And Kirbie's inability to get a scent off her?"

"I don't know. I couldn't wrap my thoughts around her hair," Alex said. "Maybe it's part of her powers. You'd think Kirbie'd want us to have all the help we can for when we go up against Cloak."

"Yes, well," Gage said. "Speaking of help, I have something for you."

He handed Alex two sheets of paper, each containing a list of addresses, along with the names of people, corporations, and notes about what each building was used for.

"What are these?" Alex asked.

"While I was taking a break from my work on the Gloom, I did some research into real estate. Each of these addresses is owned by a corporation or a dummy name that Cloak has used in the past. It looks like Cloak bought a lot of property in the months leading up to the Justice Tower attack. Probably getting ready to establish outposts once they took over the city. Many of these buildings might house legitimate businesses, but I thought it might be helpful."

"Are you kidding?" Alex asked. "This is more than helpful. It's perfect."

"I'd start by plotting them on a map," Gage said, turning

back to his work. "Maybe have Kyle search for info on the buildings. He appears to be pretty adept with computers."

Alex found Kyle at the dining room table with Misty. Both of them were hunched over a beat-up shoe box, sorting through its contents.

"Look what I found in the basement!" Misty exclaimed as Alex approached. "It's full of all kinds of flower seeds. Kyle's going to make me a bouquet, and then we're going to have fresh flowers all over the house, and it's going to smell *amazing*."

"Don't get *too* excited," Kyle said cautiously. "I have no idea how long these have been down there. I've never really worked with old seeds like this before."

Alex sat down at the table and picked up a few of the packets.

"Sounds great, Misty," he said, sliding the seeds back over to her.

"Oh! These!" Misty said, pulling a packet from the box and shoving it into Kyle's hands. "These are the ones I want first! Can you make these purple flowers?"

Kyle examined the picture on the front of the package.

"Technically these are *blue* hydrangeas," he said. "But they do kind of look purple."

"Great!" Misty said, unfazed. "And if these don't turn out right, we'll just try another packet!"

Kyle tore the edge off the package and poured the dark brown seeds onto the table. He waved his hand over them and closed his eyes, as if he were casting some sort of spell. Misty leaned on her elbows, her head dropping down close to the table. Kyle opened his eyes, grinned, and winked at her.

A few of the seeds began to tremble. Slowly, thin green shoots started to poke out of them, casting off their brown shells like old coats. Kyle waved his hands again, and the plants began to grow at an incredible rate, until small bushes threatened to overtake the dining room table completely, their roots sliding off the sides and growing toward the floor as they sought out soil. Kyle unfurled his clenched fingers, and all over the greenery, stunning patches of flowers erupted. He beckoned with his finger, and several of the flower clumps merged, the vines and leaves of the plant twisting together into a single large bouquet that floated over to Misty, who watched the whole thing in complete wonder, her eyes wide.

"Wow," Alex murmured.

"They're perfect," Misty said, her voice barely above a whisper.

"You can cut off that bouquet," Kyle said, "then if you can find some pots or something down in the basement, we can plant the rest."

"Here," Alex said, anxious to help. He reached out with his thoughts and picked up the empty seed packet, wrapping it in telekinetic energy. It floated into the air, and then tore open, until it was a flat piece of paper, a dull silver on one side. It began to shake, then folded in on itself quickly, until it was a delicate silver butterfly that landed softly on the edge of Misty's flowers.

Misty gasped.

"Thank you!" she said, grinning at Alex. He smiled back, happy he could excite her. "I'm going to go find Bug," she continued, jumping up from the table. "I bet he can call in some *real* butterflies, too! The dining room can be like an indoor garden!"

Kyle coaxed the plants into a more orderly heap.

"Hey, I could use your help if you're not busy," Alex said.

"Sure. What do you want me to grow?"

"Nothing," Alex said. "I want you to help us track down the Omegas."

He slid one of the notebook pages from Gage across to Kyle, who eyed the list of addresses.

"Gage said you're good with computers. Can you see what you can find out about these places? It's possible an Omega might be hiding out in one of these buildings. Each one has a suspicious tie to Cloak."

"Sure," Kyle said, a smile creeping over his face. "I can see if they're legit and stuff. With all the notes I've been taking on strange things in the news, maybe something will jump out at me."

"Perfect," Alex said. "Any information helps. I'm going to mark the locations on this other page on the map upstairs, then I'll come swap it out with your list."

"No sweat," Kyle said, nodding.

Alex started up the stairs.

"Hey, Alex," Kyle called after him.

"Yeah?"

"Maybe later when we have some free time, you can teach me a little bit about being stealthy," Kyle said. "Kirbie and Amp tell me you and Mallory are really good at it. We never really had to worry about hiding in shadows or anything, and I want to make sure that when the time comes, I've got all the skills I need to rescue the Rangers."

"Definitely," Alex said. "You got it."

At five o'clock, they gathered in the living room to watch the Rangers' memorial on TV. Even Gage took a break from his work to join them. Vases and pots of blue flowers dotted the floor. Despite his insistence that a memorial wasn't necessary for the Rangers, Amp leaned against the wall at the back of the room with his arms crossed.

A stage had been set up in Victory Park's statue garden—a fitting location, given the topic of the event. A dark-blue curtain was stretched across the back of the platform, bearing Sterling City's seal in white. From the sidelines, fallen Rangers cast in metal looked on. Amp's father and mother were there in the background, forever stuck in triumphant poses. At the front of the stage stood a podium, and behind it the mayor, looking solemn as he began to speak.

"Almost one month ago I awoke to news that seemed impossible. I will not pretend that unlike every citizen of Sterling City, I am not grieving. That there is not a pain in my heart when my eyes fall upon the skyline and Justice Tower is not there. We do not know what has happened to the Rangers of Justice, to our heroes, and that uncertainty is perhaps worse than anything. If we knew that they were alive, we could seek them out, and if we knew that they had fallen in battle, we could mourn them properly."

The camera pulled back to show a handful of important-looking people sitting on the stage to the side of the mayor. Among them was Misty's mother, who nodded along with a perfect impression of grief. Misty began to shiver. Mallory pulled up the corner of the girl's blanket and scooted closer to her. But Misty continued to tremble, and Mallory realized she was trying not to cry.

The mayor continued.

"But we cannot let this uncertainty rule us. After all, what would Lone Star say if he could see us now? Who's to say that he's *not* watching? Some of you are too young to remember what happened in this very spot a decade ago, when the world lost so many of its heroes. When things looked their bleakest. What did Lone Star, and Lux, and

Dr. Photon do then? They persevered. It is what they would want us to do now. I look out from this podium and I see the future of Sterling City. It is alive in the faces of our citizens. Of our youth. And in the hearts of those who have traveled here from every corner of this country to honor the Rangers. It is up to you to embody everything that the Rangers stand for. Truth. Justice. And above all, peace. Let us take a moment of silence to honor the Rangers of Justice, wherever they are now."

Alex let his gaze drift across the room. Kirbie leaned into Kyle, neither of them taking their eyes off the screen. Amp's face was solemn, jaw clenched.

"Wait. Do you see that?" Mallory asked, her eyes narrowing at the screen. "That shadow . . ."

Alex turned back to the television. The camera had zoomed out even farther, revealing a dozen wannabe heroes sitting in the first few rows, their homemade costumes shining garishly in the sun. At first he didn't see what Mallory was talking about.

And then it was obvious.

"No," he whispered.

The shadows cast by the podium and the mayor were growing, swirling together, and, as impossible as it seemed, darkening. They looked like they were moving of their own accord. Onstage, with heads bowed and eyes closed, no one realized anything odd was happening.

"They wouldn't," Kyle said. "Not now."

The shadows rose quickly, forming an inky mass behind the mayor, then melted away, revealing three figures all dressed in long, dark, hooded coats with silver bands on the shoulders. Julie. Barrage. Phantom.

Misty's mother leaped to her feet, her face contorting with fear as she pointed and screamed. Alex knew it was nothing but a performance as she pretended to be terrified of Phantom, her own sister. But the crowd at Victory Park gasped and shouted, screaming warnings to the mayor, unsure who these new figures were.

"NO!" Amp shouted, rushing a few steps forward, as if he could leap through the screen and into battle. Everyone else stayed frozen, unable to move, hardly breathing.

The mayor turned and, shocked to see the intruders onstage, stumbled back against the podium, causing the microphone to fall to the ground with a terrible *pop*. Phantom waved a hand in front of her nonchalantly, and from the ground oily shadows rose. They wrapped around the mayor, lifting him off the stage. He began to shout, but the darkness was soon covering his mouth as well, leaving only his frightened eyes visible as he floated a few feet in the air.

Chaos broke out among the crowd. Half of the Powers turned to run away, while the others tried valiantly to storm the stage, creating a mass of panicked civilians practically trampling one another. Another tendril knocked the podium out of the way, exposing the roiling darkness around Phantom's feet. The dark energy rose behind her, forming a throne of shadows, which Phantom sank into with a small smile, as if finally relaxing after a very long journey. An inky coil raised the microphone to her dark lips as she crossed one leg over the other and reclined.

"You should see your faces," she said slowly to the people in the park, savoring each word. She nodded slightly, and the mayor was tossed forward onto the grass below the stage. He gasped for air, and several citizens appeared by his side and pulled him away from the stage, out of the camera's range. "Your sad excuse for a leader is right about one thing: The future of Sterling City *is* here today."

As Phantom spoke, Barrage and Julie took a few steps away from her dark throne. Barrage's hands emanated a pulsing red glow as balls of explosive energy orbited around them. Julie let her coat fall to the ground, exposing a sleeveless version of her Beta uniform, the silver skull of Cloak gleaming in the stage lights. Her fingers grew long, transforming into talons, as her arms hardened, spikes jutting out from her elbows and shoulders. A group of police officers and Powers climbed up the side of the stage. A few of them pulled the terrified officials and Misty's mother out of the camera's view. Julie was ready for the attackers, moving quickly, slashing through their ranks with manic laughter. More police appeared at the foot of the stage, guns drawn, but a flick of Phantom's wrist disarmed them.

"What are they doing?" Mallory whispered. Alex shook his head, his eyes wide. As much as he'd talked about Cloak making a move into the public view, to actually see it was mind-blowing. Were they retaliating against Alex and the others for infiltrating the underground base? Or was this part of something bigger, part of the Society's new master plan?

And where were his parents? Where was Titan?

Onscreen, Phantom continued, ignoring the shouting masses around her.

"Allow me to put to rest any uncertainties you may have about the Rangers of Justice. It was by our hands that Justice Tower was destroyed, and your heroes left this world as cowards begging for our mercy. We are at the dawn of a golden age. Soon you will learn the new order, and whisper our names out of fear and respect. Those of you who join us will be rewarded with power beyond belief. The weak among you will fall just as Lone Star did: helpless to stop us."

She looked into the camera. It was as if she was staring through the screen and directly into Alex's eyes.

"We are the Cloak Society. Our power is unmatched. And we will not tolerate resistance."

As if on cue, another wave of Powers charged the stage. They yelled as they rushed forward, led by a girl with incredibly long auburn hair that hung in the air all around her face. Del.

"Del!" Amp said, pointing at the screen.

"Oh no," Alex said. "She has no idea what she's up against."

Two thick ropes of hair shot out from Del's head, catching Julie by the wrists. But Julie only smiled and swung her attacker to the side, sending Del across the stage. Balls of energy began to rain down from Barrage, knocking the untrained and undisciplined fighters back. The Cloak Society laughed. Phantom could not have looked more pleased on her dark throne.

Any bystanders who had stayed behind or had found themselves frozen in shock were now running away, screaming as Barrage began hurling his explosive energy out into the crowd. The injured Powers on the stage were crawling away, desperately trying to escape. Del was nowhere to be seen. The camera shook, and then fell over. Julie's gemlike arms stretched wide, the reflection of her father's explosions causing them to shimmer brilliantly.

Fire was slowly consuming the curtain decorated with Sterling City's seal. Phantom began to laugh as she fell backward into the throne, now swirling with darkness and growing into a portal to the Gloom. And then the camera cut out, and the screen went blue.

After a few moments of stunned silence, everyone in the living room began to talk at once. Or at least, everyone began to make noise. The sounds coming out of Kyle's mouth were more random syllables than words.

"What was the point of that?" Alex asked.

"I don't know," Mallory said. "They've been underground for so long."

"All those people," Kirbie said. "We should have been there to protect them."

"What's the endgame?" Gage asked no one in particular.

Amp stood behind them, soaking it all up until he couldn't take it anymore. He barged out the front door, letting it slam behind him. From the center of the yard, Alex and the others heard a deafening shout released into the dimming sky.

A WALK IN THE
PARK

Sterling City was sent into a panic. For ten long years they'd believed the Cloak Society had been destroyed by the Rangers of Justice—for many, it was hard to fathom that Cloak had ever existed at all. And now the villains had returned, casting off all shrouds of mystery and stealth and putting themselves in the center of the world's gaze. In the hours that followed their display in Victory Park, the city responded. Police officers were placed on every corner. The National Guard was on alert. Federal agents touting credentials from every agency and acronym imaginable caught late-night flights to Texas. And yet, no one knew what they were really looking for, or what level of threat Cloak posed. No one could even say for sure whose jurisdiction the Cloak Society fell under. This had always been something the Rangers of Justice had taken care of.

Back at the lake house, the kids played the scene over and over again in their heads, trying to make sense of it, and when it wasn't in their heads, it was on a loop on every television station. But they had no answers. There were only questions to obsess over. What was the point of it? Why now? Why those three Cloak members? Though they could come up with plausible answers, there was no way of knowing for certain what Cloak had in store for Sterling City. But they couldn't just sit around waiting. Once they all agreed that facing Cloak head-on was not a possibility, they turned back to something they could actively pursue: the Omegas.

Everyone gathered in the Rec Room the next morning, after a near-sleepless night. Alex and Kyle compared notes at the map of Silver Lake, now marked with the buildings Gage had identified as possible Omega hideouts. With Kyle's research crossing several possibilities off the map, there were still over a dozen different locations for the Omega base. Even if they took the utmost care, using Bug as their eyes, they'd be putting themselves in danger with each investigation. And besides, after the incident with Del surprising him at the warehouse, Alex's faith in Bug's abilities had dropped to practically zero.

They needed someone who knew Silver Lake, who

could look at the map and list of addresses and point out the ones that were suspicious, or in some way exceptional. They needed Del. Besides, she was on their side. She had fought the battle *they* should have been fighting in Victory Park—had put her life on the line for their cause. When Alex suggested they call her, no one objected.

"Hello?" Del's voice came through the phone, groggy and fractured.

"Hey, Del? It's Alex? From the warehouse?" For some reason his statements sounded like questions when they left his mouth. "Are you okay? We saw you on the news last night."

"Alex!" she exclaimed, the sleep melting off her. "Yeah, I'm fine. I mean, a little bruised up, but it could have been a lot worse. It was a real horror show down there."

"What happened? We saw everything until the portal opened, but then the camera went out. We've been trying to piece it together through news and internet reports, but it sounds like most people fled pretty early on."

"Yeah," Del said. "You pretty much saw all the action. As soon as that portal thing opened, those three got sucked into it, and they were gone. Just like that. Which is kind of great, because if they'd stayed around to fight, I think we would have gotten the crap kicked out of us."

"Was anyone killed?" Alex asked warily. "All the news sites have different info. I don't know why no one has made an official statement yet. For all we know, Cloak's using their resources to feed conflicting reports to the media."

"I have no idea. I stayed in the park and helped as long as they'd let me, but when the police and everyone arrived, they cleared the place out pretty fast." Del paused. "They're serious bad guys, Alex. Sterling City isn't safe, but I don't know what to do. Are you guys planning to retaliate?"

"Listen," Alex said. "We're working on something that we could use your help on. I can't give you many details, but if you're feeling up to it, could we meet sometime today?"

"Of course!" Del said, her voice ecstatic. "Where are you guys? I'll come right over."

"No," Alex said. "Let's meet somewhere in town. Where do you live?"

There was a brief pause on the line.

"Do you know where Permian Park is?" she asked. "It's big, and should be pretty empty."

"Sure," Alex said. He didn't actually know where the park was, but maps were something they had in abundance. "Three o'clock?"

"Perfect. I'll see you guys there."

The line cut out, and Alex returned to the Rec Room to report to the others.

"I dunno," Kirbie said. "I don't like the idea of meeting out in the open."

"Yeah," Mallory said. "But it's cold out today. You can

bundle up, and no one will be able to recognize you, if that's what you're worried about. Or you could stay here and—"

"Oh, no," Kirbie said decisively. "I'm going."

"Are we sure we can trust this girl?" Kyle asked.

"We all saw her fighting Cloak last night," Alex said. "If we're going after the Omegas, she's our best source of info right now."

"I hate to say it," Amp said, "but it's true. We could use her help—scent or no scent."

"Gage wants me and Amp to help with the Gloom device this afternoon," Mallory said. "Something about metalwork and frequencies. But we can probably get out of it if you want us to go with you."

"No, that's okay," Alex said. "The Gloom device comes first."

"I'm coming with you," Kyle said. "I've studied these maps, and if we run into trouble in a park . . . well, trees and stuff. You get the idea."

"And I can provide extra eyes while you're talking," Bug said. "I can keep a lookout."

"We've got plenty of people on this mission already," Alex said.

"Bug's coming with us," Kirbie insisted. "There's something strange about Del. If I can't smell her, I'm not holding it against Bug for not seeing her. Besides, he did a great job doing recon for you guys during the day."

"Fine," Alex said.

"And me. I'm going too." They turned to look at Misty.

"I've been stuck in this house ever since they flashed my face on TV," she said. "The trip to the underground base totally doesn't count."

"Misty—," Alex started.

"NO!" she said, shaking her head, not giving him a chance to talk her out of it. "I know exactly what you're going to say about how dangerous it is and how I'm not old enough to be going on missions and stuff with you, but I'm going. I'm a part of this group. Not just your transport when you can't take a bus somewhere."

Alex opened his mouth to argue with her but knew it wouldn't do any good. And she was right, of course.

"Besides," she said, her voice softer, "it's a park. I don't really remember the last time I was at one of those."

"Fine," Alex said hesitantly. "But you're going to have to go in disguise."

Misty inhaled a small high-pitched gasp.

"I know exactly what to wear!" she said, running for the door. She called over her shoulder as she descended the stairs. "Somebody find me some big sunglasses!"

"No more outdoor training," Amp said as he walked out of the room. "No sparklers or lanterns. From here on out, we fly as far under the radar as we can. We should look into blackout curtains and keep the lights to a minimum once it gets dark."

Alex rubbed his eyes, tired from the restless night.

"Are you okay?" Kirbie asked, coming to his side. "You're looking a little rough lately. If you want, you can sit this out. Kyle and I can take care of it."

"I'm fine," he said, forcing a smile. "Just a little worn out. That's all."

But inside, he was worried. Not just about Cloak and the Omegas and the safety of everyone around him—and of Sterling City in general, for that matter—but about what they were doing. Meeting Del. Trying to track down the Omegas. Going against Cloak. In the beginning, he had so much hope. When he promised the others that they'd rescue the Rangers and that Sterling City wouldn't fall, he'd meant it. But after so many small failures, he worried deep down in his gut that every step forward only drew them closer to doom.

When Misty emerged from her bedroom, she wore the black leggings and purple plaid skirt she'd had on the night of Justice Tower, along with an oversized gray cable-knit sweater. Her red hair was pulled back, completely hidden by a long paisley silk scarf she'd found, and huge sunglasses covered most of her face. It was a good—if dramatic—disguise.

Kirbie had on sunglasses as well, along with a gray knit cap, obscuring her features enough to not be immediately recognizable to someone on the street. Kyle grabbed a blue hoodie, which could hide his face well enough in a pinch, while Bug wore a brown bomber jacket. Alex thought about sliding his Cloak coat on over his jeans and sweater, but it felt too linked to the Society to wear during the day, even without the silver bands on the arms. He carried a backpack full of notes and maps—and the taser, just in case.

From the tunnel, they took a bus that dropped them a few blocks away from Permian Park. As they walked down the residential streets, they talked about what they could and couldn't tell Del.

"We shouldn't mention the Gloom at all," Kirbie said. "If word got out that that's where the Rangers are—or even that a place like that exists—it would cause a panic."

"You're right," Alex said. "In fact, we should probably avoid talk of Justice Tower altogether."

"Don't worry. I'm in no hurry to rehash that night," Kirbie said grimly. "But unless she's a complete idiot, she must have realized that Cloak is behind everything."

"Then we only tell her that much," Kyle said. "And absolutely no mention of the lake house. For all she knows, we could live in a tree house on the other side of Sterling City."

"With all this secrecy, she's going to feel like we don't trust her," Alex said.

"Just remember to keep your guard up," Kirbie said. "We don't know what we're walking into."

"She's already in the park," Bug said, his eyes flashing. "It's just around the next corner. Unless she's brought a handful of kids to attack us, we should be fine."

"Look at that," Alex said, happy with Bug's presence for a change. "No ambush."

"I wish it was summer," Misty said, pulling her scarf down around her face a bit more. "I bet there are ice-cream trucks here in the summer."

"Misty, I'm pretty sure we're a few degrees away from seeing our breath," Alex said. "How could you possibly be thinking about ice cream?"

Permian Park was laid out over several blocks in the middle of a well-to-do neighborhood. Unlike Victory Park, the trees here were sparse, popping up intermittently in areas not designated for sports practice fields or tennis courts. Del sat alone on one of several picnic tables beside a playground made up of dinosaur-themed equipment. Swings hung from the belly of a brontosaurus. A couple of children climbed on the arms of a tall metal T. rex.

"The park really lives up to its name," Alex said.

"Actually, dinosaurs didn't show up until the Triassic period," Bug said. "After the Great Dying, which was at the end of the Permian age. It was the largest extinction event in history. The biggest loss of insect species ever."

Alex scowled. He'd been proud of himself for recognizing "Permian" at all. His lessons with the Tutor were perhaps a bit lacking in the ancient-geological-time-periods department.

"Sorry," Bug murmured. "I used to be really into dinosaurs."

"Hey!" Del said, jumping up from the table as they approached. Her hair hung down in curls all around her, falling over her shoulders. Ringlets floated in shapes that defied physics, bobbing slightly in the still air, constantly in motion. "You guys came!"

"Of course we did," Alex said. "I told you we'd be here."

She smiled at Kirbie. "It's great to see you again. And you're Thorn, right?"

"Kyle."

"And who are you, with the pretty scarf?" Del asked, smiling at Misty.

"This is—," Alex started.

"The Mist," Misty finished, holding out her hand and speaking in a voice that was lower than her normal register. "A pleasure to make your acquaintance."

"Likewise," Del said, shaking her hand. She turned to Alex. "Just how many of you are there on this new team? At the warehouse, it sounded like you weren't taking on new recruits."

"There are plenty of us," Kirbie said, forcing a smile and

taking a seat at the picnic bench. Amp and Alex sat beside her.

Alex unzipped his backpack and took a small journal of notes out, along with a rolled-up map. Misty frowned.

"I'm going to check out the playground. You know, just to make sure there's nothing weird going on over there," she said decisively. "You want to come?" she asked, turning to Bug.

"Sure," Bug said, his eyes glinting.

"Just keep your eyes open," Kirbie said, but Bug and Misty were already walking away, Zip's silvery wings fluttering along in front of them. Alex kept one eye on Bug as he used his powers to hold the corners of the map down on the picnic table.

"So," Del said. "What can I do for the Junior Rangers?"

"Well," Alex said, ignoring the part about him being a Junior Ranger, "we'd like you to take a look at this map of Silver Lake. At all of these circled spots that aren't x-ed out. We're wondering if you can tell us anything about them. If any of the locations are . . . suspicious."

"Okaaay," Del said, drawing out the word as her eyes scanned the map. "That's not giving me a *lot* to go on."

"Just take a look and tell us what you know about any of the places," Kyle clarified. "We're tracking a criminal, and we think he may be hiding out at one of these addresses."

Del looked up at Kyle, her eyes widening slightly. "You mean the Cloak Society?" The hair framing her face moved back, exposing a purple bruise above her right temple.

"You were hurt last night?" Kyle asked, ignoring her question.

"Nothing serious," Del said. "So, really, who is it you're tracking?"

No one said anything. Del looked at their grim expressions for a moment before lowering her eyes back down to the map on the picnic table.

"Right," Del said softly, without looking up. "I know a few of the neighborhoods where you've marked addresses. They're harmless enough. This circle here is just an empty lot right now, so you can mark it off. How do you think these places might be connected to those criminals?"

"We've got really smart sources," Kirbie said.

"The best," Kyle agreed. He pulled a notebook from Alex's backpack and started to take notes.

"Hmmm," Del said, her finger falling on another circle. "I don't know this address in particular, but it's across the street from a big police station, so it seems like it'd be counterproductive as a villain's hideout. And this one is surrounded by all-night diners and hotels. It's a heavy traffic area, even at night."

Her eyes continued to bounce from circle to circle. Even with three eliminated, there were still over half a dozen possible locations left.

"I don't know what to tell you about the rest of these,"

Del said, frowning. "I don't know the specific areas well. But they're all in either high-traffic or residential neighborhoods. None of them are secluded like that warehouse was. . . . Wait, was that place a Cloak Society hideout?"

Alex let his eyes drift to Kirbie and Kyle. Kirbie inhaled deeply, her eyes never leaving Del's. Alex could detect a hint of a wolf in them.

"It's impossible to know anything about Cloak for sure," he said.

Del looked perplexed but nodded. She did a final once-over of the map, biting her bottom lip.

"Actually, I know this place," she said, pointing to one of the circled buildings near the corner of the map. "It's a theater."

"Right," Kyle said, shuffling through the notebook. "The Playhouse. Stage shows and stuff. Seems innocent enough."

"It *was*," Del said. "But the troupe in charge of it moved to a bigger venue in the city a few months ago. As far as I know, no one's using it now."

"It's secluded," Kyle said.

"And pretty big too," Del added, shrugging. "That's where I'd look first."

"Okay," Alex said. "That's a good lead. Thanks."

"So . . . ," Del began, looking back to Alex. "What else can I do for you?"

"That's all," Kirbie said. "We've got your number if we need anything else."

"Come on," Del said. "The Cloak Society? They're, like, the biggest bad guys in the history of bad guys. You need all the help you can get if you're going up against them. Trust me, I've got enough bruises from last night to know that. I'm volunteering."

"Look, you've been a big help with the map," Kirbie said. "Thank you for that, and for what you did last night. It's just that . . ."

"I'm just some girl from the outskirts of Sterling City, and you were trained by Lone Star himself?"

"No, it's not that—"

"Then you don't trust me," Del said.

Kirbie didn't say anything.

"I get it," Del said. "You have to be careful. I showed up out of nowhere and beat up one of your friends. But if what the Cloak Society said last night is true, all of us are in for trouble. I'll prove to you that I'm on your side somehow. You'll see."

"I'm sorry," Kirbie said, her face falling a bit. "I didn't mean to—"

"It's okay," Del said with a small smile. "I imagine that if I'd been through whatever it is that got you out of Justice Tower and into this park, I'd be suspicious of strangers too."

Kirbie nodded, looking like she was letting her guard down a bit.

"Thanks again for all your help," Alex said.

"I don't suppose one of you would walk me home," Del said. "It's just ten blocks from here, but I've been a little creeped out ever since last night."

"We really should be getting back," Kirbie said.

"I'll go with you," Alex blurted out before he really thought about what he was saying.

Kirbie gave him a cold stare.

"I mean, I wouldn't want to be out alone right now, either," he said. "Misty can come with me, and we'll travel back fast. You guys go ahead and start working on the investigation."

"It's just ten blocks," Del said again.

"Sure," Kyle said slowly. "Okay."

"I'll get Misty," Kirbie said without looking at Alex. She made a beeline for the playground, where Bug was hanging upside down off a pterodactyl wing while Misty swung slowly on the brontosaurus.

Kyle gathered up his notes and the map. Alex busied himself with double-checking the zippers on his backpack and making sure he didn't leave anything behind until Misty showed up at his side.

"Those swings were the worst," she said, tucking a stray strand of hair back behind her sunglasses. "Oh, and the perimeter is secure."

"Next time we'll meet somewhere with a better playground," Alex said.

"Next time we'll meet at an amusement park," Misty corrected him.

"Shall we?" Del asked.

"Yeah," Alex said. "Let's go."

Kyle gave Misty a smile before leaving to join his sister. Kirbie was talking to Bug, looking very serious, still staring at Del.

"That was awkward," Del said, shrugging. "Sorry if I caused a problem."

Alex smiled slightly.

"Don't worry about it," he said. "Lead the way."

Alex, Del, and Misty were quiet as they left the park. For several blocks, Misty stared slack-jawed at Del's hair.

"Can I touch it?" she finally asked.

"Of course," Del said. "It's just hair. It won't bite." She grinned at Misty and added, "Unless I want it to."

Misty reached out tentatively and stroked the flowing auburn hair. "It's so pretty," she cooed.

"So, how did you two get mixed up with the Junior Rangers again?" Del asked, flicking her hair back and forth to Misty's delight.

"It's a long story," Alex said before Misty could answer.

"What about that Bug guy?" Del asked. "I thought he was trekking back to Oklahoma or something."

"He just kind of . . . showed up."

"And Kirbie didn't have a problem with *him*?" Del asked, frowning slightly.

"Apparently not," Alex said. "It's like everyone fell in love with him the moment he showed up."

"You don't sound like you're sold on him."

"Not really," Alex said. "I think he might end up being more trouble than he's worth."

He caught himself before he said more, and looked over at Del, who seemed to be to hanging on his every word. When his eyes caught hers, she smiled.

"Want to see a trick?" she asked, turning her attention to Misty. Del's hair suddenly began to twist, braiding itself in complicated patterns that seemed impossible.

"Oh my gosh! That's gorgeous," Misty whispered, her eyes twinkling. She reached up to the scarf around her head. "I know what I'm doing tonight."

"If I was a Junior Ranger, I could fix your hair all the time," Del said. She turned back to Alex. "So what *do* I have to do to get in with them? Kirbie seems to have it out for me."

"I don't know if I can help you there," Alex said.

He thought about Kirbie's past, and her life before she was rescued from Victory Park by Lone Star. Of course she had problems trusting people. It was a wonder that she had ever agreed to meet with him in front of Centennial Fountain. But then, she had said she sensed good in him. And Del, well, she was someone Kirbie couldn't sense at all.

"Well, what did you do to get in? I know you weren't part of the Rangers before Justice Tower fell," Del said, pushing Alex again for his story. "At least, not that I know about."

"No. I pretty much gave up my whole world."

"What do you mean?"

"Let's just say I wasn't always the hero type."

"Alex," Del said, stopping. "We all have stuff we're ashamed of in the past. I've told you my story. You totally owe me."

Alex was quiet for a few seconds. "Maybe another time."

"Do you regret it?" she asked. "Turning your back on your whole world, I mean."

Alex thought for a moment. He'd asked himself a thousand times if he'd done the right thing by betraying Cloak, but he'd never questioned whether he regretted it, which was a different issue entirely. Instead of thinking about the underground base, or his parents, or his place on the Beta Team, he thought about how, despite everything that had gone wrong, he'd still managed to help save Kirbie, Amp, and Kyle, not to mention a big chunk of Sterling City.

"No," he said assuredly. "Not at all."

"Good," Del said. She walked a few steps into the alley, pausing beneath the low-hanging branches of a tree. "This is me. I guess I'll see you two around."

She flashed a smile as some of her hair flew up into the branches. In an instant it pulled her upward, until she was up and over the fence and into the backyard.

"She's so cool," Misty whispered.

Alex smiled, and nodded.

THE

PLAYHOUSE

"Let me get this straight," Amp said quietly as he tiptoed through the brush later that night with Alex, Mallory, Kirbie, and Bug, the others holding down base at the lake house. "The Cloak Society's secret headquarters is beneath an old drive-in, and they've got their elite squad of assassins holed up in an abandoned theater?"

"Despite their usually low profile," Alex said, "they *do* have a flair for the dramatic."

He held his arms out, motioning to his trench coat.

"You should see pictures of the old uniforms," Mallory said. "Full-on hoods and capes back in the day. And the ones from the eighties were basically spandex bodysuits with silver underwear on the outside."

"Hey," Kirbie said. "I'm pretty sure my uniform is mostly spandex."

"But that serves a purpose," Alex said. "Besides, Gage said the rest is made up of unstable molecules or something science-y, right?"

"Unstable molecules?" Kirbie asked. "That's totally not a real thing."

"Quiet, guys," Amp said. "We're coming up on the theater. Bug, do your thing."

They crouched in the dense vegetation, a few yards from where the grass and bushes gave way to a parking lot. Bug's eyes began to glow, and Zip jetted from his shoulder, flying toward the theater. The grounds were surrounded by trees on all sides, and the building itself was a simple structure, a single story in the front while the back was triple that height to accommodate the stage and lights and curtains. A garage was in the back, where scenery and unused props might have been stored.

"Two glass doors lead into the theater at the top of some stairs. They're chained together. There appears to be access from the roof," Bug said.

"That's not going to do us any good," Amp said.

"There's also a stage entrance on one side, and what looks like a ground-level entrance into the auditorium on the other. No windows."

"That does make for a smart hideout," Mallory said.

"I'm sending in some gnat scouts through a vent on the roof," Bug said. "Give me a few minutes."

Alex raised his eyes, zeroing in on power and telephone lines. He traced the lines to the theater and focused on one of the wires, pulling it from its post.

"What was that?" Amp asked.

"Just taking out the phone line. In case the place has an alarm," Alex said. "No phone, no cops."

"I doubt that the Omegas have an alarm system that would call *the cops*," Kirbie said.

"Hey, I'm just trying to cover all our bases here."

"I don't see anyone inside," Bug said. "But let me check out what's under the trapdoor onstage."

"There's a trapdoor on the stage?" Mallory asked.

"Of course there is," Bug said. "Haven't you ever been in a play before?"

They were all quiet.

"Oh . . . right," Bug said. "No time for acting when you're Rangers and Betas. Sorry. I've got nobody inside, but there's a map of Sterling City and some boxes in one of the dressing rooms. Might be worth checking out."

"Alex, you think you can pick the lock on the stage door?" Amp asked.

"No problem," Alex said.

"All right then. Let's move."

They tried to make their way across the gravel parking

lot quietly. Once they reached the building, Amp, Kirbie, and Mallory pressed up against the wall, keeping an eye out for movement, while Bug kept working with his spies inside. At the door, Alex probed the lock with his mind. It was old and stubborn, but without too much tinkering, he was able to slide the heavy dead bolt aside. He pulled open the thick metal door and its hinges creaked loudly, a sound that reverberated through the open theater auditorium.

"So much for surprise," Alex said. "You'd better be right about there not being anyone else here, Bug."

"I'm sure of it," he said.

They filed into the theater one by one, flashlights drawn. Bug led them to the greenroom, off to the side of the stage, where they found a working lamp.

"Electricity," Mallory said. "Someone's been using this place."

Kirbie's face changed as she inhaled deeply.

"No scent I recognize," she said.

"We should split up," Amp said. "We'll cover more ground that way."

"I'll take the upper level," Alex said. "The catwalk and balcony. I don't want any more surprises from above like last time."

"I'll go with you," Bug said, happy to see a way to help. "Maybe I can get the light board working so we're not in the dark."

"All right," Amp said. "Kirbie, Mallory, you check the dressing rooms and backstage areas. I'll take the lobby."

"Alone?" Kirbie asked.

"If I run into trouble, you'll hear me," Amp assured her. "Be careful."

Kirbie nodded and followed Mallory toward the stage. Amp headed in the opposite direction, out into the seats of the auditorium and into the darkness.

"This way," Bug said to Alex, heading up toward the lobby area. "There are stairs right outside this door."

They climbed up to a catwalk made of metal grating, covered unceremoniously by spare scraps of carpet and rugs. One side was screwed into the brick wall of the theater, and a thin metal pole served as a railing on the opposite side. Alex stepped carefully, a bit wary of the construction.

"Hello, friend," Bug said as Zip landed on his shoulder. "Good job."

The catwalk led them to a small room crammed full of electrical equipment. The front wall had a huge window with a full view of a thick curtain hiding the stage on the other side of the auditorium. Bug stared at a long station covered in knobs and switches.

"What do you think?" Alex asked.

"I can probably figure it out," Bug said, pressing a few buttons. A hum came from inside the station. "But it'll need a little time to warm up."

Alex saw movement out of the corner of his eye. He swung his flashlight toward it, but the beam was reflected in the glass.

"Hey," he said cautiously. "What else is up here?"

"Out there the catwalk branches out all over the auditorium," Bug replied. "It's how they adjust the lights from show to show."

"You know a lot about this place."

"I've got Zip's eyes, remember?" Bug said.

Alex nodded.

"You stay here," he said. "I'm going to check it out."

"All right, but there's nothing out there."

Alex stepped onto the metal catwalk and followed it out over the auditorium below. He walked carefully, keeping one hand on the railing, his flashlight beam falling over the dusty stage lights.

He'd almost reached the end of the catwalk when he saw movement again, this time from the left where the metal path branched out over the auditorium. He turned quickly, but his flashlight showed nothing but a dead end on the catwalk. A few hanging wires swayed. He crept forward, and the catwalk creaked. He flashed his light back and forth over the metal floor, until he came to the end. Nothing was there. He exhaled.

And then, all the lights went up.

Alex, momentarily blinded, thrust an arm up in front of

his eyes. He blinked rapidly as his pupils adjusted. Through his squinted eyes, he saw Bug, standing just a few feet behind him, unfazed by the sudden illumination.

"Jeez," Alex said. "Are you trying to kill me?" He grasped onto the railing.

"We wouldn't want that," Bug said. There was a sarcastic quality to his voice Alex had never heard before. "Who'd look after Kirbie and everyone else then?"

"What's that supposed to mean?"

"Nothing," Bug said, taking a few steps forward. "I just thought we'd have a few words while we're alone together, since you see me as competition."

"Competition?" Alex asked. "What are you talking about?"

Bug snorted.

"You don't trust me," he said, taking another step closer. "Not that I can really blame you. I mean, if I changed my allegiances on a whim like you did, I probably wouldn't trust people either."

"Just back off, Bug," Alex said slowly. "You don't want to get on my bad side any more than you already have."

"Bad side. Is that supposed to be funny coming from someone who was a supervillain a month ago?" Bug asked. "I wonder how often the others look at you and wonder if deep down, part of you still belongs to the Cloak Society."

Alex narrowed his eyes and clenched one of his fists. He

kept his mouth shut tight, afraid that he'd say something he'd regret. If only Kirbie and the others were up in the rafters now to see this side of Bug. Alex never should have accepted the outsider into their group, however hesitantly.

"Kirbie told me she's worried about you, you know? About your true loyalties. I'll be keeping an eye on you, Alex," Bug said, turning to walk away. "After all, villainy is in your blood, isn't it?"

Alex's lip pulled back into a sneer as he wrapped Bug in energy and pushed him backward, lifting him into the air and holding him so that his body leaned over the catwalk railing.

Alex looked around, his eyes burning blue.

"Where's your little green friend?" he asked. "Aren't you going to call in a swarm of gnats to fight me off? You are *useless.*"

"Finally, some of that power I keep hearing about," Bug said, not looking worried at all. "But you're just proving my point, aren't you?"

An animal howl came from somewhere on the ground level, followed by the sound of splintering wood, muffled by the red curtain drawn across the stage. Kirbie.

Alex flicked his wrist, and Bug slammed onto the metal grating.

"I'll deal with you later," he spat.

Alex ran to the center of the catwalk. He could hear

the sound of fighting behind the curtain now, and see the fabric billowing out. It was a long drop to the stage, but he was filled with anger, and he needed to get down there. Fast. He took a deep breath, sprinted, and hurtled over the metal railing at the end of the catwalk.

He let out what he hoped sounded more like a battle cry and less like a scream as he pushed energy toward the ground, slowing his descent. He landed on one knee at the edge of the stage, then tore through the split in the center of the curtain, looking for the others.

Fluorescent lights hummed overhead. Pieces of discarded plywood scenery littered the stage—a castle tower here, the wall of someone's bedroom there—dilapidated sets left behind when the troupe moved out. Mallory was thrown through a Styrofoam tree to his right, landing in front of him.

"Mal!" he exclaimed, kneeling at her side. "Are you all right?"

"Yeah," she said, jumping to her feet. "But we've got big trouble."

A kid in his teens stepped on top of the remains of the tree, the brittle Styrofoam crushing beneath his feet. He was on the short side, but sturdily built. He wore black boots and pants, and a dark jacket zipped almost all the way to his throat. His brown hair was short and pushed to one side at a slant.

"Legion," Alex growled.

Mallory thrust a palm forward and shot a bolt of super-heated air directly through Legion's stomach. He hunched over in pain and looked down at the hole in his abdomen before fading away into the air.

"Just one of his clones," Mallory said. "I can't find the real one in this mess, and these guys keep getting in my way. Kirbie's clawing through them one after the other on the other side of the stage."

"All right," Alex said. "Let's find the original."

"He's not our only problem," Mallory said, grabbing Alex's shoulders and twisting him around so he faced the fake bedroom wall.

A tall, lanky figure walked through the plywood, as if it weren't there at all. He was dressed exactly as Legion's clone had been, only his body was translucent. His skin was a chalky white, and his eyes and hair were a matching shade of faint silver. On his right hand he wore a black glove, studded with wide, heavy metal on the knuckles. Five metal points—man-made claws—protruded an inch past each of the fingers.

Ghost.

Alex shot a blast of energy at the Omega, but it went right through him, knocking the bedroom wall over onto another set piece.

"Nice try," Ghost said, his voice a rasping whisper.

"How do we fight him?" Alex asked.

"We don't." Mallory said.

They turned and ran, darting between painted plywood and scrim and trying not to trip over sandbags and weights. Ghost cut them off as they rounded the castle tower. He solidified and swiped at Alex's face with a clawed hand, but Alex blocked him with the arm of his coat, the built-in bulletproofing stopping the blades. Then, realizing that Ghost had to be tangible at that moment, he blasted the Omega with a telekinetic bolt. Ghost flew backward, fading away before sailing through the back wall of the theater.

Across the stage, a sonic blast erupted, sending a handful of Legion's clones smashing through the scenery onstage, nearly clearing it completely. Amp and Kirbie stood beside the theater's fly system, the ropes and pulleys that controlled the lights and backdrops hanging above the stage. Kirbie was in her wolf form, and she roared and charged, leaping up the back of the castle tower and pulling the real Legion from his hiding spot, then tossing him onto the stage. He bounced and tumbled on the splintered scenery, copies rolling out of him.

Alex began to charge forward, but a pale arm wrapped around his neck, choking him. Ghost had ahold of him. A strange sensation ran through Alex as he watched his hands fade away and he began to sink through the stage, like the chill that ran through his body whenever Phantom used her powers near him. His palm froze, and for a moment he could see two worlds—the brightly lit stage in Silver Lake, and the barren wasteland of the Gloom.

Ghost let him go in the near darkness beneath the stage. Thin lines of light poured in from the seams between slats of wood above him. Alex jumped forward and turned around to see the Omega, hardly visible in his intangible form.

"Little Alexander Knight," he rasped. "Thinks he's all grown up and can take on the world. I remember when you were just a Gamma, a little nuisance always following the rest of us around."

"Things change," Alex muttered, backing away, feeling behind him in the darkness for a wall or staircase, attempting to get his bearings.

"Not everything," Ghost said, stepping forward. "Not the Cloak Society."

Alex gathered all the energy he could around himself, trying to create a shield as Ghost approached. The Omega raised his hand to attack, but Alex kept the crackling blue energy pulsing close to his body, waiting for the perfect moment to strike, when he could be sure that Ghost was able to take damage.

The Omega swung his clawed fingers at Alex's throat. Just before they made contact, there was a flash in Alex's eyes, and telekinetic energy exploded from his body. It forced Ghost upward, banging his head against the ceiling, and blew open a trapdoor not far from where Alex was standing. Without hesitation, he climbed back up onto the stage and rejoined the battle.

Amp, Kirbie, and Mallory were tearing through the onslaught of duplicates stepping out of the original Legion. The clones repeatedly faded away, only to be replaced almost instantaneously. Bug stood off to the side, his eyes shining. Suddenly a small army of beetles and roaches and flies swarmed in from the open stage door, clouding around several of the copies' faces, blinding them.

Alex readied a blast of energy to take out the real Legion, when the Omega noticed him and, sneering, pulled a small gun from inside his jacket. Alex couldn't tell if it was another taser, or something far more lethal. Legion pointed it at Alex, his lip curled up in a snarl.

"I'm so tired of taking it easy on all of you," he said. "I'm sure no one would mind if just one of you was killed *accidentally*."

"Hey, loser with the gun," a voice called from across the stage.

Legion turned to see Del standing by the theater's fly system.

"Lay off my friends," she said.

Before Legion could send his clones in for an attack, she flicked her hair back. The ropes behind her were severed, sending the counterweights sailing toward the ceiling.

Onstage, a canvas backdrop plummeted from the rafters. Legion realized what was happening a moment too late, and the thick metal rod lining the bottom of the backdrop missed his head by only a few inches. It caught his right shoulder, causing him to cry out in pain. The metal and canvas kicked up dust on the stage. Legion stood with his arm hanging limply, his shoulder clearly dislocated, as Kirbie and the others dispatched his final clones.

Ghost appeared, rising from beneath the stage. He stood beside Legion, whispering something into his ear. They stared at the gathered forces around them. Amp, Alex, and Mallory had their hands poised in front of them. Kirbie was in wolf form, growling, while Del's hair floated out in a fan around her, small throwing knives glittering in the stage lights. Bug's eyes glowed, looking menacing, a swarm of insects buzzing above him.

Legion looked at Ghost, and back to Alex. He smiled smugly.

"Next time," he said.

Ghost reached out and placed a hand on the other Omega's shoulder, and the two of them sank into the floor just as simultaneous shots of telekinetic power, sound energy, and subzero temperatures converged on them, the three attacks knocking a hole into the cinder-block wall at the back of the stage. Everyone remained frozen, alert, ready for another attack. Instead they heard the sound of a car starting outside and peeling away into the night.

"Did we scare them away?" Bug asked.

"I think so," Kirbie said.

"We couldn't have," Alex said, confused. "You heard Legion. They were taking it easy on us. They could have kept fighting."

"Maybe they're not as powerful as we thought," Kirbie said hopefully.

"No. I think they just retreated until they could fight us on their terms," Mallory said. "We already know they're supposed to take us alive."

"It doesn't make sense," Alex said, shaking his head. "So what *was* their mission? Why were they here?"

"Wait, so . . . we won?" Bug asked.

What a stupid thing to ask, Alex thought. And with the Omegas gone, he remembered the anger that had surged through him on the catwalk before the fight broke out.

"You!" he said, pointing in Bug's direction. He flexed his fingers and lifted, raising Bug into the air.

"Alex!" Kirbie yelled.

"We can't trust him," Alex said. "This is the *second time* he's let someone attack us when we were supposed to be alone. And you should have heard him on the catwalk. . . ."

"What are you talking about?" Bug asked. "I wasn't even up there."

"Liar!" Alex's eyes flashed with blue energy.

"Knight!" Amp yelled, pulling at his outstretched arm. "What are you doing?"

"All I did was turn the lights on, and then I heard the fighting down here," Bug said, appealing to the others.

"Cut the act," Alex sneered. "Why are you really here?"

"Alex, the Omegas showed up in a car," Mallory said softly but firmly, trying to talk to him logically. "They obviously came *after* Bug did his sweep. That wasn't his fault."

"But still—"

"Just stop!" Kirbie yelled. She looked up at Alex with an expression he recognized immediately. He'd seen it on his mother's face time and again. Disappointment. "Do you know how crazy you sound right now? Do you know how you look? Like someone I fought on the steps of Silver Bank."

Alex looked back at Bug, helplessly kicking his feet, and Zip, buzzing around as if he might be able to help. The assembled flying insects still hovered around Bug—he hadn't tried to use them against Alex. Slowly Alex lowered his arm, and Bug.

There was an uneasiness in the air.

"On the catwalk, before you guys started fighting . . . ," Alex murmured, then shook his head. Nothing made sense to him.

"What did you find in the dressing room?" Amp asked, obviously trying to move on.

"Nothing. The map was unmarked. The boxes were full of packing peanuts," Kirbie said. Her eyes fell on Del. "It's like someone led us to a trap."

"No, I . . ." Del's eyes widened.

"I guess we're just lucky you appeared when you did to save the day," Kirbie said flatly.

"I just figured you guys would come here tonight," she said. "That's why I came."

"She was just trying to help," Alex said.

"Yeah," Kirbie said, her voice rising. "But I didn't pick up Legion's scent when we first got here, or on any of the stuff in the dressing room. Isn't it weird that they showed up for the *first time* once we were inside?"

"What are you accusing me of?" Del asked.

"She just *saved* us," Alex said.

"Hey," Amp said, taking a step between the three of them. "We're alive. They're gone. Now I say we get out of here before they come back with reinforcements, okay?"

Amp was right. They were slow to move, but eventually they began to walk out of the theater.

"Roaches, Bug?" Amp asked.

"They were all I could find on short notice."

"Next time, bring hornets."

"Kirbie . . . ," Alex started.

"No," she said, walking past him. "I don't have anything to say to you right now."

Before Alex could go after her, Del grabbed his arm, a look of desperation on her face.

"Let me go with you," she said, her eyes pleading with him. "Let me *help* you."

Alex was confused, already in trouble with the others, not knowing who to trust, not really sure what to do anymore. And as much as he understood Del's desire to help—as badly as he felt about her past—he couldn't jeopardize their cover.

"Get home safely, Del," Alex said, and he walked away.

He joined the others outside, and they made their way into the trees, starting the long trek back to one of the entrances to the underground tunnel. They had their eyes over their shoulders the whole way back home. No one spoke. Alex felt like if he uttered a single syllable, he might bring the whole world crashing down around him.

16

SHADOWS OF THE
PAST

Alex woke with a start as the sun began to creep over the horizon, staining the sky orange. He'd been having a nightmare, though he couldn't remember the specifics of the dream. He gasped for breath. It took him a few moments to realize that he was safe—relatively speaking—in his room at the lake house. He knew trying to go back to sleep would be hopeless, so he got dressed and tiptoed down the stairs. The house was cold, and he kept his blanket wrapped around him. In the kitchen, he drank a full glass of water. As he stood there, wondering what to do next, he heard a creak coming from Kirbie's room. She must have been awake as well.

He felt the sudden, overwhelming urge to do something

nice for her, remembering how upset she'd been the night before. He thought about making her breakfast, but while searching through the pantry, he came across a paisley tin of tea—chamomile tea, the same kind his mother used to drink to calm down at the end of the day. He found a mug and microwaved some water, dunking the tea bag in afterward.

He made his way to her door and rapped gently. There was no answer, so he knocked harder. Still nothing. With a sigh, he went into the living room. Through the picture window, he could see Mallory sitting on the porch steps. She didn't turn when he opened the front door but somehow knew it was him.

"You used to sleep late every morning," she said. "If it hadn't been for me as your backup alarm clock, I think Barrage would have burned your legs on every run."

"That's true," Alex said, sitting down beside her. "But the one great thing about Julie was that no matter how tired or late I was, she was always worse."

Mallory looked at his mug.

"Started drinking tea?"

"I found it in the pantry," he said. "I thought maybe Kirbie might like it."

"I don't think she's up yet."

"Yeah." He handed the mug out to Mallory. "Want it?"

She smiled and took the tea, holding it in her hands

and heating it to a near boil, until steam rose in white billows from the top. Alex could feel the warmth radiating from her hands. It was nice in the chilly morning air.

"I'm worried, Mal," he said. As soon as the words left his mouth, he felt a little better. Like admitting this to someone else took some of the burden off him.

"I know," Mallory said. "Last night was crazy in a lot of ways, but everyone will be all right."

"I feel like I'm a little out of whack lately."

"You definitely scared Bug," Mallory said. "You really should go easier on him. I've kept a close eye on him since he got here. I think he's okay. And I can see why you think Del would be a good addition to our group. You just have to give Kirbie time to warm up to her."

"It's not just last night. I'm worried about everything. I can hardly sleep because I think every creak in this stupid old house is one of the Omegas. Gage came into the room last night, and I almost knocked him out the window with a telekinetic blast."

"Alex," she said. "We're all scared."

"But you're so on top of everything," he said. "Same with Amp. You two are so calm under pressure."

"Is that what you think?" she asked, smiling with surprise. "Alex, I'm terrified. Amp is completely freaked out, too. We're just really good at putting up a strong front. Besides, thinking about what happens if we don't succeed is too much to deal with. You've always had a habit of trying to take all the responsibility on yourself. Just like on our first mission as Betas. Or at Justice Tower. But we're a *team*. Even if it is a weird one. And that means we share responsibility for everything. That's just how it works."

Alex thought about this for a few moments while Mallory sipped the scalding-hot tea.

"I should have talked to you before," he said. "You always know what to say."

"I think I'm just feeling especially old and wise today since it's . . ." She trailed off, looking away.

Alex was confused for a second before it hit him. It was Mallory's birthday—and he'd completely forgotten.

"Oh man, Mal!" he exclaimed. "I'm so sorry. I forgot. Happy birthday!"

"Shhhh," she said. "I wasn't even going to bring it up. We have plenty of other things to focus on."

"No, no," Alex said. "This is perfect. This is exactly what we need." He jumped up, patting down his hair and hoping that it didn't look like he'd just rolled out of bed. "I'm going to run into town and buy you a cake or something."

"That's *really* not necessary."

"Are you kidding me, Mal? It is *completely* necessary. You stay here. If anyone asks you to do anything, tell them I'll do it when I get back. You just relax. Keep drinking tea or something. I'll be back in no time."

Mallory started to argue with him, but it was too late. Alex was practically halfway down the basement stairs already. She was right. They were a team. And he was going to cheer them up one way or another.

Alex headed to the twenty-four-hour grocery store just a mile away from one of the underground entry points, the same store he'd gone to with Kirbie when Bug started following them. He stopped at a pay phone and searched his pockets, happy to find some loose change. He dialed Del. After several rings, she picked up.

"Yes?" she answered. Her voice was lower than usual, angry-sounding, and for a moment, Alex didn't recognize it.

"Um, Del?"

"Alex!" she said, surprised, her pitch rising. "Sorry, I'm just getting out of bed."

"Hey," he said. "I just wanted to make sure you got home okay last night. After everything that happened . . . I just wanted to check in."

"Thanks," she said. "I'm fine. How's everyone else doing?"

"Okay, I think. Honestly, I haven't seen much of anyone yet."

"Where are you?" Del asked. "Last time you called,

the number came up blocked."

"I'm at a pay phone."

"Oh," she said, sounding a little put out. "I thought maybe you guys were okay with me having your phone number now."

There was a brief moment of silence before she spoke again.

"So what's our next move?"

"I don't know," Alex said. "But we'll figure something out. We have to. Listen, I need to pick a few things up and head back to . . . base. But we'll be in touch. I'm glad you made it home all right."

"Okay," Del said. "Be safe. I hope I talk to you soon."

"And Del, thanks for last night."

Alex walked inside the grocery store and inspected the bakery counter. He found a box of a dozen cupcakes. They were chocolate, Mallory's favorite. Perfect.

The store wasn't very crowded, just a few early-morning shoppers dotting the aisles. There had been a time not too long ago on Cloak's Thursday outings when Alex had looked at people like this—browsing the cereal aisle, comparing the prices of deli meats—and quietly mocked their mundane lives and the seriousness with which they took their groceries while he, a son of the Cloak Society, was destined for such *greater* things. But now he couldn't help but envy them. These people were probably going home to families. Maybe they'd have a quiet day watching movies or reading books, or just spending time together, without much worry.

On a rack beside the checkout lane, he spotted the morning copy of the *Sterling City Chronicle*. For the first time since the fall of Justice Tower, the front-page headline didn't mention the Rangers. Instead it read CITIZENS GRIPPED BY FEAR: RIOTS REPORTED ACROSS THE CITY. Alex's heart pounded. The city was starting to crumble in on itself. They had to think of a plan. Fast.

Alex's mind raced as he left the grocery store. He needed time to clear his head, to figure out their next move, so he took the long way back, walking slowly and taking a few detours. He tried to focus and use the meditation techniques Kirbie had taught him to calm down a little, but his thoughts were still a jumble.

He ended up in an unfamiliar area comprised mostly of old buildings and stores that hadn't yet opened for the day. The wind picked up, making him shiver. Alex stared down at his right hand, just to make sure that the cold was natural, and not a reaction to Phantom's powers. Nothing there.

He was so caught up in his own thoughts that he didn't realize he was being followed. It was only after he made a sharp right turn to head toward the tunnel that he noticed a shadow moving into an alley. He froze for a moment, unsure of what to do. To continue on would lead his tail straight to the lake house. But facing whoever it was alone was dangerous. If someone was after him, they were undoubtedly sent by Cloak—it wasn't like one of the Junior Rangers' fan club members would recognize *him*—and he wasn't sure if he could take them on himself. He could always try to shake them off his trail . . . but he was tired of running.

Alex turned and marched to the alley, a grimy, narrow space between two tall buildings. There was no one there, but the alley splintered off into different routes between the structures, peppered with rusted trash cans. Alex paused, taking in the scene, noting the fire escapes and possible hiding points for enemies, and began to venture farther into the alley.

Someone approached from around the corner. His father. Volt. Dad. He stood in the center of the alley and looked Alex dead in the eyes. He said nothing, only shook his head in disappointment, and then continued walking, disappearing behind one of the buildings.

Alex dropped the bag of cupcakes. His first instinct was to call out to his father, but he had to remember that Volt was the enemy now. He took a deep breath and ran forward, gathering great masses of telekinetic energy in his hands. This was it, he thought. His final stand. It had come sooner than he expected.

He turned the corner, following Volt's path, but

instead of Volt, there was Titan.

"Pathetic," Titan sneered.

Alex released a blast of power from his hand, but Titan dodged it, rolling out of view into another alley. The blast hit the corner of one of the buildings, sending up an eruption of brick dust. Alex ran into it at full speed, holding his breath, shielding his eyes from the debris with one arm.

When he stopped he was in another short, dead-end alley. There was nowhere for Titan to run, no doors or windows for him to disappear into. Only Titan wasn't there. At the end of the alley, leaning against one of the walls with her arms crossed over her Cloak trench, was Shade. She smiled as Alex stood frozen, a stunned look on his face.

"Hello, my son," she said softly.

"Mother." He hadn't been prepared to see her, hadn't been prepared for all the emotions that her face brought boiling to the surface. His anger at her and fear of what she was capable of . . . but also, his desire to prove himself to her.

He shook his head and raised mental shields of energy, hoping to defend himself against her powers. They must have already been at work without him realizing it. Otherwise, there was no way to explain the disappearance of his father, or Titan. But he couldn't feel her powers like he usually did when she was poking around in his brain.

He dug his heels into the ground and clenched his

fists, ready to go on the offensive. He kept his eyes trained on hers, watching for flashes of silver. His whole body trembled.

"My darling Alexander," Shade continued, taking a step away from the wall. "Don't you think it's time you came home? Don't you miss your family? Your destiny?"

"What do you want?" Alex asked.

"I want what any mother would want," Shade said, taking a few more steps forward. "I want my son at home. I know we've had our differences lately, but can't we put all that behind us? The Cloak Society is on the verge of greatness. We're so close to breaking into a new age. I want you beside me when that happens."

"You just want my powers," Alex said. "You want me to be your mindless weapon."

She continued to walk toward him, slowly shortening the gap between them.

"I'm not attacking you *now*, am I? Not trying to turn off your thoughts and cause you to drift into a long nap. Though you look like you could use it, dear. Have you not been sleeping well?"

"Stop trying to play games with me," Alex said. He shouldn't have been talking to her, should have attacked while she thought she had him distracted. But he couldn't. Alex found himself wanting to hear what she had to say. Wanting to hear her voice a little bit more.

"Let's think about this rationally, Alex. It's you and your pathetic little group of lost-kid Rangers and remnants of the Beta Team against the Cloak Society, with all our power and resources. You can't hope to win against us."

There was the mother he knew. At his feet, trash and bits of brick began to float into the air. It may have been his fate to be a part of the Cloak Society—it may have been in his blood—but he wouldn't go without a fight. If the High Council wanted him back, they'd have to break through every blast of crackling blue energy he could muster.

"No," Alex admitted. "But we can try."

"Fine," Shade said, her face taking an ugly shape. She was only a few yards away from him now. "Then let's negotiate. You come back to the base with me, and I'll forget about the others. About Misty. About the she-wolf. How does that sound? You'll only get this kindness from me once, son. Turn your back on this offer, and you'll watch the rest of your friends suffer *horrors* before we're done with you."

Alex thought about this. It didn't sound so bad, trading his life for theirs. But he knew Shade, knew how the High Council worked. There was nothing keeping his mother from stripping away his thoughts and memories and then going after the others. He imagined that she'd send *him* in after Kirbie and Misty and the rest of them, just to humor the Council.

"So," Shade said, offering an open palm out to her son. "Have we got a deal?"

Alex smiled. It was a pleasant feeling to know exactly what to do for a change. He shoved both hands forward, lighting up the alley with popping blue energy. Shade flew backward, along with all the trash cans, litter, dirt, and dust in the alley. She hit the brick wall behind her and fell to the ground, the metal cans clanging down around her.

Alex darted toward the spot where she fell, ready to attack again if necessary. But he couldn't find her. There was no one there. No body. He glanced down at his palm, but there was no Cloak mark either—he hadn't felt the icy surge of Phantom's powers in use. It was as if his mother had just disappeared into thin air.

Or she was never there at all.

Alex rubbed his temples, worried about a different threat now. He hadn't been sleeping much. He'd been paranoid and tired—others had said so. He wasn't in the right frame of mind.

Had he imagined the incident with Bug the night before as well?

Alex was suddenly very scared that he was going crazy.

He backed slowly out of the alley and picked up the cupcakes. He kept his eyes sharp, but there was no sign that anyone else had been there at all.

He started for the tunnel. No one followed him. There were no shadows this time. Only a deep urge to be back with the others, where he was certain he belonged.

Alex was still confused and shaken by the alleyway ordeal when he arrived back at the lake house, just in time to meet Amp and Kirbie on the platform underneath the basement.

"You shouldn't have gone out by yourself," Amp said.

"It's Mal's birthday today. I went out for cupcakes." He raised the bag in his hand slightly.

Alex noticed that they were dressed warmly, and that Kirbie's Ranger uniform was peeking out from beneath her sweater.

"Where are you two going?" Alex asked.

"On patrol," Kirbie said. "There are a few things we want to check out."

"Oh," Alex said. "Give me a few minutes and I'll join you."

"No," Kirbie said, a little too firmly for Alex's liking. "We just need to blow off a little steam. Patrol like we used to, before everything happened. Before we ended up here."

"No offense," Amp said. "We both have communicators. We'll be in touch."

"Sure," Alex said. "I get it. This is a Rangers-only kind of thing."

"Alex . . . ," Kirbie started. She looked like she was on the verge of saying something important, but instead sighed. "Kyle's rechecking the info on those buildings, looking for anything we might have missed. You should help him. Take it easy today. You look pale."

And with that, the two of them stepped onto the transport and were whisked away through the underground tunnel. Alex watched from the platform until they were nothing but a faint speck in the distance, and then finally, nothing at all.

17

RIFT

They ate the cupcakes after lunch. Mallory was grateful, grinning widely when Alex presented them to her, but it was Misty who was really excited. She had two while Kyle triple-checked information about the possible Omega bases, and Bug went on his daily nature walk around the perimeter. Alex hid a few of the desserts in the back of the fridge for Kirbie and Amp to eat once they returned from patrol.

Alex decided not to tell Mallory—or anyone else, for that matter—about the incident with the Cloak members in town. He was feeling crazy enough already. He was afraid of how she might look at him if he told her he'd chased imaginary figures into a winding alleyway. After all, had his mother actually been there, she never would have let him escape. So he spent the afternoon alone in the Rec Room. He sat down on the couch and spread the marked map of Silver Lake out on the coffee table. His vision began to blur after a few minutes, but he didn't blink, as if the correct path might be laid out before him if he just looked at the map from a different perspective. Soon his lack of sleep over the past few days took over, and he was drifting between sleeping and waking, balancing somewhere in between. He half wondered if this was what had happened earlier in the day—if he was experiencing waking dreams. He sat on the couch like this for some time, before he felt hands shaking him. He flung his arms out, sending a low-level telekinetic pulse through the room, then opened his eyes, only to see Gage on the floor beside him, getting to his feet.

"It's only me," Gage said.

"Gage! I didn't realize I was sleeping so deeply," he said. He looked around the room, groggy with sleep.

A great, satisfied grin spread over Gage's face. His eyes were wide and wild, and his goggles were pushed up into his hair, causing his dark curls to shoot out in every direction.

"I've done it," he said proudly. "To be honest, I wasn't sure if it was even possible, but I've done it. I've found a way into the Gloom."

Alex didn't move. His heart felt like it was on fire, and it took everything in him not to scream with excitement. Just when he was feeling that failure was inevitable, Gage was providing them with a possible victory.

"Show me," he said.

Gage had rearranged the workstations in the garage so that the circular patio table stood a few yards away from one of the garage doors. On it sat the containment device Alex and the others had recovered from the underground base, only now there was something else connected to it. Metal cables and wires protruded from its top, and in a thick metal setting facing straight ahead—Mallory's work, Alex imagined—was the Excelsior diamond, aimed at the big metal door.

"How does it work?" Alex asked.

"Phantom's concentrated energy flows through the Excelsior like a filter," Gage said. "With a little surge of power, the dark energy gets pushed out of the diamond, creating an entrance. I can be more technical if you like."

"As long as it gets us in. You're sure it's safe?" Alex asked. "You seemed pretty concerned about it just a few days ago."

"I booted it up right before I came and got you," Gage said. "All the readings are stabilized."

"What about Phantom? She could sense the Umbra Gun in Justice Tower. Can she pick up on this, too?"

"We should be perfectly safe," Gage said with a small

smile. He picked up an electronic screen he'd swiped from the underground base and tapped on it. A light began to shine below the diamond on the device. It pulsed a dull golden yellow.

"Using my notes on Lone Star's energy, I installed a miniature cloaking device. . . ." Gage paused for a moment. "If you'll forgive my word choice. The device emits only slightly higher levels of Phantom's energy than your Cloak mark. And while she might be able to detect someone who is marked *inside* the Gloom, the rift in planes that this creates shouldn't draw any unwanted attention to us. The only reason she sensed the Umbra Gun was because the concentrated energy inside its container had no dampener."

Alex nodded, staring at the device.

"What do we do now?" he asked.

"We need to test it," Gage said. "I opened the portal once, but I haven't tried to pass anything through it."

"You want to test it *now*?"

"Unless you have more pressing matters," Gage said.

Alex smiled wide. "Are you kidding? Fire it up."

Gage tapped on the screen again. The dim light faded slightly as something dark colored the Excelsior. Suddenly four points of inky energy shot from the gem, forming the corners of a perfectly symmetrical diamond shape on the garage door. The darkness spread, until straight lines connected the points, and then the garage door simply melted away. It was replaced by roiling, oily shadows—energies Alex recognized from Phantom's portals.

"You genius," Alex whispered. "You actually did it."

"The Excelsior device opens a rift between our world and the Gloom," Gage said. "But once the link is established, the portal becomes self-sustaining, drawing power from the other plane."

"You mean this thing could stay open forever?"

"Under ideal circumstances, its possible. But there are other factors. Entropy, for example. And the diamond serves as a stabilizer, so moving the Excelsior too far away would cause the portal to crash. I haven't measured at what distance that sort of implosion would occur."

Alex looked around the garage and found a fishing rod leaning against one of the walls. He picked it up and walked tentatively toward the portal, his right hand growing colder with every step. He didn't even have to look—he knew that the mark of Cloak was out and gleaming on his palm.

He was a yard away from the portal when Gage stopped him. The inventor took the rod and motioned for him to step back, handing Alex the computer screen.

"I have tested my last invention on you, my friend," Gage said, turning to the gateway in front of him and pulling his goggles over his eyes. "This one is on me."

He stepped confidently to the portal and, with only a beat of hesitation, began to push the fishing rod into the darkness. It slid in easily, without resistance. He held it there for a moment, then pulled it back out, holding the end of it up for closer inspection. It seemed fine, and it *felt* normal, if a bit cold.

Gage looked up at the portal, his face determined. He dropped the rod onto the floor and began to step forward.

"Uh, Gage," Alex said, trying to mask his concern. "Maybe we should test it on something else first. I can find Bug and have him fly Zip inside."

"We don't know if his connection with insects can cross over into the Gloom," Gage said. "Trust me, I've been over the possibilities in my head. This is the only way we'll know if it works."

Without hesitation, Gage took two big steps forward and thrust one hand into the darkness. He shivered for a moment. Alex stepped forward, but Gage shook his head.

"If something goes wrong or I'm not back in a few minutes, hit the red button on the screen," Gage said.

And with that, Gage bent at the waist, pushing the upper half of his body through the portal. He stayed like that for a few seconds before stepping forward and disappearing into the garage door completely.

"Gage!" Alex shouted, but there was only the low roar of the gateway.

He stared into the portal for what felt like a very long time. Terrible scenarios began to flood his mind. He imagined the portal starting to grow, eating away at his world. He thought of Gage, never to be seen again, lost to wander the Gloom indefinitely with the Rangers of Justice, their only hope of escaping gone. Or of the skeletal monster he had seen in the Gloom before—when he'd snuck out of Cloak's base with the goal of kidnapping Kirbie and proving his loyalty to the High Council—staggering into the garage, moaning an anguished howl, coming for him.

Fortunately, none of these things came true, and Gage eventually walked out of the blackness and back into his makeshift workshop as if he were walking in through the front door. He shook his head and blinked, his eyes readjusting to the bright overhead lights.

"Right," he said. "It works. You can turn it off now."

Alex stared dumbly at Gage for a moment before hitting the red button on the screen. The lights on the device went out, and the dark energy of the portal fell away, retreating into the shadows of the garage.

"It works," Alex repeated softly. "It works! Gage, you realize you just saved Sterling City. I mean, you may have just saved the world!"

"One step at a time," Gage said, though he couldn't help but smile. "We haven't found the Rangers yet."

"Yeah, but now we *can*," Alex said, his mind reeling. "What's it like inside?"

"It's the Gloom," Gage said, confused by why Alex

would ask such a question. "It's miles of darkness and wasteland and cold."

"We have to tell the others," Alex said, putting down the screen and heading for the door.

"I'm going to stay out here," Gage said. "I'm wondering if I can create a tracking device that could home in on Lone Star's energy signature."

"Nope. Not this time, Gage," Alex said. He held open the door. "Come inside and take some credit."

Gage looked taken aback at first, but a smile began to creep across his face.

"Okay," he said, following Alex toward the house.

Alex began yelling as soon as he opened the front door, causing Kyle to spring out of his chair and the plants in the room to shake. Mallory and Misty ran down the stairs, while Bug emerged from the kitchen with a cupcake in his hand, Zip fluttering around his right shoulder.

"Gage, tell them," Alex said.

"Well," Gage said, "I've figured out a way for us to get into the Gloom."

The room was deadly quiet. Gage shifted his weight on his feet.

"You're sure?" Kyle asked.

"I was standing in the Gloom not two minutes ago," Gage said. "I'm still a little cold, to be honest."

Misty screamed and jumped on Gage, throwing her

arms around him. Gage slowly lifted one hand to pat her on the back.

"I knew you could do it!" Misty said, backing away from him. "You're the smartest person in the whole world."

Before he could respond, they were all hugging him, thanking him for offering their only possible way to defeat Cloak.

"We have to tell Kirbie and Amp," Kyle said, looking at Alex. "When will they be back?"

"I don't know," Alex said. "I haven't seen them since this morning."

All the exuberance faded away from Kyle's expression.

"I thought you would have been in contact with them," he said softly. His eyes searched everyone else's faces, but he could tell that no one else had spoken to them in hours.

"Don't freak out," Mallory said calmly. "I've got a communicator on me. Where's the locater we used to track Bug to the warehouse?"

"I think I saw it on the dining room table," Bug said, licking a bit of frosting off one of his knuckles.

They rushed into the dining room.

"Amp? Kirbie?" Mallory asked into a communicator. "Come in. Can you hear me?"

Alex watched her as Gage booted up the locater. Her eyes met Alex's. She shook her head slightly.

"That's odd," Gage said, tapping on the screen.

"What?" Kyle asked, his voice verging on panic.

"Their communicators aren't broadcasting," Gage said.

"Could the batteries have gone out?" Kyle asked.

"No, that's not possible. Kyle, would you bring me your computer? I'm going to see if I can pinpoint the last place the communicators were broadcasting from."

Kyle disappeared into the living room and returned with his laptop, pushing the others out of the way and opening his computer on the table beside Gage.

"Okay," Gage said, pulling up a map on the computer. "Here. This is where both communicators went dead at almost the exact same time. A few hours ago. It looks like some sort of office building."

They crowded around the screen to see where Gage was pointing, and Alex scanned the map. He picked out Permian Park and a few other landmarks, but none of them were very close to the place Gage had zeroed in on. It was a part of the city Alex had never been before, not too far from one of the underground stops.

"I know that place," Bug said from the back of the group. "That's where Del went after we met her in the park."

"What?" Alex asked. "No. I dropped her off over here somewhere, a mile away from there, at least." He pointed to the map. "Misty was with me."

"Right, but . . ." Bug hesitated for a moment. "Kirbie didn't trust Del, so she sort of had me follow you guys when you walked her home. Well, Zip followed you, technically. After you and Misty left, Del climbed out of the backyard and went to this office building. That's the last I saw of her. Zip was too big to get in through any of the vents, and I was too far away to connect with any other insects."

"You followed me?" Alex asked, anger tingeing his voice.

"Kirbie asked me to," Bug said.

"I . . . ," Alex started, but the implication of what Bug said was beginning to sink in. "Del lied to me."

Kirbie had been right. Of course she had been. Every instance that she or Amp or anyone had questioned Del's motives came to his mind, along with every time that he'd vouched for her.

"So Kirbie knew about this place?" Kyle asked, his voice verging on the frantic.

"Well, yeah," Bug said. "She had me write down the address for her and everything."

"That's what they were doing this morning," Alex said. "They were going to investigate Del."

"We need to move," Mallory said, her face very serious. "If the signal went down a few hours ago, they could still be there."

"You're right," Alex said. "Get ready to go. We leave in one minute."

"I'm coming with you," Kyle said, his jaw set. Behind him, the plants in the living room thrashed about in their pots. "I'm not losing my sister again."

Alex nodded and turned to Misty. "With Kyle gone, I need you to help protect the house. Gage has created something that could save Sterling City, and I need you to keep it safe. If this is bad—if my mother has gotten to them—then Cloak knows where we are."

"Right." Misty nodded firmly.

"If there's even a *hint* of anything strange, you take the device and Gage and you mist out of here. If that happens, we'll regroup at . . . Permian Park. Okay?"

"I won't let you down," she said.

"I know you won't."

Kyle found a black peacoat in the living room closet and buttoned it up. Bug's steps could be heard in his room upstairs. Alex's mind was spinning. Nothing made sense, no matter how he tried to piece things together. Why would Del turn against them? Had everything, even her attack against Cloak in Victory Park, been a lie? Or was there something else at play that he just wasn't seeing?

Gage uttered a small curse at the computer screen.

"What's wrong?" Alex asked, terrified of what this new crisis might be.

"The building Bug tracked Del back to," Gage said, shaking his head. "It's been owned by an entity called the Zener Corporation for years. I don't know why I didn't catch this when I did my first sweep of the map."

Alex thought of his room at the underground base, where he'd had a wall covered in Cloak-related newspaper clippings and photos. There in the center was a portrait of his grandfather—his mother's father—the man who had run the High Council before the present generation took over. He had called himself "Grim," but before that he'd had a real name. *Charles Zener.*

"It's a Cloak building. That means Del . . . ," Alex murmured, backing out of the room slowly, then sprinting up the stairs.

He threw on the Beta uniform that Misty had given him. He'd need to be able to move. To fight. For a moment, it looked as though the grinning silver skull on his chest was laughing at him. From his backpack, he grabbed a few items that might come in useful and shoved them into his pockets. Mallory was waiting for him at the bottom of the stairs in her Cloak uniform as well, ready to fight if necessary. Bug and Kyle joined them as Alex quickly brought everyone up to speed, warning them that this could be bad—that they were about to enter Cloak's territory.

"This is it," Alex said. "We have to be prepared for anything."

"What do we do if Del's there?" Mallory asked.

"We have to assume she's an enemy," Alex said.

In the back of his mind, he was still trying to piece together how, exactly, Del had gotten involved with Cloak.

Had she always been working for them, or had his mother gotten to her and made her some sort of drone?

"Alex," Bug said, "I know I probably shouldn't have followed you without—"

"Bug," Alex interrupted. He stared at him gravely for a second before speaking again. "When we get there, give me a tight perimeter, and move your insects in as quickly as you can. I want to know what's waiting in that building before we storm inside."

"Of course," Bug said, nodding.

Alex started down the steps and into the basement, the others following behind him. He held open the hatch in the cement floor as the rest of his team climbed down. Misty and Gage watched from the top of the stairs.

"We have communicators," Alex said. "We'll keep in touch."

"Be careful," Misty said.

"You too."

And with that, he climbed down into the darkness, shutting the hatch behind him.

18

A FAMILIAR
FACE

They flew through the city streets, running as if chased by beasts, until they crouched in a parking lot across from the office building where the signals had stopped broadcasting. The sun had just set. Night enveloped the town. Bug sent Zip ahead as he, Alex, Mallory, and Kyle hid behind a row of hedges. The building looked like any other office building, with a single floor of office space, the windows all tinted dark, reflecting the world outside. Kyle brought the shrubs up around them, shielding everyone from view.

"What have we got?" Alex asked Bug.

"Glass front door. Back entrance as well. I've got gnats inside, but they're slow," Bug said. "The entire floor is a bunch of cubes and empty offices. I'm not seeing any movement, and the place is completely dark."

"Look," Mallory said, pointing. "On the side of the building. There's a tiny basement window with light pouring through it."

"Okay," Bug said. "I'm sending Zip to check it out. No good. The window's frosted. Doesn't look too thick, but it's too small for us to get through. Wait! One of the gnats is inside. . . . I think I've found what might be a door, but it's completely sealed. I can't get anyone through there."

"All right," Alex said. "Then we go in through the back, quietly. Once we're in there, we'll figure out this sealed door. Kyle and Mal, cover me while I work the locks. Bug, keep close to us and report any movement. Remember to watch the floors—I don't want Ghost taking us by surprise."

"We could be walking into a trap," Mallory said.

"I know," Alex said. "But this is all we have. We can't lose Amp and Kirbie."

"Let's *go*," Kyle said. "If my sister is in there, that's where I need to be."

They jogged across the empty street. Alex paused only once, as they passed the frosted basement window. He thought he saw a shadow move behind the glass, but he couldn't be sure.

Alex made short work of the locks on the back door, and soon they were inside, tiptoeing on the Berber carpeting. The desk furniture and upholstery were all dusty.

Spiderwebs had been spun between the arms of chairs. No one had used the office building for its intended purpose in many years. It was nothing more than a cover for whatever was below them.

Bug led them into what must have been the office break room. Inside was the sealed door the gnat had found. There was no knob or hinges, just a tall rectangular panel on the wall.

"What do you think?" Bug asked.

"How do we even know this is a door?" Kyle asked.

"Trust me," Alex said. "It's a door." The square screen to the left of the panel was identical to the electronic screens in the underground base.

"Be on guard," Mallory said.

Alex stepped forward and raised his right palm to the screen. It flashed, and the panel slid away, revealing a staircase leading down into a brightly lit hallway.

"Bug?" Alex asked.

Zip flew past them.

"It's a single long hallway," Bug whispered. "Rooms on either side. Windows in each door. They look empty. There's one that looks like it's being used as a bedroom. It's got a map and computer and stuff. . . ." Suddenly Bug took off, bolting down the stairs.

"Bug!" Alex whispered urgently, as loud as he could. "What are you doing?"

"Kirbie's tied up in the last room," Bug called over his shoulder. "She's the only person here."

Kyle stormed down the stairs, running through the hallway until he saw Kirbie through one of the door windows. Her mouth was gagged, her arms bound behind her in a chair, her legs chained. Alex was right behind him and ripped the door from its hinges with a single thought.

Kyle ran inside, pulled the cloth from his sister's mouth, and hugged her.

"Get me out of here," she whispered anxiously.

"Just give me a second," Alex said. Her hands and feet were held in metal cuffs. They were simple locks—he was surprised she hadn't gotten out of them herself, knowing how she'd once escaped from the metal chair in Cloak's underground cell—and the bonds clinked open and onto the floor with just a little nudging from his mind.

Kirbie jumped up out of the chair and embraced Kyle.

"I knew you'd come for me," she said. "How did you find me?"

"The communicators," Kyle said. "We just tracked their last broadcast."

"Of course," Kirbie said, smiling broadly. "So smart."

"You're okay?" Alex asked.

"Yeah," Kirbie said.

"Where's Amp?"

"He's not here," Kirbie said. "Just let me catch my

breath for a second and think."

"I was so worried," Kyle started. "When you didn't respond . . ."

He kept talking as Alex went out to investigate the rest of the hall. He entered the room across from them—the bedroom Bug had noted. On one of the walls was a large map of Silver Lake. Like the maps at the lake house Rec Room, it was covered in notes. There was a bunch of circles on it, mostly places Alex recognized—Permian Park, the warehouse where they'd first met Del, and the grocery store where they shopped, the place where Alex had gone to buy cupcakes earlier that day. Beside the store, written in red pen, was a phone number. Lines were drawn all over the map in places where he knew he'd been, paths he had taken.

He was looking at the map the Omegas were using to find them.

His head pounded. On a desk beneath the map were a laptop and several notebooks. He traced his finger over one of them lightly.

"Alex," Kirbie called from across the hall, "come back in here, please. I need you."

He looked into the other room. Kirbie's expression was frantic.

There was something odd about the way she was acting. He'd seen her in worse circumstances, watched as her whole world fell apart in Justice Tower, and never had she looked that scared.

"Where's Amp?" he asked again, walking back into the room.

"I don't know," she said, her eyes getting dewy. "We came in here to look around and we were attacked so fast that I'm not sure what happened. When I woke up, I was cuffed in that chair. That was right before you got here."

She walked over to Alex and gave him a long hug.

"Thank you," she said.

"What do we do now?" Bug asked.

"We can't stay here," Mallory said.

"If he's not here, we should go back to base," Kirbie said. "Regroup, then search for him. I'll try to remember anything that might be helpful."

Slowly Alex was putting everything together. Things finally started to make sense. The disappearing Cloak members in the alley that morning. The way Del always showed up exactly where they were. He began to realize that all of them had made a grave mistake when they started chasing after the Omegas. That all this time, they thought they were on the Omegas' trail, when really someone else had been on theirs. Watching their moves. Guiding them. Trying to infiltrate their ranks and discover their whereabouts.

All these thoughts became a mess in his head, until

they were practically screaming at him, and then, he *stopped* thinking. He breathed deep and cleared his mind, just like Kirbie had taught him to do on the lawn of the lake house. Adrenaline rushed through his veins. He had a terrible suspicion and had to be absolutely focused. The blue of his world fell away, and color faded in. The ache in his head disappeared.

"Don't you think?" Kirbie asked again. "Back home?"

"Kirbie . . . ," Alex said, looking at her closely before letting the blue energy filter back into his world. He took a deep breath. "If I'm wrong, please forgive me."

Before she could question him, he thrust his palms forward, sending a blast of blue energy sailing at her. She moved as if the rest of the world were in slow motion, her right shoulder twisting over as she bent backward, her body taking an inhuman position that should have broken her back. The telekinetic bolt shot past, missing her torso by less than an inch, and smacked into the wall between Bug and Kyle, crumbling the plaster.

"Kirbie!" Kyle shouted, stepping forward.

Slowly Kirbie's body twisted up, but now all hints of tears or fright were replaced by pure anger.

"What gave me away?" she asked, her voice low. "I was perfect."

"You didn't give her enough credit." Alex smirked. "She would have been out of those cuffs in no time."

Kirbie's lip curled up in a snarl.

"And the eyes," Alex said. "Kirbie's hazel eyes were the first thing I saw in color after three years of nothing but blue."

"What are you doing?" Kyle asked, his words frantic. He stepped forward, but Mallory pulled him back. Things were falling into place for her, too.

"This isn't your sister," Alex said, never taking his eyes off the girl in front of him. He let his thoughts creep down into his coat pocket, holding on to one of the items he'd brought from the lake house. "She's been playing us all along."

"Alexander Knight," the girl said, her voice full of scorn. "The prodigal son of Cloak. I expected more from you, but you're nothing but a scared little boy who's lost his way, aren't you? Practically helpless."

"I wouldn't say helpless," Alex said.

He thrust his hands out once more, and again Kirbie's body twisted down and over at a sharp angle. But this time, the attack wasn't a telekinetic bolt. Instead a small Cloak weapon emerged from Alex's pocket, wrapped in blue energy. The taser. Alex clenched his thoughts around the trigger. The girl saw it too late, and the electronic blast caught her on the side.

She fell to the floor and began to shake. Kyle burst forward, pushing Alex out of the way and kneeling beside his sister. Her body began to change. One moment she was Kirbie, and then she was Del. But she didn't stay in that form for long. She was Shade. And Titan. And Volt. Even Bug, much to the *real* Bug's shock. He jumped back, nearly tumbling over the chair in the room.

"Kirbie!" Kyle shouted as Mallory and Alex pulled him away from the shape-shifting body.

Finally the girl was nothing at all, just a blank gray mannequin. It melted down, forming a small pool on the floor, then began to reform itself, a female figure growing toward the ceiling. Her color returned. In front of them stood a tall, thin girl dressed all in black, just as Legion and Ghost had been at the theater. Her hair was blond, slicked back. Her eyes were a penetrating blue. She sneered at Alex.

"The girl from the warehouse," Bug murmured.

"Novo," Mallory said furiously.

"I can't believe it took you so long to figure out," Novo said. When she spoke, her voice rang with higher and lower tones, as if echoed by several other people. "I thought I was being so *obvious* at times."

"That was you in the alley this morning," Alex said. "And it was you on the catwalk—not Bug. You were at the theater the whole time. No scent. Easy to blend in with the shadows."

"Just trying to shake things up a little bit," Novo said. "I had to keep you on your toes. Fracturing your little team was surprisingly easy. But then, allegiance isn't really something you value, is it, Alex?"

Alex tried to wrap his thoughts around her, but they slipped right off, just as they had with Del's hair—with *Novo's* hair. Mallory took a step, slowly making her way behind Novo, ready to attack, but the Omega's arm shot out, stretching twice its normal length, until it was a long blade pointed directly at Mallory's neck.

"No, no, no," Novo said. "Play nice or I disappear and you never find your friends."

"Where are they?" Bug asked, his eyes shining. Alex hoped he was calling in an army of bees or something.

"We underestimated how far your powers developed," Alex said. "The hair was a nice touch. Was that your idea, or is there a real Del somewhere?"

"There was someone like Del once," Novo said with a smile. "But she's long since left this world."

"Your mission wasn't just to track us down," Mallory said, frost forming in the air around her hands. "You've been keeping us distracted. You're nothing but a diversion."

"Every mission given by the High Council is imperative to Cloak's future glory," Novo spat.

"Where's my sister?" Kyle shouted.

"Gone," Novo said. "With the other Ranger. They were so arrogant, storming in here to confront me, as if they had any idea what was really going on. They thought they'd interrogate poor little Del and find out what she was doing in an abandoned office all alone. You should have seen their surprise when Ghost walked through the wall."

"Tell us where they are," Kyle yelled, his fists shaking. His eyes searched the room, looking for anything his powers might be able to manipulate.

"My teammates are making them feel at home far from here." Novo grinned and took a few steps toward Alex. "Turn yourselves in to the Cloak Society at the underground base by tomorrow at midnight. All of you, the Uniband inventor and the little girl as well. Or your friends die."

"You think—," Alex started, but Novo's fist shot forward, connecting with Alex's jaw and knocking him to the ground. At the same time, one of her legs shot back, catching Mallory in the stomach. Her mass shifted, and her right arm became a thick club knocking Bug and Kyle backward. Then Novo sprinted for the door, jumping over Alex, and ran into the bedroom. In a single swipe, she collected the notebooks and laptop. Her body was scarcely more solid than a liquid as it flew through the air, smashing through the frosted window and seeping out onto the sidewalk.

"I can't get ahold of her with my powers," Alex said, getting to his feet.

"Kyle," Mallory said quickly, trying to catch her breath. "Can you stop her?"

"No," he cried, running to the window. "There aren't

any plants close enough."

Alex ran out the door and up the stairs, making his way to the first floor just in time to see a black car turn the corner and disappear into the night. Mallory and Kyle were right behind him.

"We're doomed," Kyle said, destroyed. "Kirbs . . ."

"South," Bug whispered.

"Huh?" Alex asked.

They all turned to Bug, who was only now climbing the stairs. His eyes were glowing a brilliant, golden green.

"She's headed south on Main Street," Bug said. "She's on the phone. Angry. Wait . . . now she's merging onto the loop."

His eyes met Alex's, looking both at him and *through* him, at something else.

"Zip is tucked into the bottom of the back windshield," he said. "If she's on her way to Kirbie and Amp, I can track her."

"Bug," Alex said. "You're amazing."

Bug smiled.

"We need to get back to Gage and Misty," Mallory said. "If Kirbie's at the underground base, the lake house is compromised."

"Right," Alex said. "Radio them now."

"She's on the loop now, headed east," Bug said. "Someone should probably start writing this down."

* * *

By the time they crawled into the basement of the lake house, it was clear by the directions Bug continued spouting that Novo wasn't headed toward the Big Sky Drive-In or the tunnel behind Phil's Fill-Up that led to the underground base. In fact, she seemed to be headed in the *opposite* direction of Cloak's headquarters.

They tore through the house and to the garage, where Gage stood hunched over a map in his lab coat, goggles on top of his head, tracing Novo's route as Misty looked on. They crowded around the map, trying to guess where she might be going.

"Why aren't they headed to the Big Sky?" Alex asked. "Wouldn't that be the smartest place to go?"

"I suspect it's likely a case of pride," Gage said, continuing to map Bug's directions. "The Omegas are supposed to be Cloak's elite squad, and you discovered their Silver Lake base, then foiled Novo's plans to infiltrate our ranks. They may have used this to their advantage by giving us an ultimatum, but it obviously wasn't their original plan. If we don't turn ourselves in—and they can't really be sure that we will—they lose. And there's no way they want the High Council to see that. So it's better for them to capture us away from the base and bring us all in at once."

"But wait. If Novo's going somewhere else—if *Kirbie* is somewhere else, we can take the fight to them," Kyle said. "We'll show up and get the drop on them. For real, this time."

"Yes!" Alex said. "They expected us to raid the warehouse and the theater, but this time it's different."

"I can mist us in!" Misty said. "They wouldn't know we were there until we were *right there*."

"The only question is where they're headed," Kyle said. "She's close to the edge of the city as it is."

"Okay," Bug said. "She's turning off onto a private road. There's no sign. Just a lot of dense trees."

Everyone turned their attention back to the map.

"She's come to a giant wrought-iron gate. It's got to be twenty feet tall, all spikes at the end," Bug continued. "Now she's exiting a tree-lined gravel path and turning onto a circle driveway. This place is gigantic. It's this creepy dark stone building with—"

"Two towerlike structures framing a giant wooden door," Alex said, finishing the sentence for him, his eyes wide. "Stained glass in the tower windows. A peaked roof. Stone dragons on either side of the entrance."

"Wait. How did you know that?" Bug asked, his eyebrows scrunching together.

"It's the old Cloak Society mansion. That was their headquarters before they moved underground," Alex said. Energy welled up inside him. "I've never been there—never even knew where it was, exactly—but I've seen pictures."

"I think I can get us that far," Misty said, looking at the map doubtfully. "But it might wipe me out."

"I don't want to risk that. We'll probably need your help getting into the mansion," Alex said. "Gage, can you figure out a way to get us there?"

"Maybe," Gage said, studying the map. "There's a tributary of Silver Lake that looks like it runs straight up to the back of this stretch of land." He turned his attention to the tarp-covered boat sitting on a trailer in the corner of the garage. "If we take *that*, we can sneak in from behind."

"Misty," Kyle said, "will you go grab the seed box? I don't want to be caught without plants again, wherever it is we're going."

She nodded quickly, darting off into the lake house.

"All right," Alex said, looking at Gage. "We're going on offense. Pack up anything that might be helpful for us. Blackout Bombs, laser pistols—all of it. Including that device that nearly took my hand off. The Umbra Magnet."

"Umbra Magnet. I like that," Gage said. "I'll keep it close. But we should treat it as a last resort, since we can't be sure of its effects."

"You're coming?" Alex asked.

"Of course I am," Gage said. "You have no idea what security they have at the mansion. Plus, you may recall that I'm not a terrible shot."

"Good," Alex said. "Bug, get Zip to figure out every

possible entrance to the mansion."

"I'm already on it. I may not be able to get her in, but I'll scope it out."

"And . . . ," Alex said quietly, "I'm sorry about yesterday and the theater. Even with Novo messing with my mind, I should have had more trust in you, and Kirbie."

Bug smiled. "No worries, friend," he said.

"We have to get this thing down to the water," Mallory said, pulling the tarp off the boat.

"I've got it," Alex said, his eyes filled with crackling energy.

He motioned with a hand and the garage door rose, then he gathered all his energy, fueling it with emotion. He thought of Kirbie and Amp, locked away in the old Cloak mansion somewhere, and of how Novo had deceived him for the past week—even causing him to question his own sanity. He poured all those powerful thoughts into the blazing blue energy surrounding the boat trailer and pushed it out onto the front lawn. He followed it out of the garage, raised his arms, and gave it another powerful push, sending it rolling down the slight incline of the lawn. It picked up speed and splashed into the cove. The boat floated just off the shore, and the trailer sank beneath the water.

"Wow," Bug said, stepping up beside him.

"Yeah," Alex said. "I'll . . . get the trailer out later."

"Here!" Misty said, running back out of the lake house, carrying a box with her. "I've got the seeds!"

"Thanks," Kyle said. He flipped through the box and shoved several of the packages into his coat pockets.

Mallory and Gage emerged from the garage, the latter carrying a small black duffel bag and the map that would lead them to the Cloak mansion. Together, the six of them walked toward the water.

"I've hidden the gateway into the Gloom in a cooler and placed it in the rafters," Gage said. "It's not much, but it couldn't hurt. Should something happen to me—"

"Don't talk like that," Alex said, cutting him off. "We'll all be back in time for breakfast."

He pulled the boat to them as they walked out onto the dock. They climbed in, Alex sitting behind the wheel, and started it up. Gage took the passenger seat, spreading the map out in front of him.

"Okay," Alex said. "Let's go."

He gunned the throttle, and the boat was off, skimming across the glasslike surface of Silver Lake into the black night.

A CAGE AND A
PADDED ROOM

The water became too shallow for the boat about a mile from the mansion, forcing Alex and the others to travel the rest of the way on foot through the dense woods that butted up against the muddy banks of the river. Zip met them on the shore, guiding their path.

As soon as they were close enough, Bug sent out more scouts, surrounding the Gothic mansion.

"Novo's upstairs in a study," Bug said. "She looks angry, throwing her arms around as she talks. Ghost is sitting in a chair in the middle of the room, reading a book. He doesn't seem to be paying much attention to her."

"Good," Alex said. "They're not expecting us."

"Amp!" Bug whisper-shouted. "I've found him."

"Where is he?" Kyle asked. "Is my sister with him?"

"He's in a strange room on the first floor. Looks like it's bolted from the outside, and there's just a small sliver of a window cut into the door. The entire room is padded with foam and gray panels of some sort. He's just pacing back and forth inside."

"Acoustic tiles," Gage said. "They made him a sound-proof room. Brilliant."

"There's probably a cell for each of us in that house," Mallory said.

Bug continued, "Legion is in the kitchen on the other side of the first floor. I think he's making a sandwich."

"What about my sister?" Kyle asked again.

"I don't see her on the top two floors, but there's a basement. I'm sending a fly down there. One nice thing about this old house, there are plenty of cracks."

"I can set a Blackout Bomb to take out any electronic devices or alarms on the back lawn leading up to the house," Gage said, digging in his bag. "But if we're going to play this stealthily, I assume you don't want to take out the house lights."

"Right," Alex said. "Let's try to get in and out undetected."

"Kirbie . . . ," Bug murmured.

"What?" Alex asked, his voice urgent.

"They have her in a big cage in the basement."

"Oh, Kirbs," Kyle said. His top lip curled back, exposing gritted teeth. The trees around him began to shake. "We need to get in there."

"I've got a fly going in loops in front of her, trying to get her attention," Bug said. "Okay, she sees me! She's happy but . . . she's waving her hands in front of her and telling me to move backward. I think the bars are electrified."

"Of course they are," Mallory said.

They stopped at the edge of the woods. An expansive lawn led up to the back of a huge, dark house that looked like something out of an old horror movie. The rear grounds were almost completely open, with only a few tall trees dotting the clearing. A fairly steep incline led down to a pond that the tributary trickled into. To the side of the mansion, a few stone benches sat on a gravel path, leading to a large fountain, long since dried up. There was a deck and an outdoor seating area at the back of the house, but judging by the sad state of the furniture, it hadn't been used in some time.

"What's the plan?" Gage asked.

"Is there a way into the basement from outside?" Alex asked.

"There's a small window on the other side of the house," Bug said.

"Misty, use your powers to take Mallory over there. She can melt a hole in the window for you, then the two of you can sublimate in, rescue Kirbie, and come right back here. Okay?"

"Got it," Misty said, though she didn't sound nearly as confident as she had earlier in the evening. Mallory nodded an affirmative.

"Gage, after you black out the lawn, we'll make a run for a first-floor window. You keep an eye out for alarms, and keep that Umbra Magnet ready. If we get in over our heads, we can use it to stun one of the Omegas. Bug, can you have Zip meet us there and show the way to Amp's room?"

"You got it. The window closest to us will take you straight to him."

"Good. You and Kyle wait out here and keep an eye on what's happening inside. If we get in a jam, Kyle, you're our rescue."

"Let me go with them to get my sister," Kyle said. "I have to make sure she's safe."

"I promise we'll bring her back," Mallory said. "Alex is right. We'll need you out here in your element as backup."

Alex took a deep breath and exhaled slowly. "If we work together, we can do this," he said. "Gage?"

The inventor handed a Blackout Bomb over to Alex— a small, pen-shaped gadget capable of short-circuiting electrical devices.

"Plant it at the base of the third tree to the left," Gage said. "Then set it off."

Alex wrapped the pen in blue energy and floated it across the yard, stabbing it into the ground where Gage instructed and clicking its top. A small spotlight near the old fountain went out.

"All right, everyone," Alex said. "Let's go."

Misty grabbed Mallory's hand and they broke apart, drifting through the air, traveling across the lawn just above the ground. Alex turned to Gage.

"Follow me," he said. "Light, quick steps. Stay in the darkness when you can."

Gage took off his white lab coat and tossed it onto the ground, revealing all-black clothing underneath.

"I'm with you," he said.

Alex darted out of the clearing and made for the shadows of the first tree. The moon was nearly full, and the sky virtually cloudless, much to Alex's disappointment. He made his way to the next tree shadow, and continued like this until he and Gage were crouched below a window, looking into a dark hallway at the end of the mansion. Alex slowly brought his head up, peeking through a crack in the drapes, looking for signs of movement.

"I can't see much," Alex said. "Can you detect any security systems?"

"One second," Gage said quietly, pulling his goggles over his eyes. "I was hoping I'd get a chance to try these out." He twisted the frames, and they went dark.

"It looks like there's a standard proximity sensor on the window. I'm sure it was state-of-the-art at some time or another, but it's outdated now. Luckily, I brought a magnet with me."

He dug around in his bag and produced a slim black strip.

"And that helps?" Alex asked.

"These old sensors use a magnet to keep a closed circuit," Gage explained. "As long as you don't open the window more than a few millimeters, I can slide *this* magnet in to trick it, which will keep the alarm from going off. I'm surprised they never covered this in your training."

"We dealt mostly with lasers and motion sensors when it came to this sort of thing," Alex said as he unclasped the locks at the top of the window with his powers and raised it just a crack. "I doubt the Council ever thought we'd be breaking into many houses."

"All done," Gage said, smiling. "How Cloak ever felt safe with such rudimentary security, I'll never understand."

Alex raised the window all the way and stuck his head inside. The hallway was dark and still. He paused for a moment just to make sure they hadn't tripped any other alarms, then climbed inside. Gage followed, throwing his bag in to Alex first.

Zip flew toward them, fluttering around at eye level.

Alex gave the bug a thumbs-up, then followed her down the hall, happy to find that the dark wooden floors weren't as creaky as they looked. They tiptoed past several closed doors, Alex silently willing them to remain shut. He kept his ears cocked and eyes straight ahead, power welling around his fists. Halfway down the hall, they came to a heavy metal door. There was no knob, only a dead bolt and a steel bar across the outside. About three-quarters of the way up was a slim piece of sturdy glass, an inch high and six inches across. Alex peeked through and saw Amp sitting against a corner. Wavy gray acoustic tiles lined the walls, while egg-crate foam padded the floor and ceiling. A battery-powered lantern sat against one wall, casting long shadows of Amp's figure behind him. Alex tapped softly on the glass.

"Soundproof, remember?" Gage said, handing Alex a small flashlight.

Alex clicked the light on and off a few times in the window before catching Amp's attention. The Ranger was up in a flash, pressing his eyes against the slit of glass. Alex held up one finger, telling Amp to hold on, and crouched down beside Gage.

"What do you think?" Alex asked. "Any secondary security?"

"It looks simple enough to me," Gage said.

Alex took off the outside bar while his thoughts probed the lock. There was a click, and he pulled open the door a bit and stuck his head in, putting a finger over his lips. Amp nodded and stepped out into the hallway.

"I don't know where they took Kirbie," he whispered.

"She's downstairs," Alex said quietly. "Mal and Misty are there now."

"Del is one of the Omegas."

"Yeah, we figured that out," Alex said glumly. "Just a little too late."

Zip suddenly began to fly in circles above their heads, then jetted a few feet away from them, toward the window. When none of the three boys moved, she flew back to them, ramming herself into Alex's forehead twice and then taking off again, down the hallway.

"Go," Gage whispered. "Quickly."

The three of them hustled down the hall on their toes, every tiny creak ringing in their ears like an alarm. Alex went through the window first, followed by Gage. Alex began pulling it shut with his powers as Amp climbed out onto the lawn. The window was almost closed when Legion appeared at the opposite end of the hallway, walking toward Amp's room.

Alex ducked down and used his powers to open the drapes very slightly, just enough to allow him a better look inside. He noticed the bar from the cell door leaning against the hallway wall at the same time as Legion.

"Bad news," Alex said, turning to the others. "The whole in-and-out-without-being-noticed plan is kind of not an option now."

Inside, Legion started yelling. Gage adjusted his goggles, squinting across the lawn and into the night.

"Bug and Kyle are still alone," he said. "And looking quite concerned."

"Misty and Mallory aren't back with Kirbie yet," Alex said.

"What do we do?" Gage asked.

Alex looked back and forth between Gage and Amp.

"Feel up to getting back at these guys?" he asked Amp.

"You have no idea," he said.

"Then let's make sure they're focused on us and not Kirbie and the others," Alex said.

They ran around the back of the mansion. Alex was unsure of what they should do to get the Omegas' attentions, but he didn't have to wonder long. Legion was already on the back deck, surveying the area. When he saw them, he grunted and started to sprint, copies stepping out of him one after the other, while the original never lost his stride. Alex forced four of them backward with a telekinetic wave, sending them toppling head over foot. Amp let out an angry cry and two more, including the original, flew through the air.

"I think he maxes out at about six or seven," Amp said. "If we can just keep pushing them back, we're good."

There was the slightest gust of air above them. Novo landed in front of Alex and Gage, a ripple running through her body as she hit the ground. A sweeping kick took them both down. She stood above them, tall and imposing.

"I didn't think you'd find this place, or have the gall to come here," she said. "I'm afraid that next you're actually going to impress me."

Alex tried to wrap his thoughts around her, but again, there was something about her powers that made her too slippery to hold on to. He shot a strong telekinetic burst straight at her face, but her head just whipped back, melting into her shoulders before sprouting from her neck again.

"You're becoming a real nuisance, Knight," she said. "Nothing would make me happier than to take care of you right now."

"Go on," Alex said. "Try."

Off to the their side, Alex kept one eye on Amp, who continued to fend off hordes of Legion copies.

"You still don't understand, do you?" she asked. "I had you running all over Silver Lake, from warehouse to park to theater to office building. We could have captured one of you at any time. Could have taken you to Shade and had her pry the location of your hideout from your mind. Could have slaughtered you one by one if we'd liked."

"So why didn't you?" Alex asked.

"Because our mission was to keep you *busy*," she said. "To keep you from meddling with the Council's plans. They have much bigger things to worry about than a few deserters hiding out on the outskirts of the city."

Alex let out a short, antagonistic laugh. Novo had a distinct pride in her voice that could only have come from being raised in the Cloak Society. Gage had been right when he'd speculated that the Omegas were ashamed of their failures.

"Then it must be embarrassing to have us mess up your plans, right?" he asked. "The great Novo, unable to handle a few kids."

"You don't know anything about the Omegas!" she shouted, pointing her finger at him, her voice taking a deep, terrifying tone. She composed herself and continued. "You and the rest of the Betas have no idea what it was like for us. You had every privilege available to you *and* your parents on the High Council."

Her face contorted with anger, her hands shifting between bludgeons and blade-shaped appendages.

"They were going to give you everything," she continued. "But you turned your back on it. Joined the weak, petty Rangers, of all people. As if you could ever just *leave* Cloak."

"Hey, *Del*," Kirbie's voice called from the other side of the lawn. She stood beside Mallory and Misty. "Say the part about the Rangers being weak again."

Before Novo could turn around, Kirbie was on top of her in her she-wolf form, howling furiously, claws ripping into the Omega.

TEAMWORK

Alex and Gage backed away from Kirbie and Novo, surprised by the brutality of Kirbie's attack.

A figure rose from the earth behind Misty—silver hair followed by pale white skin. In an instant he stood at his full height, one clawed hand raised above her.

"Misty!" Gage yelled.

She turned and disintegrated just as Ghost's hand fell down at her. Ghost turned, glaring at Gage, and started toward him, running straight through Novo and Kirbie as if they weren't even there. Misty reappeared between Gage and Alex and grabbed their arms. Before either of them could say anything, they were hovering in particles, flying through the air and beneath the crack left open in the hall-way window.

"Sorry," Misty said, as they solidified inside. "I kind of freaked out."

"That's okay," Gage said, stepping away from the window. "But that window's not going to stop him."

"Run," Alex said.

As he spoke, Ghost's head popped through the glass. He spotted them, gave a sickly smile, and began to sprint down the hallway after them, chasing them into the dark confines of the mansion.

They came to the entryway of the house, where twin sets of stairs ran up opposite sides of the room, converging at a landing on the second floor. There a silver, hooded skull was mounted on the wall, grinning down at them.

Alex started up the left stairway while Gage opened the front door, pushing Misty out.

"Stay sublimated," he told her. "And hide. Rescue anyone in trouble on the lawn, okay?"

"But—"

"Go!" Gage shouted. It was such an unusual thing for him to do that Misty complied immediately, falling to pieces and floating away.

Ghost ran into the entryway and stopped at the bottom of the stairs, grinning maniacally before starting after Alex.

"Show me what you've got," Alex said. He poured his energy into a great blue shield, creating a barrier between them on the staircase. But Ghost went right through it, as if there was nothing there.

"Crap," Alex muttered.

"Undeserving," Ghost rasped as he swiped at Alex.

Alex dodged, but the claws of Ghost's right hand caught him at the chest, digging into his skin. This was Alex's chance—Ghost had to be solid to attack, but it also meant that he could be harmed. Alex quickly gathered a small sphere of telekinetic energy between the two of them. He let the ball explode when Ghost attacked again, sending crackling blue bursting in every direction. Ghost slammed back against the wall, his clawed hand ripping the silver skull from Alex's Beta uniform. But the power pushed Alex back as well, and he fell over the railing and hit the marble floor below.

"Hey, Ghost!" Gage shouted, halfway up the right staircase.

"The unpowered one," Ghost said, fading back into his intangible form. "You're hardly worth my attention."

"Alex, back away," Gage said, pulling something from his bag as he reached the top of the stairs. "We may not be able to touch him, but at least part of him is in this world."

Alex slid across the floor, putting distance between them. The Omega charged at Gage, his clawed fingers out and ready. He was a second away from striking when the inventor held out the Umbra Magnet and switched it on. It hummed slightly as the convex metal bubble on its top opened.

Ghost's mouth twisted with a pained moan. Phantom's dark energy surfaced on his skin in the form of an omega covering his right eye. His body thrashed for a moment, before he focused himself enough to swipe a hand at Gage. The inventor's lips parted with a gasp.

He looked down. Ghost's arm was sticking straight through him. Intangible.

Ghost's mouth fell open and his faced scrunched in worry as he lost control over his powers. His limbs twitched in reaction to the device in Gage's hands. Ghost looked down at himself, his mouth moving but no words coming out as he continued to grow fainter, until he was only a wisp, and then, finally, nothing at all.

When Gage exhaled, it was in a long, shaking sigh.

"What just happened?" Alex asked.

"His Umbra powers reacted in the same way yours did," Gage said quietly, astonished. "They overcharged and fought to keep Phantom's mark, and that took him completely into the Gloom, where the Umbra Magnet couldn't reach him."

"Can he come back?"

Gage shrugged. "I'm sure he'll figure out how to use

his powers to cross planes, or Phantom will pluck him out. Either way, we just bought ourselves some time." He looked at Alex's chest, where the silver skull had once been. Four shallow red cuts now filled the space. "Are you all right?"

"I'll be fine," Alex said, turning to the front door. "The skull didn't really suit me much anyway. Let's find the others."

They burst back outside, into the night. Misty was nowhere to be seen, and Alex and Gage sprinted around the side of the house toward the sounds of snapping foliage and bursts of sonic energy.

In the grassy area on the side of the house, they found Amp and Kyle fighting half a dozen copies of Legion. Kyle ripped open a seed packet from his pocket and waved the package in front of him, then thrust his other hand forward, fingers spread wide. The plants began to grow in midair, prickly vines forming out of nowhere and tendrils unfurling into the night air, latching onto a trio of clones and snaring them. Then Kyle used the limbs of a nearby tree to smash into the attackers. When the branches rose, there was nothing but a mass of snaking vines left on the ground.

Alex and Gage ran to Amp, who was holding yet another trio off with sonic blasts. Farther down by the water, Novo and Kirbie continued to fight each other brutally as Mallory shot supercharged blasts of heat and cold at Novo when she could get a clear shot. Bug's eyes blazed in the darkness beside them as he sent torrents of insects into the fray.

"This guy's re-spawning every five seconds!" Amp yelled, picking off another of the clones. "I can't tell who the original is anymore!"

"I have an idea," Gage said, pulling a laser pistol from his bag. "Alex, stay back. Cover me."

Gage cranked the Umbra Magnet up to its highest setting and ran toward the clump of clones, firing the pistol ahead of him. One of the bunch reacted, crying out in pain as Gage approached, the same omega mark surfacing over his right eye that had appeared on Ghost's.

"That one!" Gage shouted. "He's the target."

But before Gage could turn the device off, one of the duplicates collided with him, tossed through the air by a giant tomato plant under Kyle's control. The Umbra Magnet went sailing, landing right in front of the actual Legion. He howled, shaking, and then suddenly there were four, eight, twelve more Legions on the ground, multiplying rapidly as his powers went into overdrive, until one of the clones accidentally stepped on Gage's device, crushing it.

There were now at least two dozen Legions slowly getting to their feet, dark omega symbols over each of their right eyes.

"What did you do?" Kyle shouted.

"It was an accident," Gage said, backing away from them.

Among the veritable army of Legions, the original was slowly standing. The duplicates waited for his mental commands. He raised a trembling hand to his face and touched the omega. He opened his mouth and let out a shout of pure rage. His clones yelled along with him.

"Pitch modulations," Amp said quietly, soaking up the sound. "Everyone get behind me." His voice was already getting louder, his body beginning to vibrate.

"Time to go back into your quiet room, Amp," Legion's dozens of voices said in unison, forming their many hands into fists and preparing to charge.

Amp let out a short, booming laugh.

"Your every word gives me power."

He spread his hands out wide, and instead of focusing his absorbed sonic energy into a concentrated blast, let a single note pour out of him—just like he'd done with the music in Gage's workshop. Then he increased the decibel level, focusing all that sound energy on the army before him. He was so skilled at directing the noise that behind him, the others could hardly hear it.

The duplicates started to sprint toward Amp just as he began to raise the pitch and frequency of the tone, until it was a high, shrill whine that should have brought them to their knees.

"It's not working," Kyle said.

"Yes." Gage pointed. "It is."

Behind the army of clones, the actual Legion was on the ground, his hands clamped over his ears. As he lost focus, the members of his army began to fade away.

Gage turned to Alex.

"Go help Kirbie," he said, pulling something else from his bag. "We'll be fine here." He turned and handed a red object to Kyle. "This is something I call a *Gasser*."

Alex sprinted toward the water where Kirbie and Novo battled, striking violently at each other over and over again. Novo's training far surpassed anything Alex could have imagined. Her body twisted and flattened and solidified and liquefied at a feverish pace, one moment putty, the next solid and striking out at Kirbie's wolf form with bladelike appendages. Mallory shot carefully aimed subzero blasts, but they were quickly absorbed into Novo's body, along with any insects Bug sent in to attack her.

Kirbie was fighting with pure animal rage. The ferocity of her attacks was like nothing Alex had ever seen from her before. She tore into Novo, swipe after swipe, ripping the girl apart, only to have each piece of her opponent's body ooze over the ground and merge back into the same fighting mass.

"Kirbie!" Alex shouted as he neared them.

The golden wolf turned to him, glaring through diamond pupils, and roared. Alex took a few steps back, unable to find any trace of Kirbie in the beast. Novo suddenly wrapped herself around the she-wolf. Mallory took the opening and leaped onto the Omega's back, her hands sizzling against the amorphous mass. Novo's face appeared directly in front of Mallory's, crying out in pain.

"Stupid girl," she said. And then Novo's oversized fist swung around, hitting Mallory hard in the gut, sending her flying. She landed in the water several yards away. Steam rose from the surface of the pond. Mallory emerged slowly, scowling, the liquid vaporizing off her as she walked to shore. In the shallows, the water boiled around her legs.

"Mal!" Alex shouted as he and Bug ran to her side.

"I'm fine," Mallory said, never taking her eyes off Novo. "I think she's weak against extreme temperatures, but she's never in one form long enough for me to do any real damage. If I can just get her to stay in one place, I can freeze her until we figure out what to do with her. I don't know how much longer Kirbie can keep this up. Can you hold her with your powers, Alex?"

"I've been trying," Alex said, "but there's something about her viscosity. She slips right through my thoughts. And she's moving too fast on land for me to trap her. We need to get her away from Kirbie and into the air or something."

"What if we got her into the water?" Bug suggested.

"Yeah . . . ," Alex said, his eyes brightening, "If I could create an energy bubble—or better yet, a whirlpool—she'd be trapped by the force of it, even if I couldn't hold her directly."

"Even if she liquefied," Mallory said. "Then I could just freeze the whole thing."

"We just have to get her to the water somehow."

"No problem!" Misty said, assembling beside them. She lowered her voice to a whisper. "I'll just mist her over the water and drop her in."

"Yes!" Alex exclaimed. "That's perfect."

"We need to get her away from Kirbie," Bug said.

"Bug, the first thing you should know about dealing with supervillains is that they've all got oversized egos and short tempers. I have an idea." Alex turned to Mallory. "Feel like pushing her buttons?"

Mallory grinned, nodding.

"Good," Alex continued. "See if you can draw her attention to you. Misty, get Kirbie out of there, then wait for my signal to take care of Novo."

"Got it."

"I'll see what I can do about keeping her distracted when Misty goes in," Bug said.

Alex nodded and turned to Mallory. "She's all yours."

"What's the matter, Novo?" Mallory asked, turning toward the brawling girls. "I thought you were supposed to be the best there was, but you and your team are losing to a bunch of kids who've barely even worked together before.

It's probably a good idea to just go into hiding instead of reporting your failure to the High Council. Don't you think?"

Novo turned her head, glaring at Mallory. A cylinder of mass shot out from her stomach, hardening just as it hit Kirbie, sending the she-wolf flying backward, howling. So much for having to separate the two of them. She landed near Kyle, Amp, and Gage, who were coming down the slope toward the water, and reverted to her human form. Kyle ran to his sister's side.

"I'm okay," she said, struggling to catch her breath from the fight.

"You ungrateful little girl," Novo said to Mallory, her body shifting into her natural state once again. "You don't even care about the sacrifices that were made for *generations* so that you could exist today."

Alex turned his attention to the pond, imagining a wide turbine spinning. The liquid was resistant, but he kept working it, gritting his teeth, drawing energy from the depths of his mind and body. Finally the water began to flow in a clockwise motion.

"Sacrifices?" Mallory asked, her breath visible as the temperature lowered around her. "Cloak killed my parents, then Shade took my memories of them. Don't lecture me on sacrifices."

"You're unworthy of the mercy Cloak is showing you,"

Novo snapped. "But once I deliver all of you to the Council, I'll be able to take my place beside them. They will lavish me with gifts and titles in the new Sterling City. They'll realize that I'm a worthy heir. And you . . . You'll serve me mindlessly."

"You sure about that?" Mallory asked. "You Omegas were nothing but tools to them. They didn't even let you stay at the base. Titan and Julie are their favorites now."

A growing hole formed in the center of the water as the whirlpool picked up speed. Alex grunted as his hands shook in front of him, energy streaming from his eyes. He raised his arms, pulling the swirling water up into the air, until it rose from the pond like a miniature tornado.

Behind him, one of Novo's arms molded into the shape of a razor as she stepped toward Mallory.

"We're supposed to take you alive, but I don't know. . . . You may just have to be collateral damage," Novo said.

"Now!" Alex yelled through clenched teeth, looking over his shoulder.

Bug's eyes lit up, and a swarm of dragonflies and beetles descended on Novo, led by Zip. They flew around her in tight circles, causing her to stumble. Misty appeared behind her and wrapped her arms around the Omega's waist.

"What?" Novo sneered, spitting out a mouthful of gnats. "They've sent in a child after me now? The terrifying Mist?"

"The terrifying Mist," Misty repeated as her body fell apart. "I *told* everyone the name worked."

And with that both girls were nothing but particles in the air, flying over the spinning column of water. They reappeared for an instant, and then Misty was gone again, drifting away as Novo fell through the sky.

She was caught in the rotating water, spinning around wildly. Mallory stood beside Alex, raising her hands beside his. She started freezing the trap from the base, ice forming on the surface of the pond in thick sheets, radiating out from the column.

"Yes!" Bug yelled. "You've got her! Keep going!"

But just as the top of the column began to solidify, a mass shot out—Novo had managed to shape her body into a form that could fight against the vortex's pull. Instinctively Mallory focused her freezing blasts directly on the Omega, who was in the middle of changing back into her human form and had no way of dodging the attack. The girl's transformation slowed, until finally it stopped completely, and Novo was frozen solid by Mallory's powers.

Amp let out a sonic blast, hitting the now-frozen Omega in midair with such force that Novo shattered and rained down on them in pieces.

Alex turned to see Amp standing a few yards from the banks of the water, one arm still thrust out. Gage was beside him, as was Kyle, who was helping Kirbie walk down to meet the others.

"I didn't mean to—I mean, I didn't know . . . ," Amp said, horrified by what he'd just done.

"It's okay," Alex said, breathing heavily from the exertion of creating a small tornado. "She's not dead. Just frozen."

"Oh," Amp said. "Well, good then."

"Legion?" Mallory asked.

"Sleeping," Gage said.

"We should all probably start carrying Gassers around with us," Amp said. "Those things are amazing."

"Oh, wow," Kirbie said, limping forward and staring at the frozen column of water on the pond. What Alex and Mallory had created was truly a spectacular sight.

"Are you all right?" Alex asked, looking at Kirbie. "You were crazy ferocious against Novo."

"Yeah," Kirbie said, looking down at the ground. "I'm fine. Just a sprained ankle, I think. I don't know what came over me."

"It was incredible," Alex said. "Next time you don't trust someone and I don't listen, just wolf out and I'll definitely change my mind."

"Um, and you're never sparring against me again," Kyle said to his sister.

"Kirbie," Alex said. "Listen, I'm sorry about Del and not—"

"Alex," she interrupted. "We're a team. It's part of our

job to help each other out, and to forgive each other quickly. Otherwise, we'd never get anything done."

Alex nodded gratefully. In the back of his mind, he could almost hear his mother laughing at such a notion.

"So," Kirbie said, changing the subject. "When she thaws, is she just going to put herself back together?"

"Undoubtedly," Gage said.

"Then why don't we make it harder for her? Bug, do you think you could summon a swarm of something? The farther apart her pieces are, the longer it'll take her to re-form, right?"

"That shouldn't be a problem," Bug said. "I can spread her out over a mile or two. Maybe more."

Kirbie looked down at a big chunk of Novo's frozen body, featureless, like a big gray ice cube. She brought her boot down, smashing it into tiny fragments.

"Do it then," Alex said to Bug. "Amp, will you help me take care of Legion? Everyone else, do a quick sweep of the mansion. Bring back anything that looks useful, or like it may connect to Cloak. We'll regroup here in five minutes."

Alex walked away, Amp in tow, as hordes of dragonflies, flying beetles, and other buzzing, dark insects converged on the soggy banks.

Legion was sleeping soundly on the open grass.

"What should we do with him?" Alex asked. "He's an enemy. A fierce one. We could always—"

"Rangers don't kill," Amp said, cutting him off.

"That's not what I was going to suggest," Alex said. "Besides, I'm not a Ranger."

"Maybe not," Amp said, turning to look at Alex. "But I think you'd make a good one."

Alex didn't know what to say, which seemed to suit Amp just fine.

"So, I was going to say maybe we should just tie him up," Alex said. "He'll escape as soon as he's conscious, but it's not like we have anywhere to take him."

Amp patted Legion down, removing a cell phone from the inside pocket of the Omega's jacket.

"I'm calling the police," he said, "and telling them that we've discovered one of the Cloak Society's bases."

"But Cloak has so much sway with everyone, especially the police . . . ," Alex started.

"They can't own everyone. Not every officer," Amp said. "Legion may not stay locked up, but at least we'll have done something. *Someone* will start asking questions. Especially now that Cloak has gone public."

"Help me get him inside first," Alex said. "We'll leave him where he'll be easy to find."

They carried the Omega into the entryway and tossed him onto the ground, in the space between the two staircases. Alex used a lamp cord to bind Legion's wrists, as Amp slid open the phone and walked into the hallway.

Alex looked up at the gleaming, hooded skull mounted at the top of the stairs, an emblem that had once been such a source of pride for him. It blazed blue in his vision. He narrowed his eyes, and without so much as a twitch of his body, the skull collapsed in on itself, the metal screeching, until it was nothing more than a crumpled piece of silver stuck to the wall.

"The cops are on their way," Amp said, walking back into the entryway.

"Good," Alex replied. "Let's go home."

21

RETURN OF THE
RANGERS

The eastern sky was lightening to a cobalt blue by the time Alex and the rest of the team got back to the lake house. They left the boat docked at the beach. Gage started to open the door to the garage, but Kyle pulled him away from it.

"You have to sleep sometime," he said, fighting back a yawn. "I'm not going into the Gloom with a kid who's crazy from being awake for a week."

Gage hesitated, but eventually stepped away from the door, following everyone inside. They shed their coats in the living room, letting them fall to the ground, their sore bodies revealing every future bruise, every scrape that had gone unnoticed during the fight and the cold ride home. Then they crawled into their beds. All of them slept soundly for the first time in weeks, partly because they were exhausted, both physically and mentally, and partly because they felt safer, knowing they had finally accomplished something. The Omegas weren't gone for good, but they were gone for now, and though they would surely come together again— when Ghost found his way back to the normal world and when Novo reconstituted—they had been beaten. Alex and the others knew they could do it again. In the meantime, their safe house had not been discovered, and they had a way into the Gloom. They were going to get the Rangers back.

It was late afternoon before Alex woke, his eyes greedy for more sleep, sore against the light as he finally opened them. He showered quickly, the hot water stinging the cuts on his chest. He stumbled downstairs, his stomach growling audibly, and grabbed a bowl of cereal from the kitchen before joining the others in the living room.

"You're just in time," Kirbie said, scooting closer to Mallory on the couch to make room for him. "The news is about to come on. We're hoping they mention Legion and the mansion."

Alex took a seat, shoveling spoonfuls of cereal into his mouth as the opening to the five o'clock news began. He wondered halfheartedly if Julie and Titan and the High Council were gathered around a television in the underground base somewhere, watching the same program.

"Our top story tonight involves a mysterious police call that led to what may be the first break in the investigation against the much-sought-after 'Cloak Society,'" the anchor began. "Early this morning police received—"

The anchor paused, looked confused for a beat, and then continued speaking.

"Ladies and gentlemen, our newsroom has just received *breaking* news from city officials. We now go live to the steps of city hall, where the mayor has called an emergency press conference."

"What?" Alex mumbled through a mouthful of cereal.

The video cut to the front of city hall, all off-white limestone and pillars. The mayor stood behind a dark wooden podium. Several cameras flashed as he began to speak.

"Citizens of Sterling City and beyond: It was not long ago that I stood before you with a heavy heart. Without news of our departed heroes. And in our time of need, we were attacked by maniacal forces who threatened the welfare of our glorious city. Ladies and gentlemen, I am here today to tell you that our fears can be put to rest."

He stopped speaking and lifted his head to the sky. The camera tilted up. At first there was nothing to see but a glare of light. And then a figure began to float down, as if from the sun itself. His boots and sleeves were white. Set against the blue material on his chest was a golden starburst.

"It can't be," Kirbie whispered.

As the figure got closer to the ground, his face came into view. His hair and eyes were dark, his skin olive. He wore thick-rimmed black glasses. The expression on his face was one of restrained joy.

"Photon," Gage stated flatly. "But how . . ." He looked as confused as he ever had in his life.

"We have to go," Kyle said, already scrambling toward the coat closet. "We have to get down there to see him."

"Shhhh," Amp whispered.

"It must be a trick," Mallory said. "It must be Novo."

"There's no way it could be her," Bug said. "My insects scattered her too far. She couldn't have put herself back together so quickly."

"Besides," Gage said, "Novo isn't a flier."

The man onscreen landed beside the mayor. The crowd roared, and it took several moments of coaxing from both men before there was enough quiet for anyone to speak. Finally Photon bent his face toward the microphone.

"Good evening, citizens," he said. "I am Dr. Photon of the Rangers of Justice."

More applause and cheering. In the lake house, no one dared to breathe.

Photon continued, his voice a smooth, even tone. "A little over a month ago, the villainous organization known as the Cloak Society laid siege to Justice Tower. A battle raged there in the dark hours of the night. Lux and Lone Star were lost to us, captured by Cloak's terrible powers and swept away to an unknown location. I don't know if they're alive or dead, but I will not rest until I find them, and the Cloak Society is crushed."

The crowd roared.

"It's really him," Amp said, his bottom lip quivering as he spoke. "There's no shape-shifter or android or magic power that could copy him so perfectly."

"I, too, would have been lost," Photon continued, "were it not for intervening forces—a group of individuals who arrived in the eleventh hour, in the moments before Justice Tower fell, and rescued me from the same terrible fate."

"Is he talking about us?" Alex asked quietly. "That can't be right. . . ."

"Ladies and gentlemen," Photon said, "it is with the utmost pleasure and deepest gratitude that I introduce you to my lifesavers, the people who have been nursing me back to health this last month, and the newest members of the Rangers of Justice."

He stepped to the side of the podium and smiled widely. From the audience three people emerged, walking proudly to the podium.

There, in front of the cameras, stood Titan, Volt, and Shade, wearing the same Ranger uniform as Photon. Alex's mother wore large, dark sunglasses that completely obscured her eyes, but as she reached the podium and placed a hand on Photon's shoulder, Alex was sure he could see a flash of silver behind them.

"These three are the true saviors of Sterling City," Photon said over thundering applause. "You will soon cheer for them as you have cheered for me, and for my lost comrades. But for now, know this: We are the Rangers of Justice. Let no criminal walk free among our streets. Let no villain go undefeated. For we will strike down any who stand in the way of peace. This is our promise to you as the protectors of Sterling City. A golden age is upon us."

He stepped away from the platform and slipped his hand into Shade's. Together, the four of them raised their fists into the sky. The clamoring of shouts and applause from the crowd at the steps turned into an unintelligible roar.

"What's going on?" Kirbie asked.

"My mother. She did this," Alex said. "They took him out of the Gloom, and my mother rewrote his mind. Made him their pawn. *That's* what she's been working on. That's why the Omegas didn't just capture one of us and take us to her."

"Photon," Kyle whispered. Plants in the living room trembled as he tried to control his emotions.

"If they have Photon, they have the city now," Kirbie said through clenched teeth. "The people are desperate for heroes. They'll follow them blindly."

"They'll be able to impose whatever restrictions they want as the threat of Cloak grows, manipulating everyone's fear," Gage said. "Curfews. Martial law. They'll lock down the city." He lowered his voice. "It is an excellent strategy."

"No," Amp said. "Photon has to remember who he is. Who *they* are. There's no way they wiped away all of him."

Alex placed his bowl on the table and stood, his thoughts racing. He walked to the window overlooking the front yard and garage, where Gage's newest creation sat hidden in the rafters. He stared down at his right palm for a moment, searching for signs of dark energy and bracing himself for the dark wastelands ahead of them.

"All right," he said, curling his right hand into a fist and turning to his teammates. "It's time we rescue the rest of the Rangers of Justice. It's time we enter the Gloom."

EVERY HERO'S JOURNEY
HAS A BEGINNING....

Don't miss the first book in
the Cloak Society trilogy!